A BIT OF EARTH

Rebecca Smith

BLOOMSBURY

First published in Great Britain in 2006
This paperback edition published 2007

Bloomsbury Publishing Plc,
36 Soho Square,
London W1D 3QY

A CIP catalogue record for this book
is available from the British Library

ISBN-13 9780747585886

10 9 8 7 6 5 4 3 2 1

Typeset by Hewer Text UK Ltd, Edinburgh
Printed in Great Britain by Clays Ltd, St Ives plc

All papers used by Bloomsbury Publishing are natural,
recyclable products made from wood grown in well-managed
forests. The manufacturing processes conform to the
environmental regulations of the country of origin.

www.bloomsbury.com/rebeccasmith

To S.M.

AN ORGAN WOULD BE too loud for a child's funeral. As the pianist played *Morningtown Ride* the coffin was carried out, tiny and horribly small. He was a slight boy. Couldn't have made it past three stone.

> *Maybe it is raining*
> *Where our train shall ride,*
> *All the little travellers are warm and snug inside.*
> *Rocking, rolling, riding . . .*

Or never warm and never snug ever again. There were flower arrangements of a yellow digger and the White Rabbit from *Alice in Wonderland* with a watch that had now stopped for ever. The sun streamed through the stained glass, casting lozenges of light in sweetie-wrapper colours across the flagstones.

Susannah woke, clawing at the pillow, finding that here it was sunshine and day. She lurched out of bed and across the landing to Felix's bedroom. He was asleep. The sunshine couldn't penetrate the curtains she had made for his room.

They had thermal as well as black-out linings, for Susannah was a worrier. She gently sat down on the end of his bed, and picked up Marmalade, his toy cat. Felix woke.

'Hello Mummy. Is it morning?'

'Just about. You can stay in bed for a while longer if you like.' She hugged him and wondered, yet again, why he always smelled faintly of mice. 'I'm going to make your Ready Brek. I'll call you. We don't want to be late.'

Susannah and Felix were never late for nursery. They took a short cut across the university and the botanical garden, often walking that far with Daddy, whose name was Guy. He was Professor Guy Misselthwaite, head of Botany, a department that was really only a side shoot of Biology and numbered just one and a half staff, himself and Jeanette, the secretary.

Quarter to eleven. They would probably be playing outside on the bikes and trikes by now. Susannah tried to blink away the images of her dream. Perhaps she had stayed too long in Victorian Literature. She wheeled her trolley of books to be re-shelved into the Gothic Architecture section. Felix would be fine. Felix was safe. He was probably playing in the sandpit, or on the climbing frame or, most likely, making friends with some woodlice or gazing in awe at the woolly caterpillars that had colonised the tree next to the nursery playground.

Professor Judy Lovage (History of Art), neat in her customary colours of a Siamese cat, smiled a 'good morning' as Susannah shelved the last of the books and pushed the trolley back towards the lifts.

Susannah Misselthwaite, part-time university library assistant, wife of Professor Guy Misselthwaite, and mother of

Felix (aged four and a half) sometimes forgot that she was an MA herself. She was mostly very content. Her morning was nearly over. She decided to catch the bus into town that afternoon. Felix needed some plain white polo shirts (five would be a good idea) before he started school. No point taking the car. It would be quicker and easier by bus.

Susannah had sometimes wished that she was one of those feckless mothers, like the ones in books or films. Perhaps she should try to be like the mother in *Hideous Kinky* and give Felix a nomadic childhood of heat and dust, unsuitable friends and adult company. Then she thought of threadbare monkeys cruelly forced to perform, and of snake charmers. She had once seen a French documentary about a snake charmer. He went into the Sahara and dug snakes from their holes. She hadn't really thought about it until then; hadn't imagined that snakes who were charmed had once been wild.

Susannah didn't realise that her international background already gave her a low-level but enduring glamour in the queue outside the nursery.

'Susannah,' they said, 'oh, she's half-Swedish.'

'I thought it was German.'

'No, but her family live in Germany.'

'She speaks five languages.'

'And Felix is learning most of them.'

The chorus shrugged and gave half-smiles at yet another instance of their own maternal inadequacy.

Felix's nursery session finished at 3 p.m. Some mummies would arrive early and stand outside juggling fractious babies or swaying from one Birkenstock to the other. Susannah would be one of these (minus the baby and sometimes the Birkenstocks). Then there were the 'on time' ones who always arrived exactly as the doors opened. There was also the late late crowd, who either sprinted in apologising every day, or most often sauntered in, unaware of the possible shame and anxiety caused to their offspring, who were left alone on the story mat or hiding under the climbing frame. Susannah would never have been one of these late ones. She thought that she had detected an edge, a barb, in the nursery ladies' voices.

'Oh, I expect Mummy's just caught in a traffic jam, again . . .'

'Don't worry, Bethany, Daddy's probably just in a long queue at the supermarket, like last week . . .'

Felix had once burst into tears at a book read on *Tweenies*. A little boy's mummy is late and he imagines she has gone to buy another boy or been eaten by a crocodile. She would never, ever, put Felix through that.

What if one day the nursery ladies said something like 'Daddy's in the pub' or 'Mummy prefers being at the gym to being with you'? But she could see that they just wanted to get the sand swept up, and get home to make their own children's tea.

There were stern warnings issued in writing when children were enrolled. If you were twenty minutes late they would telephone the emergency contacts you had given. If those people weren't available, the duty officer at Social Services would be informed, and if you still hadn't arrived after half an hour, your child would be handed over to the authorities. Would they really do that? Surely one of them would just take the uncollected child home with them. She hadn't discussed this possibility with any of the other mothers. After all, who would be more than twenty minutes late with their emergency contacts uncontactable? And who but Susannah, Library Lady, Uber-Organised Person Extraordinaire, would have bothered to read this small print anyway?

As she reached the stop she saw a bus pulling away. Never mind. It wouldn't matter. She had plenty of time. She could get right round the shops and be back in time to collect Felix. She sat down on one of the mean little flip-down seats, the only person waiting. Perhaps it was worth missing the bus so as not to have to stand in a crowd of students. Professor Lovage was walking towards her, smiling and swinging her bag in a girlish, carefree way. Susannah smiled too.

'Off into town?' Professor Lovage asked.

'I just need the last few things for Felix starting school, some white polo shirts.'

'A big step,' said Professor Lovage. 'Is he looking forward to it?'

'I'm not sure. He doesn't seem to have much sense of time, so I don't think he holds the idea in his head much. But some of the children he knows from nursery will be going.'

'I'm sure he'll be all right then. Good luck with the shopping.'

'Thank you.'

Professor Lovage walked on, thinking that she should

really go into town too. There were a lot of things she needed to do, birthdays coming up and so on. But the thought of her garden in summer was just too tempting. She would rather expend her energies there. The watering and tying back and hoeing, and sitting on her little bench, seemed much more important than shopping.

Susannah stared up the road. Still no sign of a bus. Students were starting to gather and bunch up at the stop. When it finally came it would be crowded after all.

'Oh look, a backhoe loader!' she told herself as one passed. It might take her a long time to break the habit of commenting on all the heavy plant and construction vehicles she saw. Felix was now old enough not only to name them all accurately himself, but to be unimpressed by all but the most enormous or unusual. Here at the university, with its constant expansion and improvements, even giant wheel loaders were two a penny.

She quietly wished that there was another little boy, a brother for Felix, to continue the hobby with. Or a little sister. But no more babies had arrived, and she and Guy would have found any kind of treatment too intrusive. They no longer talked about it.

A car of astonishing beauty pulled up, an Alfa Romeo Spider in a metallic Mediterranean blue. The driver was Julius East, Head of Spanish.

'Where are you off to, Susannah?'

'Just shopping in the city.'

'Fancy a ride?'

She paused, too polite to accept eagerly, too polite to refuse.

'I'm sure my bus will be along soon . . .'

6

'You prefer a bus to this?' He smiled at her slowly, knowing that she would accept. She stood there on the pavement, unsure, whilst he got out and came round to open the passenger door. It was a long time since anyone had done that for her.

'In you get.'

'Thank you.'

The seats were made of the softest leather that Susannah had ever felt. She supposed that there was some glossy brochure/car-showroom name for that colour. 'Tan' sounded too pedestrian. And what kind of animal had it once been? Susannah worried that she might mark the seats somehow. So lucky she hadn't been wearing jeans. What if the rivets had ripped them? But she supposed that people who drove cars like this must sometimes wear trousers with rivets too.

The seats were so low that she felt as though she were sitting on the road.

'Relax,' he said. 'You have your knees all pulled up. You're hugging them as though you're a schoolgirl. Perhaps you are. You do look so young, Susannah. Too young to be married to a professor of botany.'

'Oh, I'm really very old,' said Susannah. But she stretched out her legs. 'This is a beautiful car.'

'It's new. If you have time, we'll just take a detour, then you'll see what it's really like.'

Her hair was whipped back and then forwards again into her eyes. It might be turned to string by the time they arrived. She pushed it behind her ears again and again.

'In there,' he indicated the glove compartment with a slight thrust of his chin, 'there's a scarf you can borrow.' She wouldn't have been surprised if he kept a pair of gloves there too. The thought of gloves in a glove compartment pleased her, and she smiled. The scarf was a long thin rectangle of heavy white silk. She placed it over her hair and knotted it at the nape of her neck, wondering who it belonged to. Perhaps he just kept it there for whichever woman (or more likely, pretty student) he happened to pick up. She could feel his eyes on her legs. She placed her bag primly on her knees.

They were in the forest now. She wondered when they would turn back.

'I have to get some polo shirts for Felix. He's starting school soon.'

'You will have time on your hands.'

She looked down at her hands, as though she might see time growing there, some sort of silky golden fur. Or perhaps it would be thyme, with pretty little stems coiling around her fingers. But her hands were unchanged, slim, neat and pink. She had a French manicure. The idea of having your nails painted so that they looked like nails pleased her as well.

She looked out of the window – fields, ponies, more trees, and hedgerows gorgeous with butterflies, betony, ragwort, chamomile, and sun spurge. They zoomed past cow parsnip and earthnut pea, so much prettier than their names. The sky was much brighter out here.

'The sky is bluer out here, don't you think?' she said, gazing upwards. There were three aeroplanes leaving wonderful paths across the sky. 'Once when Felix saw some of those vapour trails he said, "Mummy, the clouds are lining up!"'

He smiled. She could tell that he was smiling, but she didn't look across, she just kept looking up. And that was why Susannah didn't see the deer, or know that he was going to swerve to avoid it. She never knew what had happened.

2

HIS MUMMY HAD NEVER been late before. Felix sat on the carpet and waited. Soon all the other children were gone.

'Your mummy's a bit late today, Felix,' said one of the ladies. 'Don't worry, she'll soon be here. Why don't you do this puzzle whilst we just finish sweeping up?'

He finished the puzzle.

'Would you like to help sort out these Stickle Bricks and Mega Bloks, they've got a bit mixed up.'

Felix tipped them all out onto the floor and then helped put them into the right boxes.

'Well, I think I'll just try ringing your daddy instead.'

'My mummy has a mobile phone.'

'I know, sweetie, but sometimes if you're in a really busy shop you don't hear it ringing if it's at the bottom of your bag.'

They gave him two biscuits out of the tin that was just for grown-ups. He was thirsty, but he could see that they had already put the cups away. They let him eat the biscuits sitting on the carpet. He heard the lady talking to somebody on the phone.

'Don't worry,' she said. 'Daddy said that he'd come and collect you. He won't be long. You can look at the books if you like.'

The other ladies went home.

Felix stood by the door and waited there. Daddy had hardly ever collected him. He wished he had come earlier, he could have shown him the bikes and how fast some of them could go.

When Daddy arrived he didn't look happy.

'I'm so sorry,' he said, but not to Felix. 'I really don't know where my wife can have got to. Perhaps I was meant to be getting him all along, and I forgot. Maybe she thought some other mother was taking him home. Sorry.'

'That's all right. Bye Felix.' The nursery lady was holding a big bunch of keys. She followed them out and locked the door behind them.

'Oh good, it's the car,' said Felix.

'Felix, were you meant to be going to tea with somebody and they didn't come to nursery? Was I meant to be getting you today?'

'I don't know. But Dad, they have this big tyre thing on wheels. You can sit inside it and somebody, it has to be a grown-up, pulls you round. You could pull me round in that if you came before they put it away.' But all his dad said was 'Maybe she's at home.'

When they got back home Mummy wasn't there either. Felix watched TV and had some juice, not diluted. His dad kept going to look out of the window and trying to ring her. After a while Felix knelt on the sofa so that he could look out of the window too.

'Dad, a police car is coming. It hasn't got its light on so it can't be an emergency.'

'Oh no,' said his dad. 'Oh no.'

Two policemen came in. One was a lady. His dad started crying. Felix had never seen his dad cry. His face looked horrible, as though it was coming off. Felix started to cry as well. He ran to the mirror in the hall to see what his face looked like when he was crying. Did it look as though it was coming off too? The policewoman came after him. He asked her why his dad was crying.

Was this the bag of an adulterer? Here were tissues; a make-up bag with a cornflower design containing two lipsticks, a compact, mascara (brown not black), a miniature toothbrush and a tiny tube of toothpaste, and a brown tortoiseshell hairclip; a diary containing almost nothing but dates of nursery events and meetings for work; two blue rollerballs; a tube (bent and almost cracked) of anti-histamine cream; a tin containing plasters that were khaki camouflage instead of so-called skin colour, presumably for diminutive wounded soldiers; a letter from the school saying when Felix was due to start and what he would need: a copy of *Mr Golightly's Holiday*; a pigeon feather ('Mum, will you look after this?'); a packet of lemon-flavoured mints, and her keys with the photo-fob of Felix in his nursery sweatshirt against a background of clouds. The only thing that was a mystery was the old postcard she had been using as a bookmark — toy boats in the Tuileries gardens with the sky an improbable blue. It was captioned 'Bassin dans les jardins des Tuileries, à l'arrière plan, l'Arc du Carrousel.'

They had never been to Paris. But Susannah had travelled a lot when she was a teenager and student, before they had been together. After all, she was a European.

This bag could have been tipped upside down in public, on any headmaster's desk or live on TV. It seemed that there was little here to be revealed, and nothing to shame her. There had been a once-white silk scarf too, now horribly stained. They hadn't even offered it to him. He had seen it though. Guy did not know that silk scarf. Was it a present? Had it been given to her that day? Perhaps it had been kept secretly somewhere. A once-white silk scarf.

Professor Lovage sat on her pale yellow sofa, drinking a cup of chamomile and spearmint tea. She had been reading a book about Stanley Spencer and resolving that this summer she would take a trip to Cookham. She was looking at one of her favourite pictures, which was of people lying on the pebbly beach at Southwold. She had just turned to the *Resurrections* when she noticed the time, and put on the TV to catch the end of the news and the weather. Ah, the local news. She was constantly impressed by the stories that they floated as local headlines, and astonished by the fixation with disputes between travellers and local residents; but so often she had to switch off something about a case involving cruelty to animals. Today her scalding tisane sloshed onto her lap.

'A university professor and his companion were killed this afternoon in a horrific crash. Police have named the pair who died as Professor Julius East, and Susannah

Misselthwaite who worked at the university library. Experts at the scene of the crash say that no other cars were involved. It appears that Professor East may have swerved to avoid something, probably an animal, and this caused their car, an Alfa Romeo Spider, to crash into a tree. The police are appealing for any witnesses to come forward.'

Judy gasped. It could not be true. It really could not be true. Her book fell to the floor. Surely there must be a mistake. She could not think of anyone to ring. She knew Professor East only by sight. She didn't know Susannah's husband at all. She had occasionally said 'Good morning' to him in the botanical garden, but that was all. Oh, that poor little boy. That poor man.

The next day it still appeared to be true. She wrote to Susannah's husband, saying how sorry she was, and sent it (really very tackily, she thought) through the internal mail, because she didn't have his address. She tried to think of something she could do to help. Presumably relatives would arrive to help look after Felix. It was all too appalling.

A few days later she went to a toy shop and, after much deliberation, bought a puzzle for Felix. It had thirty-six pieces. The box said that it was for ages four and over, she remembered that he was about to start school. The picture was of an arctic landscape with an improbable number of species visible. She thought that there couldn't be anything too upsetting in that. So many of the puzzles were too jolly, or of the emergency services, or both. She put it in a jiffy bag and sent it through the internal post to Professor Misselthwaite. She enclosed a note saying that she hoped Felix would like it, and that she did not need any acknowledgement. It seemed so pathetically inadequate. What use was a new puzzle to a little boy who had lost his mother? Afterwards she wondered if she should have sent Felix something for starting school.

It was a week after the crash, but still before the funeral (and how dreadful to think of her lying there, the terrible cold wait in the mortuary; it should be done, as in some other cultures, the next day, before sundown). Guy thought that he should see where it had happened. Perhaps if he went there he could undo it, turn back time, find some secret switch to unhappen it. He could not believe that it was permanent, that there was no negotiation with its finality. Felix was taken to nursery by another child's mother. This woman was also going to collect him and have him for what remained of the afternoon. Guy could not remember her name. He saw that she had a sad, blotchy face and frizzy hair. He understood that he was to trust her with Felix. He didn't tell the woman where he was going.

When Felix had been taken away (Guy noticed with relief that they were on foot) he went out into the garden and picked some flowers, some Susannah herself had planted, and others that had been there when they moved in – forget-me-nots, French marigolds, roses, sweet williams, standard suburban garden fare – and tied them into a bunch with twine. Then he got into the car. He drove through the city and out towards the forest. This must have been the way they came. What was she doing? What the hell was she doing with that lecher? Good God, Guy thought, even I know about him. Julius East, whose tastes had often run to final-year students. Susannah was several years older than his usual prey. What the hell had been going on? And for how long? Always the last to know, they say, always the last to know.

Guy realised that he could hardly see the road. He pulled over and punched himself in the thigh to stop himself from crying. He drove on a bit and stopped at a garage. Got petrol and some vile coffee. He scalded his mouth and his fingers as he drove.

Now he was in the forest. They must have come this way. The limit was forty, but people always went faster. Some animal, probably a deer. He expected that was it. The bastard probably swerved to miss one and went into the tree. If he weren't dead, Guy would kill him. He thought of the joke that parents make to their children: 'Come back safely or I'll kill you.' Of course, it didn't make him smile. He drove on through a village. This must have been one of the last places she saw, these houses and shops, the shop selling beach things where she always wanted them to stop, but somehow they never had.

Soon he was through the village and driving past fields and hedgerows. Suddenly he saw it – he saw the bright colours first – oh God, a bloody roadside shrine. He saw the tree. A hateful sycamore, the trunk hideously dented and broken.

The tree itself was now bleeding to death. You would think that the authorities would have come and cut it down straight away and taken it off to be burnt. It seemed central to the horror, and all around it, the floral tributes.

He stopped the car on the verge and, gasping and sobbing, loped over to it. He began to tear down the stiff, plasticky ribbons. There were florists' cheap vile bows in all colours, loops and loops of the stuff. The villagers must have done it out of spite, they must have thought it was funny. And there were carnations and chrysanthemums, some hideously dyed, too bright, and some with their petals turning brown already. Some were in supermarket and garage cellophane, with prices and sachets of flower food still attached. He tore at them and began throwing them over the hedge. He was unaware of the cars going by, some slowing slightly, some speeding up to get away from the madman who was shouting and crying and howling. Then he was grabbed from behind and he felt his face hit the mud.

'Says he's the poor woman's husband,' the policeman said as he accompanied Guy into the station.

'Reckon he must be, by the state of him. Better get psych over here and give him something.'

'I do not need to be given something,' said Guy. 'It was disrespectful.'

'With all due respect, mate, looked like you were the one being disrespectful. A lot of local people spent good money on those flowers and teddies.'

'There weren't any teddies,' said Guy. 'I really don't think there were teddies.'

'Probably been nicked. It happens.'

'And you don't understand,' said Guy. 'My wife, Susannah, she, she . . . hated flowers in cellophane.'

They pushed a box of Kleenex Mansize across the desk to him, and ten minutes later a mug of tea.

At last Guy looked up.

'I have to be back for my little boy,' he said. 'Can I go?'

The original officers had now gone.

'Can you just show us some identification?' said their replacement.

'I do have ID. I'm a lecturer at the university.' Guy felt for his wallet and realised it must be on the floor of the car, which presumably was still there, open on the verge. 'I have to go. My little boy . . .'

'All right, mate. Take care. Check out with the guy on the desk. We're all really sorry for your loss.'

It seemed that they didn't have the officers available to drive him back to his car, not for at least three hours. It was a three-mile walk. When he got there a council lorry was taking away the sycamore. What remained of the flowers had been piled on the stump. When no cars were passing he flung them over the hedge. His own flowers were wilting on the passenger seat. His wallet was there too, and his keys were still in the ignition. He quietly put the dying flowers beside the stump and drove away.

When he got home, the frizzy-haired woman was waiting outside in a car with Felix and three other children.

'Only been here ten minutes!' she cried, all bright and breezy.

'I'm so sorry,' said Guy, 'I am so sorry for the trouble.' He held Felix very tight.

'No problem!' she said, and drove away. He went into the empty, dusty house. Letters of condolence were piling up, opened but unread, on top of the silent piano, on the kitchen table, and on the floor in the hall, just where they had fallen from his hands.

3

SUSANNAH'S MOTHER ELFIE HAD been Swedish. Her name had been Elfrida, but with her cropped blonde hair (which turned to thistledown as her final illness took hold) and her slightly sticky-out ears, Elfie had suited her more and more. She had died a year before Guy and Susannah had met. But now Guy remembered how, when he'd been shown photos, he had wondered if she might be half elfin, a changeling who had belatedly been reclaimed. He had always got on well enough with Susannah's father, Kenneth Ingram, a research chemist whose beard looked as though it had been knitted from the unravelled grey wool of school jumpers. Originally from Northumberland, work had taken Kenneth to Sweden, and then to Germany where he had remained. Guy also remembered remarking to Susannah that Sweden and Northumberland were not that far apart, and how she had laughed and said that her father was a constant pickle-eater, that he had wanted to immerse himself in a culture that had raw fish for breakfast, but then discovered a place where cheese and salami were standard wake-up fare.

If only Guy could hear her laugh, her voice again. Often it was too painful to think, but sometimes he sat and tried to think of things she had said — exact words, her accent and inflexions — if he could recall things exactly, might she come back?

Susannah's brother Jon was a research botanist, and a much higher flier than Guy. Resolutely single, he lived in Geneva and took energetic, purposeful holidays. Guy had never got to know him that well. Once, before Felix was born, they had joined him on a skiing holiday. Guy still felt diminished by it. Before they went, he had resolved to try to like skiing, but how could he really enjoy anything that involved such silly outfits and day-long bonhomie? On the first day he had ventured onto the slopes with them, but the snow had been much too slippery, and he'd had to take an ignominious ride back down on the lift and in an empty cable car. For the rest of the holiday he had walked in the forests and looked at mosses. Susannah had just laughed and said it didn't matter.

Although they had rarely seen Jon, Susannah had had long telephone conversations with him, usually in German or Swedish, conversations that Guy would never have been able to keep up with.

Now contact with Jon would be reduced to presents sent to Felix at random times of the year. Jon wasn't a rememberer or observer of other people's birthdays, or even Christmas. But Felix loved the presents: a book about rocks and minerals; a book of maps of the Alps (perhaps Jon was imagining that he might take Felix on holiday with him one day); a box of huge seed pods (which Guy and Felix worked out were from starnut palm, Mary's bean, crabwood, and sea coconut); the shed skin of a viper; an Amazonian soldier ant pickled in a bottle (Guy said it was lucky that Grandpa Kenneth hadn't seen it first); some sharks' teeth from a sailing holiday off Australia . . .

'Do you think Uncle Jon will ever come and visit us?' Felix would ask each time something arrived.

'Maybe,' said Guy, but he couldn't imagine what might bring Jon to their dull city, their shire-bound backwater. There were no dangerous sports to be had, no rapids to shoot.

'Then maybe we could go and visit him,' said Felix.

'Maybe.'

After the funeral, Kenneth would stay in touch only by letter, often enclosing some Euros for Felix. Guy knew that Kenneth had his own swallowed grief to cope with – first his wife, then his daughter – and that they should be sticking together. Perhaps Kenneth blamed him for the accident, thought that he could not have been taking proper care of Susannah. Words seemed to turn to pebbles in their mouths.

There must have been other relatives of Felix somewhere in Sweden. Elfie had had siblings. There must have been cousins somewhere, but Guy gave them no thought. He and Felix might appear as an English Misselthwaite dead end on that branch of the Swedish family tree. It didn't occur to him to be concerned.

*　　*　　*

Guy's parents and his sister Jenny arrived for the funeral. They only mentioned the cost of their last-minute flights from New Zealand a few times. They stayed in the same Travelodge as Jon and Kenneth, and all carefully avoided having breakfast together. Guy was deeply grateful that nobody stayed with him, and didn't mind that Susannah's family made their stay as short as possible. He found Jon's physical resemblance to Susannah disturbing.

Jenny's usual heartiness was muted, but only slightly. She found it hard to step out of her role as a tour leader of trekking holidays in the Tongariro National Park, the sort of vacations that are advertised in the back of the weekend papers and are supposedly designed for intrepid souls. Footloose in walking boots. Guy didn't think that it had been very independent to follow your retiring parents halfway across the world, and set up in their spare bedroom. He didn't hear his mother persuading Jenny not to wear her cargo shorts to the funeral.

They only stayed a week, and they hardly mentioned Susannah. They had all thought that she was so nice. They kept remembering the wedding, when they had been so impressed; it had been as though a Misselthwaite had managed to bag the blonde one from Abba. On the last night of their stay Guy's mother cornered him in the kitchen.

'But will you and Felix be all right? Would you like to come and stay with us? Maybe you could have a year's sabbatical? Compassionate leave? I'm sure your department would be very flexible.'

'Um,' said Guy. He didn't want to say that actually he more or less *was* the department, and that if he left there probably wouldn't be anything to come back to. 'Felix is starting school in September. It's all organised.' Pictures of Susannah smiling as Felix modelled his new school sweat-shirt flashed into his head. She had made him a PE bag already. 'I guess for, um, continuity for Felix, it would be better to stay here.' Even as he said this he thought, continuity, how could this be continuity? And what would be so good about continuity here anyway?

'Well, let me stay then.'

'Mum, it's really kind of you, but we'll be all right.' He knew that they had a holiday in Australia booked, that they had a whole life on the other side of the world. His mum had a part-time job as a museum guide, which she loved. His dad would be worrying about the garden. Their dogs were in kennels.

'Well, you must promise to come and visit us.'

'OK,' said Guy, but he really couldn't see the point.

'I don't want Felix growing up not knowing his grand-parents.'

'No. Of course not.'

'There is email,' said his dad coming in, hoping for a little something savoury on crackers.

Jenny joined them.

'You could get a web cam rigged up.'

'Good idea,' said Guy. He imagined the pictures it would send: himself and Felix standing there against the backdrop of his dingy study, opening and shutting their mouths but not being able to think of anything to say.

One of the things that Guy did manage to keep up after Susannah died was the bedtime story. It had always been

23

one of his duties, and was often then, at fifteen or so minutes, the longest time that he spent alone with Felix each day. Felix chose the book, and there were many to pick from. Books for Felix had been one of Susannah's few extravagances, they were one of her priorities. Susannah and Felix had made regular trips to the local library, something that Guy would find out, to his cost in fines, some weeks after she died. There had been no stories on those first few days (those days that Guy could now barely recall, that had passed in a fug of tears and disbelief, and noisy, uncomprehending, half-strangled grief). But then, on what must have been the fourth or fifth day, sometime before the funeral anyway, Felix had reappeared in his pyjamas, which were stained with cereal and who knew what else. He was holding a book. It was ten o'clock. Guy hadn't seen Felix for several hours. It was a 'biggest, tallest, fastest' book of facts about animals.

'Please, Dad. We haven't had any bedtime books.'

It wouldn't have been possible for Felix to choose something where emotions were flatter and more absent. Eventually Felix fell asleep and Guy carried him up to bed, then lay down with him and slept too.

A day or so later a health visitor called with some leaflets for Guy and an illustrated book for them, as she said, to share. It was called *When a Parent Dies*. Guy couldn't bring himself to look at any of it, he couldn't even open it. Just the cover was bad enough. He remembered how Susannah had once referred to those sorts of colours as 'bright pastels'. The bedtime books continued, and they were one of the closest connections that they had each day. Usually it was some non-fiction. Guy wondered if Felix was making deliberately tactful choices; unlikely, he knew, in a four-year-old. If it wasn't animals, vehicles or dinosaurs, it might be *Thomas the Tank Engine*. Suddenly Guy was grateful to the Rev. W. Awdry for his plodding prose and plots, the engines' banal expressions and characters. Sometimes Guy would think he was being cowardly, and failing Felix in what they were reading, but he would still stick to Felix's choices. There was so much to be avoided. As they climbed the stairs at bedtime, and Felix brushed his teeth, the words

> *James James*
> *Morrison Morrison*
> *Weatherby George Dupree*
> *Took great*
> *Care of his Mother,*
> *Though he was only three . . .*

would sound so loudly in his head that he feared Felix might hear them. How could A.A. Milne have written such a poem? Huh, The wisdom of bloody Pooh.

Then he thought, perhaps I'm doing this all wrong. Perhaps I should be choosing books that will make us cry. And there were many. At least when Felix was a bit older most parents in books would be dead, absent or dysfunctional. Guy reckoned that in books for seven-year-olds and above it was deemed to make for a better story. Bring them on!

Lots of new books had arrived, and so had some puzzles, stickers and drawing things. Felix liked opening the presents, but he didn't really want to read any of the new books. He liked his old books better. Some of the puzzles were too easy and some were a bit too hard. He hated it if people gave you things that were too hard and you were going to have to wait until you were older, or things that were too big that you had to grow into.

One of the presents was a kit for making a dinosaur skeleton out of wood. His dad said that they would do it later, or another day. Felix was bored of always waiting. He pressed the pieces out all by himself. The trouble was that some of them had splinters, and then he couldn't see how they all went together. He tried to build it, but it didn't look much like a brachiosaurus. He thought that his dad might be cross that he hadn't waited. He smashed it up and hid the bits in a bag under his bed. He had a go at drawing a brachiosaurus instead, but it kept going wrong. He tried out all the new pens, and then left their tops off to see if his dad noticed. He drew tiny pictures on the wall beside his bed. Dad didn't even notice that either. The next day he put all the lids back on the pens because he didn't really want them to run out. He watched videos. Dad didn't mind if he watched them again and again.

Guy tried to talk sense to himself. Terrible, stupid, random things happened. And one had happened to them. If Felix had been the one to die then at least Susannah and he could have swiftly killed themselves. Everything hung by a thread, all life, all happiness.

Sometimes the thoughts bored him, but he could not stop them. He wondered whether anyone had ever managed any original thoughts when something like this happened to them.

The world was full of stupid random events.

He remembered a friend of Jenny's who broke her neck when she slipped on a pencil, and a case he saw in the paper of some poor soul being accidentally electrocuted in a metal-walled public loo on a seaside promenade.

Think of history, the untimely demise of so many kings and queens in so many ridiculous ways, to say nothing of all the millions of ordinary, undocumented people. Tennessee Williams choked to death on a bottle cap. Everything was an accident. One big cosmic accident. These sorts of things were to be expected. They fitted. In this universe, the nonsensical and the random were to be expected. They should not even be remarked upon.

Guy hadn't seen the piece on *South Today*. Somehow he was aware that there had been articles about the crash in the local paper, but he didn't read them, and would never have deliberately kept them. Worst of all for Guy, there was an article in the university's own glossy publication. A short account of what happened, then a long glowing obituary of Julius East. It seemed that he was a professor in his prime, with a long list of publications and contributions to text books and journals. There was a short piece about Susannah who, the reader was left to surmise, had just a minor part in the tragedy; after all she had only been a part-time university library assistant, and had no publications at all to her name. She was only an MA. And wife of Professor Guy Misselthwaite, Department of Botany. It added that she had left a four-year-old son. The publication extended its sincerest condolences to both of the families involved.

Ah, the families involved. Perhaps there was somebody who could tell Guy something. Perhaps East had had a brother, a confidant, or a sister who gave him advice or admonished him on his affairs. Or maybe the brother had a wife, the indulgent sister-in-law who would know all the secrets. He imagined these Easts sitting outside at some riverside pub, discussing things. There must be somebody who knew and could tell him the truth. Whatever they were like, however appalling, he would have to ask if they had known anything.

Guy rang Personnel.

'Yes, Professor Misselthwaite. I do understand that these are special circumstances, but I really cannot release the personal details of one, albeit late, member of staff to another.'

'My wife was a member of your staff too. I'm only trying to . . . I want to express my, you know, share our troubles . . .'

'I'm so sorry for your loss, Professor Misselthwaite. I really am. Susannah was a lovely person.'

Guy ground his teeth. Then help me! he felt like screaming. Instead he picked at something, probably mud, that was engrained in the fabric of his trousers.

'Well, how about you get in touch with his next of kin, and ask if you can give me their phone number?' he asked.

'Of course I'd be very happy to do that for you. I'll call you back, whatever their answer is.'

'Thank you,' said Guy. 'Thank you.'

Felix was at nursery. There was stuff that Guy should

have been doing in the lab. There were reports that he should have been writing.

Guy should have gone shopping, or tidied or hoovered. He should have been sorting out more of Susannah's things. Felix's room was in the state that Susannah had called 'a sty of pigs'. Guy went in, thinking that he might at least pick up the animals and put the books back in the bookcase. The house was in chaos. Everything was always lost now. Susannah had been so good at finding things. She had always known where everything was. He lay down on Felix's bed and stared at the glow-in-the-dark stars on the ceiling, which by day were a nasty shade of ivory. Suddenly it was time to go and fetch Felix back.

The woman on the door at the nursery asked him if he would 'stay behind for a chat'. Felix was sitting meekly on the carpet holding Marmalade. It took an age for the other children and their parents to leave. Why on earth did they want to spend so long standing around chatting and looking at the unidentifiable things that their offspring had made? Eventually one of the nursery women gestured for him to sit down in a miniature chair. She was not the oldest, but her green sweatshirt was the most faded. Guy decided that this must betoken rank and experience.

'Would you like a cup of tea, Mr Misselthwaite?'

'Guy,' he said. 'No thanks.' He imagined it would be served in a tiny cup from the scratched red plastic tea-set that another of the women was busy stowing in a crate with some imitation fruit and vegetables.

'We just wanted to ask how you are.'

'Fine,' Guy almost barked back.

'And just let you know how Felix has been doing.'

'Yes,' said Guy. 'I am grateful that he's still been coming.'

'Of course he has been very quiet, but then he always was very quiet. He's been taking his toy cat round to any of the activities he does. And he often seems very tired.'

'Well, neither of us is sleeping that well,' Guy said. He stared down at the table, not wanting to say that Felix woke up in the night sometimes and cried, and that if he didn't get there quickly enough the crying got more eerie, and then louder because Felix had frightened himself. Or that three times now Felix had wandered around asleep, looking and looking in all of the rooms. He had seemed to want to go up and down the hall again and again as though it were a long corridor. Guy hadn't been sure what to do the first time, but then he realised that he should just guide Felix back to bed and tuck him in again, and wait and wait until Felix was properly settled.

'It must be very hard for both of you,' she went on. 'Also, he does seem to avoid doing the worksheets, but of course we haven't been pushing him. Plenty of time for all that at school. We've got some for you here, these are ones he's missed.'

She pushed the folder across the table towards Guy. He opened it and flicked through. He tried very hard to focus, and to put all thoughts but those of the present, those of this very moment, out of his mind.

Give these six mice a tail. What, he thought, one to share? He pinched himself in the thigh, fearing that he was about to give a great honk, like some big crazy goose, or start guffawing. *Cut out the washing and stick it on the line.* The idea here was to put things in numerical order. *Billie is five. Draw some candles on the cake.* Did they know that Felix could read? *Draw a ring round the things that begin with 'M'. What else can you think of that begins with 'M'?*

'Sometimes he's been a bit tearful, and he was once very vocal to Diane about the bikes and trikes. We just took him aside until he calmed down. He doesn't seem to want to join in with any imaginary play at the moment either. He is quite withdrawn from the other children.'

'I suppose that's all to be expected,' said Guy.

'There was one incident today, he hid another child's toy, Milo from the Tweenies, in the sandpit. That's partly why we wanted to have a little chat.'

'Oh,' said Guy. It was a terrible image. He tried to blink it away. 'Well, we'd better be going. Come on, Felix.'

'Well . . .' She seemed about to say some more. Guy got up. Felix had disappeared.

'He's in the outdoor area. He does like digging in our cocoa shells tray. Probably the smell.'

'Thank you,' said Guy. Outside Felix was pushing a tiny fire engine through a landscape of cocoa chips in a raised sandpit-type tray. 'Time to go, Felix. You'll be coming back tomorrow.'

'Don't forget the worksheets!' the leader called after them, but they seemed not to hear. She stowed the folder in the cupboard. Perhaps she should find out who the Misselthwaites' health visitor was and have a chat with her. Perhaps what she should have been giving Guy was a Lexicon of Pre-School Ladies' Words and Phrases.

A little chat – something appalling to bring to your attention.

A bit tearful – sobs uncontrollably.

Very quiet – miserable/friendless.

Quite withdrawn – catatonic.

Very vocal – crazy with anger.

Stephanie from Personnel rang back whilst he was making some scrambled eggs for tea. Professor East's mother would not mind him telephoning her. He wrote down the number (it was a local one), gave all the eggs to Felix, and set him to eat them in front of *Art Attack*.

The phone rang and rang. He was about to hang up when she answered.

'Mrs East?'

'Yes?' It was a quavering voice, grief-stricken, he supposed, or a very old lady, considering the time she'd taken to get to the phone.

'Mrs East. My name is Professor Guy Misselthwaite. My wife was in the car, in the accident, with your son. I am sorry you lost your son. I'm sure you know that my wife died too.'

'Oh yes.'

Silence.

'Well,' Guy ploughed on, 'as I said, I'm very sorry about your son. And I wondered if I might come and see you. I think we should meet. There are some . . .'

'If this is about insurance . . .'

'No, no,' said Guy, 'it's nothing to do with that at all. I just wanted, thought that we should meet, pay my respects . . .'

'That would be all right. I'm in most of the time. But my brother-in-law, he's been very good, sorting things out, he said, but if it isn't about any insurance . . .'

'Really, it's not. It's, well, our families are linked now, and I just wanted to . . . It's a very difficult time, isn't it? Could I have your address?'

'It's Flat 26, Greenacres, Market Street.'

'Oh, I know where that is.'

'Julius bought it for me. He was a good son to me.'

'I'll come tomorrow morning if that's all right. Maybe about ten.'

Tomorrow came. Guy dropped Felix off at nursery and managed to avoid any conversation with the woman in charge. He drove to the supermarket for milk, bread and cereal. He abandoned his place in a checkout queue to go back for some flowers. The late summer flowers had arrived. He didn't want gladioli. For once chrysanthemums seemed appropriate, white ones. How unpleasant they smelled. They promised a vase life of at least two weeks. He decided to take a bunch of yellow button ones too. As he queued up again he noticed that their sell-by date was even longer than that of the white ones.

He had once loved sell-by dates. As a boy he'd felt a shiver of excitement at the appearance of any sell-by date that reached beyond his birthday or Christmas. You could ignore the ones on things that lasted practically for ever, but when it was some sort of medium-length-life thing, say a block of cheese or a tub of margarine, it started to get really interesting.

'Look!' he'd tell his family. 'We have to eat this by Boxing Day.' Or 'Guess what? We can even eat these ginger nuts on my birthday!' He had liked the way sell-by dates proved that time was marching on, and that other people were

33

guaranteeing that it would pass. It had pleased him that there was nothing that he could do to stop it. Nowadays, 'sell by' was more often 'use by', or just 'exp', and he was mocked by the dates on packets and tins and tubs and jars in the cupboards at home; all the things that Susannah had bought, but would never use.

Greenacres in Market Street was easy to find. The market was a pay-and-display car park most of the time. Greenacres looked like a new block of old people's flats, new flats for old people, new flats for the old and the newly old – Guy couldn't think how to put it. He pressed the buzzer for Flat 26.

'Hello?'

'It's Professor Misselthwaite,' he said, 'I rang you yesterday.' He thought that the use of 'Professor' would help, that it would make her think that he was to be trusted, as presumably she had trusted her own son, or that his visit was in some sort of official capacity, and that she should answer his questions.

The door was buzzed open. In he went through the lobby, past an empty umbrella stand and some everlasting aspidistras. Weren't aspidistras unpleasant and depressing enough without being made everlasting? They were protruding from fake brown compost with fake white plastic balls in it. He went up in the lift.

She was waiting just inside her open front door. She was tiny, must have been less than five foot and, he guessed, in her late seventies. Her hair was exactly the same shade of pale grey as her trousers and sweatshirt. They looked like clothes for being miserable in. He could see no resemblance at all between Julius East and this woman.

A thick, transparent carpet protector led past a shoe rack that held just one pair of shoes (wide, black lace-ups with a pale blue towelling lining), past the open door of a bathroom, to the sitting room. Here the carpet protector ended, but the same carpet continued, pristine and creamy, and flecked with all the colours of sandwich spread. Guy felt very ill. He needed some coffee.

'Julius bought this flat for me. I used to live in Swansea. My husband was Welsh. But after he died, Julius wanted me nearer. It's nice for the shops. It's a pity the market went. It was regular before I moved in. They do have a French one sometimes. He used to come on those days, and if the farmers' market was on. He'd come then.' Guy smiled and nodded. 'There's no point having a great big sack of something if you're all by yourself most of the time though, is there? How would I get through a whole carrier bag of rhubarb with the leaves still on?'

Guy could see into the kitchenette where there was a tiny pedal bin. The poor woman must have filled it and re-filled it with rhubarb leaves. He nodded and tried to smile some more.

'Anyway,' she said, 'would you like a cup of tea? Or I've got some of this special coffee. Julius would never drink instant like other people. He always brought some of this with him. I don't like it, but we might as well use it up.'

Let his superior coffee turn to bitter dust in the cupboard.

'I would prefer tea,' said Guy. 'Definitely tea.'

'It's all tea, tea, tea for a while, isn't it? Everybody giving you tea. And I'll put these in water.' She put the chrysanthemums into a cut-glass vase. They were much too tall for it. Guy wondered if that was how she liked them to look,

35

or whether he should trim the stalks for her. They were very woody, and probably too tough for her to manage with her own lignified hands. The wrappings from the flowers filled the pedal bin.

Guy pretended to look out of the window whilst she made the tea. There was nothing much to look at, just people parking and looking for the best spaces. She had a small balcony with tubs of trailing carnations (mail order, low maintenance, extended flowering period). He went over to a glass-fronted cabinet. Amongst the legions of china animals and dolls in elaborate costumes were framed photographs.

A family group, 1960s, a seaside holiday. The parents looked old for parents. Here was Julius East, unmistakeable, holding his shrimping net. He looked like a Roman soldier. Beside him a little girl, a younger sister, dumpy in a wrongly buttoned cardigan over her bathing costume. She was eating an ice cream, but looked sulky. A barrette failed to keep her hair from blowing into her eyes, and probably into the ice cream. Had Julius already finished his? Did he forgo them? Perhaps the flavours available on Welsh beaches in the 1960s weren't to his liking. And here he was in a graduation shot, his hair all slicked back. He looked like a young Tory politician, self-basting.

Now Mrs East was coming back with the tray.

'It's an unusual name, Julius. He grew up in Swansea?'

'That's right.'

'It must have been a very unusual name there, back then.'

A saucer rattled against the milk bottle as she put the tray down.

'Oh, he came to us with it, he was adopted, you see. It didn't seem right to change it. It was all he had. We'd given up hoping for any of our own. It was often the way. But then along came Jenny.'

'I have a sister called Jenny too. Your Jenny, she must have been devastated, I mean about the accident.'

'Well, they've never been that close, and she's very busy with her career. She's a hospital administrator, and not even married. No grandchildren for me.'

'I'm sorry.'

'She lives in Reading. They said it's not that far if you can drive, but I can't. Now I wish I'd stayed in Swansea. At least I knew people there. And I had my own garden. All I've got here is my balcony . . .'

'I've seen. Those are nice Alpine carnations.'

'Thank you. Here's your tea.'

'My sister used to collect those little china animals. They had a name . . .'

'Whimsies.'

'Oh, yes. Whimsies.' Guy sipped his milky tea. 'Mrs East, my wife was in the car with your son, in the accident. She died too.'

'I'm sorry for your loss too.'

'Thank you.' Guy stirred his tea, even though he didn't take sugar. 'Mrs East, did your son ever talk about my wife? Her name was Susannah. Susannah Misselthwaite. She worked in the university library. You see, I'm trying to find out. I don't even know why she was with him in the car. I don't know . . .'

'Susannah, you say?'

'Yes, Susannah.'

'No. I didn't know about any Susannah. I don't remember anyone called Susannah.'

'Did he bring his girlfriends to meet you?' Guy asked. How could he be asking this? He winced, closed his eyes for a few seconds, felt his stomach lurch. That tea.

'He did have lots of girlfriends, but they didn't really come to see me. But you said this Susannah was your wife.'

'Yes, my wife. People always remembered her if they'd met her. She was very pretty. Half-Swedish.'

'Oh. All his girlfriends were pretty. He was engaged once, in Spain. But they broke it off. I don't know why. I don't know all the answers.' She began to cry, very quietly.

'Mrs East, I'm so sorry. I didn't mean to upset you.' He fetched some kitchen roll, each sheet had a border of purple leaves, but when he tried to give it to her he saw that she already had a hanky balled up in her fist. 'Would you like me to call somebody to be with you?'

'No, that's all right. I'm used to being on my own.'

'I think I'd better go. I'm sorry.'

She just nodded.

'I'm really sorry,' said Guy.

The lift was still there. Down he went, and out past the aspidistras.

He thought that he might as well go in to work. When he got to the lab, he wished that he had just gone home. What was he to do now? At least as it was the middle of summer there were hardly any students about.

There didn't seem any point in trying to contact East's adoptive sister – he was hardly likely to have confided in a sulky hospital administrator from Reading.

Guy considered his options. He could go sniffing around

Languages, and try to find some friend of East who might know something and be prepared to tell him. He didn't know anybody in Languages. What would he do, email the whole department? Stand in the corridor where they all had their offices and yell?

A mug of tea appeared in front of him.

'Guy,' said Jeanette. 'You looked like you could do with this. Are you OK? What are you doing?'

'Nothing,' said Guy. 'I am doing nothing.'

When he looked up again he saw that she was gone. A cheese and tomato sandwich had appeared on a paper plate beside him. He ate it and then did some paperwork.

Guy was aware that everybody felt sorry for him. He might as well have had his own pathetic obituary printed in the university magazine. Now he might as well be wearing a sandwich board saying, 'Yes, I am he.' He might as well have a set of horns attached to his head.

He carried on going in to work when he could, but he kept his head down. He avoided gazes. People came and told him how sorry they were . . . if there was anything they could do . . . help with Felix . . . anything at all. He nodded, dumbly. Colleagues from the Biology department asked if he would like to go out for a drink, or come over for a meal. Sometimes he did, and took Felix with him. They only had to go once to each family.

There were so many things that Susannah hadn't told him. Why hadn't she mentioned that the sandpit lid leaked, and that the sand would become almost instantly green in its stagnant pools of trapped rainwater, that it must be bailed out regularly with Felix's bucket? She might at least have mentioned, just out of scientific interest, that tiny but many-celled organisms would appear in this water if he neglected his duties for even a week.

She might also have mentioned the tiny flies that would spontaneously generate if one of Felix's flannels was left by the kitchen sink for too long. He decided that flannels were pretty unsavoury things and chucked the lot away. Why had they needed so many anyway? He taught Felix how to wash himself with his paws alone. No flies on us, he thought, ha ha, hollow laughter.

Everything about Susannah had been so pristine, or so he had once thought. He wondered what else he was failing to see.

He made all the mistakes, and forgot all the things that people, and probably Susannah, would have expected him to. He dyed the washing pink and blue and grey. They ran out of everything constantly: cereal, bread, fruit, milk, clean clothes. He was glad that they had no pets. Then one day he remembered Felix's sea monkeys. Oh God. The tank would be a dried-out graveyard or an algae-coated prison by now. He sprinted up the stairs. The sea monkeys were alive and well, perhaps even reaching a demographic crisis. Felix had been looking after them all by himself. He must have been carrying tiny quantities of cooled, boiled water up the stairs, and standing on a chair to keep the tank topped up and feed them. There in a cup from a dollies' tea set was the tiny little algae-scraper-tank-cleaning tool that Susannah had got him mail order. Behind the sea monkeys' tank was the optical screwdriver he had been missing for weeks. He pocketed it and lay down on Felix's bed. What was that crunchiness under the sheet? He pulled out some minutes of a faculty meeting and three student assignments. Perhaps Felix had drawn on them by mistake and then been too worried to say. Of course he wouldn't have been cross. But no, they were unmarked.

He waited until teatime to talk to Felix about it.

'Felix, you do know that it is wrong to take things that don't belong to you, don't you?'

'Yes, Dad.'

'Well, I found some things in your room, and I wondered how they could have got there.'

'But Dad, those things weren't stolen out of your bag. They were lost.'

'Felix! Then you did take them. And what about my little screwdriver?'

'Lost too.'

'And is anything else lost?'

'I don't know.'

'Felix, if you take something and put it somewhere, then that thing isn't lost, it's taken, stolen.'

'I wanted them to be lost.'

'Why did you take them?' Felix started to cry. 'Oh, come here, have a hug. I'm not cross now.'

'When things got lost Mummy always found them for us. I thought if some things were lost, she might, she might . . .'

Guy was crying too now.

'Felix, I wish it would. But it wouldn't work. She can't come back.'

4

JUST A FEW WEEKS later Felix started school, a stumbling start, it seemed to Guy, a terrible parody of what starting school should be like. On the first day Guy waited in the playground to collect Felix, desperately hoping that it had all gone well, that Felix would have been happy and making friends and feeling a part of things. At last Felix appeared, near the back of the line, with his coat trailing on the ground. He looked beyond Guy, stared wildly about the playground, and then burst into tears. Guy knew at once that Felix had been hoping or even expecting that Susannah would be there to meet him.

Several times a week Felix would bring home notes. Often the teachers wrote Guy messages on sticky labels and stuck them to Felix's sweatshirt so that they could not be missed. Perhaps they suspected him of wilfully ignoring the notes.

Clean non-leaking water bottle required!

No dinner money! Send in on Mondays for the whole week please!

Plimsoles too small. New ones ASAP!

20p required for biscuit-making!

Small packet of tissues needed for Felix's tray!

Occasionally the notes were complimentary.

Felix made a lovely junk boat today!

'Well done, Felix. Those Chinese boats are beautiful, aren't they?' Guy said. 'How did you do the sails?' Felix just looked at him.

And all these exclamation marks! Were they meant to emphasise what was being said, or an attempt to make it appear less bossy?

One day the sticker said, *Please check Felix for little visitors!*

What the hell did that mean? Guy accosted the nearest playground mummy.

'He's probably got nits!'

Oh hell.

But it turned out that this was an eventuality Susannah had planned for. There was an unopened bottle of special herbal shampoo and an electronic combing device on top of the bathroom cabinet. As he stood there electrocuting the tiny parasites, he begged Felix:

'Please, Felix, tell me when you need something. Tell me when I am meant to do something I don't know about. Just ask! Please! I won't be cross. If they say you have to have something, just tell me. I'll do it. I promise to do it.'

Felix was silent. They both listened to the buzzes of the nit-nuker.

'Isn't it a bit cruel, Dad?'

'We have to do it.'

'If I've got them, you might too.'

'Were you listening to me just now, Felix?'

'Yes, Dad.'

'Say you promise to tell me, and to ask when you need things.'

'OK. I promise.'

'Thanks.' Guy kissed him on the shoulder.

'Well, can you cut my toenails? They keep breaking and hurting. And can we have the video of *Atlantis*?'

When Guy sat there late at night, looking and looking at the photos, searching, dredging for clues, it seemed there was nothing. What a dolt he was. A bloody dolt, his dad would have said. And too bloody lazy to have taken many photos. They were nearly all of Felix and himself in locations, and of the locations themselves.

Occasionally he had said, 'Here let me take one of you.' Sometimes he'd remembered, but usually Susannah had had to ask him to take one of her. The only photos he had taken on his own initiative had been of trees and plants. And these he had kept separately in his own private, selfish little albums. What on earth had he been thinking of? That was how he had recorded holidays and outings. The names, pictures, habitats and exact locations of plants. And he hadn't even needed to write any of it down. He would have been able to recall it all perfectly anyway. He still had all of these notebooks; hateful, self-indulgent little note-books with waterproof covers.

Back then, Susannah had laughed at him.

'You are a gatherer, I think, not a hunter.' How he had loved it when her speech had halted slightly, a sign that she was thinking in another language. 'Your ancestors must have been the magic herb-finders. Mine too, I expect.' Yes, he thought, her dad was interested in plant chemistry, her brother was a botanist, and her mother had been a botanical illustrator. She must have loved botanists, and thought that they were normal.

There had been a brief time when he had done his fair share of the photography. The albums changed and multiplied suddenly when Felix was born, as though when Felix arrived time had slowed down. From a few films a year there were suddenly dozens. He had taken the 'mother and baby in the hospital' shots, and those of the very first days, and of when Felix met the few relatives they could muster.

But Susannah had resumed her role as family photographer soon after the 'first trip out' pictures. First piece of toast, first tooth, first crawl, first steps, first birthday, and so on, and so on. The photographer had been Susannah. Yet another failing on his part. The photos stopped suddenly. And so, Guy realised, had the holidays and the parties and the trips.

Perhaps Felix was old enough for a camera of his own. Felix would love that. Or, Guy wondered, was he just so lazy that he wanted his son to take all the photos of his own childhood?

Guy loved it now if some celebrity admitted to bad times.

'And tell me,' the interviewer always asked, with a drop in tone to the ultra-empathetic, 'were there ever times when you considered suicide?'

'Well, once or twice, in my very darkest hours . . .' was the invariable reply.

'Ha!' thought Guy. 'Once or twice! Once or twice a bloody minute, more like.'

But of course he couldn't. There was Felix.

One night, up late, drinking too many cans of beer again, unable to sleep for tiredness, he watched *Once Upon a Time in America*. There was Robert De Niro, all goodness spent, all alone, lying for days on end on a bed, smoking opium, completely lost and oblivious to the world. That's what I want, thought Guy, a holiday in an opium den, complete oblivion. He fell asleep on the sofa and woke up at 4 a.m., freezing and with a crick in his neck. He shuffled up the stairs, and stood for a while watching Felix breathe. The sky was turning grey. He thought he might just go outside and do a bit of gardening. The realisation that he would look like someone digging a secret grave almost made him smile. He went to bed instead. The next morning he was up again at the usual time, showered, shaved, dressed in the usual clothes, making Felix the usual breakfast. What else could he do?

Erica Grey knocked very lightly on the frame of the greenhouse door. The paint was peeling into sharp little flakes. Erica's knuckles were tough and shiny from summers of horse-riding and dry-stone walling, sailing and environmental projects, but she still had to suck a splinter out of her middle finger. Professor Misselthwaite didn't seem to hear her. He was staring hard out into the botanical garden. She followed his gaze, wanting to know exactly what it was that interested him. The wind was sighing in the bamboo. Two yellow wagtails were dipping at the edge of the stream. She would have loved to rig up a time-lapse video camera to record the growth and collapse of that gunnera. Perhaps now one day she would.

She knocked lightly again. For some reason he had an old-fashioned, zinc-white alarm clock on the bench beside him. She stepped lightly around the side of the greenhouse and saw that his eyes were closed. He couldn't really be sleeping, sitting up like that. Erica knew that Professor Misselthwaite's wife had been killed in an accident. She would not intrude. She walked across the meadow and sat down on a bench to write him a note.

Dear Professor Misselthwaite,
    I have been told that I have got the funding for my PhD.
    Erica Grey.

So what was she going to do now? Tiptoe back in, leave the note on the bench, and possibly disturb and embarrass him? She might as well just send him an email and arrange to go and see him some time when he wasn't so, well, out of it.

Then the alarm clock went off. Too loudly. Anybody else, or a person in a cartoon, would have jumped a foot, but she saw him reach out slowly and switch it off. He rubbed his eyes and put the clock in his big leather bag, the one he always had at lectures. It was the sort of bag carried by doctors in story books.

Then he was coming across the meadow towards her. She got up and smiled.

'Ah, Erica,' he said, 'Erica Grey.'

'The letter came today,' she said. 'I got my funding.'

'Oh, good. Well done. And where was it you were going?'

'Here. I'm staying here.'

'You are? Oh, that's excellent. I thought you would have wanted to go somewhere else, Cambridge, the States . . .' He seemed to have forgotten that he had helped her with the application. 'Are you sure you want to stay here? It is a bit of a backwater in some ways.'

'I like it here. Lots of freedom. No interference.' She looked around at the garden.

'Good. Well, come and see me and we can talk about getting started. I have to go and collect my son. My watch is lost at the moment. You don't have the time, do you? I'm not sure if the clock I've got is very accurate.'

'Five to three.'

'I have to go. I'm late. I have to collect my son.'

She nodded.

She watched him go, up the zigzag path and towards the secret gate.

Before the accident Guy had made occasional forays to the shops if something had been forgotten or was needed last minute, especially when Felix was a baby. But he had left most of the shopping to Susannah. Now he wondered if maybe she had been bored out of her skull. All this constant needing of things. Surely it should be the case that you did things once, and then they didn't need doing again?

Not so, it seemed. Now that he had reached a point of thinking, at least a little, about what he was doing, rather than just crawling through the fog each day, he decided to try to make his housekeeping as streamlined as possible. Really, the shops were full of things that nobody could possibly need. He would just zip round. He couldn't decide which was worse though, wasting precious work time whilst Felix was at school, or going with Felix in tow. Yes, he would zip round. This was what he resolved. Every time.

Somehow he would find himself snarled up in the Homewares section, staring at plastic racks to go on draining boards or DVD players for £39.99. Move on! Speed up! he told himself. If Felix was with him they would then get snagged at some unseasonal display of seasonal geegaws. It would take them half an hour even to make it as far as the fruit and veg.

Then one day Felix said, 'Dad, why don't I have slippers any more? They have slippers here. Only £4.99.' And they were sunk.

He couldn't remember what size Felix's feet were. When Felix took off his shoes the insides were so worn that no number was visible. None of the slippers seemed to fit anyway. In the end they gave up.

'Felix. We'll have to go to a proper shoe shop and get your feet measured.'

'OK, Dad.' Felix looked longingly at the slippers, their bright, brushed-nylon colours and motifs of animals and cartoon characters. He would have loved some of the frog ones.

A week or so later they would get a pair of the most boring shoes in the history of the world and some brown checked slippers like the ones old men had on TV. These slippers would dwell for all eternity unworn under Felix's bed. He would never ask for slippers again.

Distractions like the slippers came up every week. It was no wonder that they ended up hardly buying any food, and often they would get home and Guy wouldn't be able to think of anything much for tea.

There had been another time when Felix had said that Marmalade had been stolen out of the trolley. They had spent twenty-five minutes queuing at Customer Services to fill out a form, and then been too tired to do much shopping. When they got back (without eggs, milk or Cheerios), Marmalade had mysteriously magicked himself back home and was sitting on the stairs.

They would often meet people Felix knew from school who said hello to them; at least the parents said hello. The children seemed to have a policy of not even acknowledging each other's existence, although when he quizzed Felix later it would emerge that this was some child he sat next to in Literacy, or opposite in Numeracy, or on the same table with at lunchtime.

Even so, just meeting a person who said hello at the supermarket made Guy feel, at least temporarily, that he had a footing in the real world, and was perhaps a real person. He didn't get the same feeling from dealings with his students at all. He could barely remember their names. They were all getting younger and they all looked the same. It was lucky that Erica, his PhD student, was taking on some of the teaching. She was very friendly to Felix too, whenever he was hanging around in the garden or the lab. She would chat to him and sometimes play a game of boxes or hangman. Guy had seen them fishing in the stream with bits of bamboo.

The other day Guy had seen Erica walking across the campus, her tall figure, like a young poplar, striding along, talking animatedly with some young fellow who was even taller than she was. They were both carrying motorbike helmets, swinging them as they walked. Perhaps she had other reasons for staying around. No, he thought, she's far too sensible to be swayed by anything like that. Watching them walk away made him remember a damp holiday he and Susannah had once taken. Why on earth had they wanted to go to Herefordshire? All he could remember about it now was the chill of the mattress and the line of poplars that marked the boundary of the farm. Had they been happy? He had thought so. Perhaps he had been too preoccupied, his thoughts as usual elsewhere, to notice. And had Susannah been happy? She had seemed it. He had never been in the habit of asking her. Did that mean that she was? Was that a sign of a good marriage, or of happiness, not having to ask these things?

Professor Judy Lovage sat in her office looking through some of the year's applications for undergraduate places. Of all the extra duties one had to undertake, this was one of those she minded the least. There were so many dreadful committees and sub-committees that one might be manoeuvred onto instead.

Each year she was surprised at how recently her potential students had been born. It was interesting to see how names came into and then fell out of fashion. She always found some of the forms touching. Unfortunately plenty of others would be irritating. Surely somebody at each candidate's school could take it upon themselves to check their students' grammar and spelling? Talk about not putting your best foot forward. At the moment the department received far more applications than there were places. She had to be scrupulously fair. Here was one from a Madeleine Jones. So many of the students came from Sussex and Surrey . . .

Madeleine Jones tried to imagine Gatwick as being glamorous. There were posters from about a hundred years ago of an aerodrome and people in flying jackets and silk scarves. Her mum had told her how, when she'd been a teenager, they'd gone there in the evenings to drink delicious freshly squeezed orange juice and eat ice cream from the new American café that had thirty-six flavours and gave you free tasters on little spoons. Her mum couldn't remember if it had been called something like Dayvilles or Baskin Robbins. Anyway, it had been exciting.

London Gatwick. How could they call it London Gatwick? It was a million miles from London, a halting train ride through sodden Surrey fields. She hated the stupid way that cows didn't stare when a train went by. But Gatwick was all right sometimes.

Sometimes she stayed on the train through Gatwick, all the way to Brighton. Ideal destination, as her mum put it, for a bit of bunking off. (Her mum used to bunk off to Brighton too.) But when Madeleine got there, she wandered the Lanes, and each time she couldn't quite believe that she had found it all, that that was it. She had a feeling that there were a whole lot of other Lanes she couldn't find or was being denied admittance to. She always seemed to get caught in the same loop, going past the same antique shops (closed) and clothes shops where she couldn't have afforded anything, the same cafés, and the same bars. She always ended up in the proper shopping centre, looking at the same things she had looked at in the same shops (but nearer home) the weekend before. Sometimes she bought an ice cream and ate it in the garden of the Brighton Pavilion (she was doing the Regency for A level). What she needed was more money. Then she could really buy stuff.

The next time she had a day off she just got the train as far as Gatwick. Loads of people at college worked there. There were signs in almost every window. She could have her pick of jobs. She would never do anything fast food. She quite fancied Lush but maybe the smell would get to her after a while. A few years ago she'd imagined that every branch of Lush had people out the back making all the scrubs and soaps and stuff. She would have loved doing that, she really liked cooking. No, if she worked at Lush it might put her off nice things.

How about Accessorize? She really liked Accessorize. Her mum would love it if she had a staff discount there. But there had been that time in the Croydon branch. She'd been about to put a pair of earrings up her sleeve when Raquel Palmer had been caught putting some gloves into her bag. They'd taken all of their names, and they probably had a database. She didn't want to work anywhere that sold shortbread and Union Jack stuff. What she should really do was go round and see where they paid the most. She went into BagelExpress to think about it over a Danish. There were only two other people in there, and the guy behind the counter who looked like Dr Kovac, her favourite doctor in *ER*.

This one might be all right.

Dr Kovac gave her an application form, and she filled it out there and then. The manager was on his break.

The manager had rung her on her mobile before she even got home. Yes, she could do Saturdays and some Sundays, even some evenings. She could do bank holidays and school holidays. Would she go for an interview on Saturday and maybe start then too if it all went well?

When she went on the Saturday she thought it must be Dr Kovac's day off. It turned out that he'd left. Her shifts seemed to coincide with those of two Dutch students. They were quite nice, but they kept lapsing into their private language. She and the Dutch girls were very clean, but she kept wondering about all the stages before them, and all the stages before any food anywhere reached anybody. Imagine all the processes, the ingredients, the production, refrigeration, the transport. Too many people involved; and yet the customers ate up every scrap.

Then she got bored. She kept accidentally going shopping in her breaks and spending almost as much as she was earning. Sometimes she hardly had anything left for shopping with her friends. Her mum said that she shouldn't be working so many shifts, and that she should be saving up, anyway. She kept saying that Madeleine would earn much more in the long term if she went to university. And she'd meet some really nice people. And somebody special.

Madeleine Jones's application was very average, but 'Visiting the Brighton Pavilion' was listed as an interest, and even though it came after 'jazz dance' and 'baking', Professor Lovage put it on the 'Offers' pile.

It was around this time that somebody on the Estates and Grounds Sub-Committee thought of the botanical garden. Funding had been identified and sponsorship was in the process of being secured for the new sports science facilities; facilities that would include a 400-station gym and a sports injuries treatment centre. There was nobody from the department of Botany on the committee, nobody on the committee who even knew of the department of Botany's interest in the garden; so when the garden was suggested as a potential development site, there was nobody there to raise a hand or even a word in protest. Minutes were taken and sent up to be ratified. A working party was formed of members of the Acquisitions, Developments and Maintenance Committee. Professor Swatridge (Modern History) was to chair it. The wheels began to turn.

5

F ELIX NO LONGER REMEMBERED the phase he'd gone
through when his globe had been new. Every bedtime,
after his story, he'd begged his mum or dad, 'Show me some
things on the world.'

He had really wanted to know, it hadn't just been a way
of making them stay, and keeping the light on for a few
more minutes.

'Show me some things on the world!'

'Where do komodo dragons live?' they'd ask. 'Where
do pangolins live?' 'Where do polar bears live? And
penguins?' Felix would point to the place and get it right
every time.

'Tell me all the scary things that live in South America,'
he'd implore them.

'Where was Mummy born?'

'Where do we live?'

'Where does Uncle Jon live?'

'Where is the highest mountain in the world? And in
Europe? And in Africa? South America? Scotland?'

Felix knew all the answers.

The game had turned into 'Where shall we go tomorrow?' They would spin the globe and Felix would close his eyes and point. They were usually going to end up in the ocean or in Indonesia.

Now, a year since Susannah had died, they hardly ever went anywhere. Their whole world had shrunk to the botanical garden, Guy's work, school and home. Their orbit was predictable and tiny. They shopped at the same shop and bought the same things week after week. They went nowhere. Once Felix was in bed Guy would work, or just sit in silence. He found that if he hummed on one note, almost constantly, it was comforting. He had never been much of a whistler. Felix picked up the humming habit too, so that they often couldn't tell which one of them was doing it.

Guy hardly ever fell asleep for the night in bed. He would doze off on the sofa, or at his desk, or on Felix's floor. One night he fell asleep sitting on his own bedroom floor in front of the wardrobe with its looking-glass door. He startled himself back to wide awake. There he was, sitting alone in his room. With his muddy trousers and crazy needing-a-cut hair, he looked like an intruder, or someone on the run from an institution. Behind him in the mirror was the blue, green and white patchwork bedspread made by Elfie and Susannah when Susannah had been a girl. Guy never bothered to make the bed now – it was perpetually rumpled, the sheets were soft with dust mites – a disgrace to the quilt's Scandinavian ancestry.

He saw too that he'd spent the day with his shirt buttoned up wrong. Dear God. He exchanged his clothes for another, equally crumpled set, pyjamas that Susannah had bought him, it seemed ten thousand years ago. He got into bed. Of course he couldn't sleep.

Here I am, he thought, alone in my room. He got up again and padded through to see Felix. He had his duvet right over his head. Guy pulled it back. Felix's hair had been turned into hot damp feathers. Guy went back to bed with a glass of whisky. He turned on the World Service . . .

What good, he thought, is sitting alone in my room? He smiled grimly as he remembered the school production of *Cabaret*. He had played his oboe in the band. The girl who'd played Sally Bowles had been fearsome and stunning, in character and on the stage and on the athletics field. Strange, he thought, that a combination of fishnet stockings and shorts, plus a waistcoat and a bow tie worn without a collar, could ever be considered alluring. What was the girl's name? Oh yes, Sandra Johnson. A good all-rounder. Had she carried on being wholesome, but into amateur dramatics? Was she living in Berlin, or perhaps sharing some sordid rooms in Chelsea with a girlfriend known as Elsie?

Eventually he slept. He dreamt that he was searching for his oboe. He kept discovering its case in different places, but each time he opened it he found that the oboe was missing.

The next morning, the first thing Guy did was look for his oboe. He hadn't played it in ages. How could he have let it go that long? He took it out, cleaned it and pieced it together. The reed was dry and looked about to crack. It made his lip sore. It was just how it had been when he'd first been learning, and was sometimes too lazy to practise. His fingers were stiff. Oil can, he thought, oil can! He was like the Tin Man in *The Wizard of Oz*, all rusted up. What was it the Tin Man said at the end? Oh yes. 'Now I know I've got a heart because it's breaking.'

He'd been in the band for a production of *The Wizard of Oz* too. He played a few bars of 'Over the Rainbow'. Much too maudlin. Back to *Cabaret*. Felix came in.

'What'cha doing, Dad?'

'Come hear the music play!' said Guy.

Felix sat on the bed and listened. Guy played 'Yellow Submarine' (rather badly) for him, then 'How Much is that Doggy in the Window?' Felix fetched a pile of music books. 'My Bonny Lies Over the Ocean', no thanks. 'Oh Susannah'. Oh hell, thought Guy. Why did everything, all his stupid thoughts, come back to this? If only he could stop having thoughts, if only they could get away. Get away! What a dolt, what a dunderhead, what a dunce not to have thought of it before!

Susannah had spent hours poring over brochures of holiday cottages, circling some in coloured felt pen and then making longlists and finally shortlists. She consulted Guy and would let him pick from the list she had drawn up. It was very strange that his first choice always turned out to have been booked already, and that the one she favoured always happened to be free. This time Guy would draw up the shortlist and let Felix decide on the first choice. There was still a pile of brochures behind the sofa, now several years out of date. Guy rang up for new ones. Wales, Cornwall, Devon, Dorset. He wasn't sure which was best. Maybe North Wales was the place for a father and son holiday. He pictured them climbing mountains, placing a small rock each on the cairn at every summit, maybe a bit of kayaking . . . or at least playing football or Frisbee on some almost empty golden beaches. Maybe they should borrow a dog to take along.

'This one is in Wales, and Wales is the one with the dragon on the flag, right?' said Felix when Guy showed him the brochures and the shortlist.

'Right,' said Guy.

'I like this one,' said Felix. 'It has a swing in the front garden.'

That settled it.

They crawled along the A5.

'We would have got there quicker if we'd walked,' said Felix. He was feeling sick. At Little Chef they'd been told it was a three-quarters-of-an-hour wait for hot food. They'd ordered chocolate cake. It had been damp and heavy. And now that they were in Wales . . .

'It doesn't always rain in Wales,' said Guy. It had the ring of 'You Don't Have to Be Mad to Work Here . . .'

Oh, the A5, thought Guy. The A5. If only it were as small and neat as a piece of A5. How they would zip across that. If only the journey to the holiday house could be as smooth and frictionless as tearing along the diagonal folded valley of a sheet of A5. If only they could just zoom along the hypotenuse . . . but they were stuck in a long line of traffic. The Misselthwaites' old Golf, though reliable and fast enough, was woefully inadequate for this trip. It had no top box, no bikes on the back, and seats for just five people, only two of which were occupied. And their luggage! Well,

Guy had tried, but even with a football and a plastic cricket set it didn't amount to much, and the view through the rear window was hardly blocked at all.

This doesn't look anything like a holiday car, Guy thought. We are impostors in the land of holidays. They had been stuck behind the same car since somewhere around Oswestry. It was a big red SUV. The large, fair, healthy heads of at least six people, a brace of cycle helmets, and many rucksacks and body boards were visible from the Misselthwaites' position below and behind them. Some French loaves were also there in silhouette, ready to make a convenient but tasty supper for the first night of the holiday. Guy had forgotten to plan anything for supper, but had thought of the next day's breakfast. So that was OK, they could have cereal for dinner – it would make them feel at home.

'Daddy, why do all the other cars have boats on top?'

'Boats? They don't have boats.'

'Those canoe things,' said Felix. 'We're the only car without one of those.' He was pointing at the roof of the SUV ahead of them. He could never remember that Guy wouldn't be able to look at what he was pointing at.

'Oh those,' said Guy, realising what he meant. 'They're sort of roof-racks with lids.'

'What's a roof-rack?'

'In the olden days people had these metal bar things on the roofs of their cars for strapping stuff to, mattresses or bikes or bits of bedroom furniture or suitcases. Then they would cover it up with a tarpaulin thing which would flap in the wind as they drove along, and sometimes blow away altogether. Now they have those canoe things.'

'But why haven't we got one? I wish we had one.'

'They're just for extra stuff. I guess we don't need to take as much with us as other people.'

'They look like those Egyptian things, but plain.'

'Plastic sarcophaguses, sarcophagi. Well, they might be. There's no way of telling what all those families have inside them.' Could well be mummified remains, thought Guy. Perhaps the paterfamilias, instigator of outdoorsy holidays, or perhaps the bodies of the fallen. Perhaps friends or relatives who had perished in sandboarding accidents were being taken on holiday, transported aloft as though by giant wood ants. He smiled grimly.

'What's funny, Dad?'

'Nothing,' said Guy. 'We're nearly there. We turn off soon. I have to concentrate now. It'll be after the next little town.'

It was easy to spot the turning because the red SUV slowed and took it first.

'No escaping them,' said Guy. They followed them at the next junction and the next.

'They must be going to the same place as us,' said Felix.

'We're almost there,' said Guy. He had memorised the directions. 'There should be a white house and a garage called Conwy Morgan Motors . . .'

'White house!' shouted Felix. 'Garage!'

'Then it's the next turning on the right. With a post box.'

'There, Dad!' yelled Felix.

The SUV had got there first and was through the five-bar gate and heading up the drive.

Oh, thought Guy, there must be a number of cottages on the farm. He had been hoping for complete isolation.

There was just one cottage with an annexe. He saw Mrs SUV jump out and beat them to the key, which he had been looking forward to telling Felix would be under the flower-pot beside the boot-scraper. The over-sized SUV children were switching off their in-car DVD players and piling out of their vehicle with what looked to Guy like exaggerated, self-indulgent stretches. How could they possibly feel cramped in that huge conveyance? Mrs SUV had the cottage door open.

'Not damp!' she sang out.

Bikes were being unstrapped, rucksacks were flung across the yard. Then they noticed Guy.

'Can we help you?' How skinny and baggy-kneed he felt next to them. The mummy stood with her arms crossed defensively over her pink and green stripy chest. She had travelled in shorts, getting in the holiday spirit back in Guildford, or St Albans or wherever. She probably thinks I'm the cleaner, thought Guy, or a mad axeman in an old Golf with a small boy. Felix might look like a hostage.

'Um, there seems to have been a mix-up,' he said. 'This is our cottage for the week. I booked it with Lleyn & District holidays.'

'Well, we've got it for the fortnight!' she countered.

Oh dear, thought Guy, they might punch me.

'Stay in the car,' he yelled to Felix.

Mr SUV and two of the sons came over.

'Now look here. You were following us and we were here first.'

'He probably tries this on all the time,' said one of the boys.

'Well, we booked it, and I have the details right here,' said Mrs. 'Now I'm sure we can sort this out in a civilised fashion.'

'I've got my confirmation too,' said Guy.

He pulled it out of his wallet with a flourish. 'There!'

'Ha! You're twenty-seventh of the ninth! We're the ones who are twenty-ninth of the seventh, and for two weeks. Sorry, mate. Your mistake.'

'What? Oh, sorry,' said Guy. 'Sorry.'

'No need to apologise,' said the mummy, with the most pleased-with-herself smile Guy had ever seen. The two big boys went sniggering back to the car to unload some more stuff. Guy looked forlornly after them. They were biffing each other, their shoulders shaking with laughter.

'Well, I'll be off. Sorry about that.'

'No need to apologise. No harm done,' said Mrs.

'Sorry,' said Guy.

'You're the one with a problem, mate,' said Mr.

'Well, we'll be off then.'

'Won't you stay for a cup of tea?' asked Mrs. One of the children was, at that moment, bringing in a flagon of Waitrose organic milk.

'Um, no thanks. No. We'd better be off.'

'Come a long way, did you?'

'No. Not far,' said Guy, backing away. 'Stupid of me, really stupid . . .'

He got back in the car.

'Daddy, what are those people doing in our house?' Felix asked.

'Well, there's been a mix-up and they've got it for the week.'

'But it was our house. I chose it. I wanted to go on that swing.' Felix began to cry. Guy could have joined him.

'Just a mistake. Oh, don't cry, Felix. We'll find somewhere else. Maybe we could stay in a hotel. Maybe right by the sea. Right opposite a beach. We'll find swings. Don't cry. Please, please don't cry . . .'

'I hate those people,' said Felix.

'So do I.'

Guy drove back down the drive and, he hoped, off into the distance. There would be no sunset. Another depression was racing in across the Irish Sea. How could he have been such a dunderhead? Why hadn't he checked it and checked it again. Why hadn't he been paying attention? He couldn't even organise a week in bloody North Wales without getting it wrong. No wonder, no wonder . . .

The dates on the booking confirmation were in his handwriting. It was all his fault.

But an hour later they were sitting on twin beds in the Gwesty Rhosyn, looking at a view of the sea.

'I've always wanted to have a go on a balcony,' said Felix.

'Now you can.'

They unpacked their few belongings.

'Let's try to keep our room really neat all the time,' said Guy. He loved the empty perfection of hotel rooms, the uncluttered, anonymous and unsullied look of them when you arrived.

'Shall we dine in or out tonight?' What Guy would really have liked was room service, but he had the feeling that not much would be forthcoming.

'Out,' said Felix. 'Maybe there will be a chip shop café.'

'I'd say that's very likely.'

They put on their cagoules and headed out into the rain.

An hour later they were back, full and happy with the taste of old, cheap fat on their lips, and many butties under their belts. Felix had fistfuls of leaflets from the hotel lobby. Now what should they do? Guy turned on the TV. Nothing at all worth watching. It was half past six. Still too early for bed.

'Fancy a bath in a hotel bathroom?' he asked Felix.

'Maybe tomorrow, Dad. I'm going to make a list of all the things I want to do on holiday.'

Guy's spirits seemed to rise, and his heart to sink at the same time. The list would contain things that Felix had spotted that were far too old for him, or that Guy was too inadequate to cope with. Susannah, he remembered with a pang, had always been the one to make a 'To Do' list on holiday.

'Couldn't we just go for walks and muck about on the beach?' he said feebly.

Felix was already sifting through the leaflets. He had spotted yet more in a folder on the bedside table.

'Pan for Welsh Gold,' he read out loud.

'We could do that,' said Guy. That sounded fine.

'Pony Trekking . . . Mountain Adventure Centre . . . The King Arthur Ex, um, something.'

'Experience,' said Guy. 'I thought King Arthur was Cornish.'

'Maybe he went pony trekking,' said Felix. 'Paintball,' he went on, 'I'd love to do paintballing. Please, Dad, I saw it on TV. It's really cool.'

Didn't Felix realise that they just weren't the paintball type?

'We'll see,' said Guy.

'Can we go to that place with machines by the beach?' said Felix. 'I've always wanted to go in one of those.'

'Um, I think you have to be twelve or something,' said Guy.

'Some of those kids in there looked my age.'

'I expect they just weren't very tall,' said Guy.

'Dad!'

'Maybe.' Guy unfolded the OS map and spread it out on the bed. 'Come and look at this. Now this is where we're staying. These tracks are footpaths . . . We could walk in a big circle, start here, it's just by the beach, then along this path, this is a waterfall. Looks like a big one too. Then if we carry on up here, I don't think it'll be too tricky for us, we should get a really great view. Then along here . . . This tells you how high up you are, and how close these pinkish lines are to each other tells you how steep . . .' His voice trailed off. How he loved looking at OS maps. He really could spend the rest of his life doing it. You could really lose yourself in one. Look at it for hours and hours. Imagine being one of the people who first drew them . . . There were so many walks that he and Felix could tackle, of course he would have to make some allowances for Felix's little legs.

He looked up from the map. Where was Felix? Oh, asleep. Asleep in his clothes on top of the bed. Guy found Felix's pyjamas. He thought that he had packed two pairs, but he could only seem to find the blue and green stripy bottoms and the top of a pair that Uncle Jon had sent from Australia, a print of jolly kangaroos in boxing gloves holding flags. He managed to get Felix undressed and into the crunchy hotel bed (did he detect a waterproof sheet?) without really waking him. Then what to do? Guy could eat the complimentary Highland Shortbread biscuits, or make himself a cup of tea in the little stainless-steel pot. He could watch TV with the sound turned down. He could take a bath and then watch the rain falling on the balcony. He opened the doors very slightly, just so that he could hear the sound of the sea.

The next morning it was still raining. They had the hotel breakfast, and by eight forty-five were all ready to go. Guy wondered how to fill the impossible hours. They walked along the sea front. Nothing was open yet.

'I think the rain might be stopping,' said Felix.

'Maybe,' said Guy. They found the terminus of a steam railway and spent a long time looking at the timetable. If they rode all the way to the end of the line and back three times it would use up the whole day. The first train left in less than an hour. They walked back along the sea front and found that a baker's had opened. They bought cartons of juice and Chelsea buns. They ate them on the train, waiting for it to go. They waited and waited. Eventually it went. Soon they were crossing an estuary, then into the woods and heading for the mountains. Felix had picked up leaflets about all the little steam railways in North Wales. There were enough for them to go on a different one each day. It seemed like a good enough plan to Guy.

* * *

Erica was delighted with her postcard. She didn't even realise that it was the only one they'd sent to someone in England: 'We have been on a different train but eaten the same cakes every day. It has rained a lot. From Felix.' Guy hadn't signed it. They also sent cards to their few relatives. Guy thought that it would create an impression of coping. He was in contact with them all so rarely that he had to improvise the addresses.

At last the week was over and they could go home again, back along the A5, a small, errant bead on a broken necklace of caravans, MPVs and SUVs.

6

AFTER SUSANNAH HAD GONE, most things stayed the same in the house, not by design but by omission. The pictures that Felix had most recently done at nursery, optimistic sunbursts and skyscapes of pinks and reds stayed up on the walls until the Blu-Tack hardened and they slipped, corner by corner. At seven, Felix pulled them all down in irritation. The bags of work he brought home from school – worksheets on weighing and measuring; hand-writing books; pages and pages of tedious (and in Felix's case always correct) numeracy problems; poems; more art; cookies baked at school and sent home wrapped in paper towels; one bag even contained a baby tooth lost at morning play, safe inside a margarine tub, never to be collected by a tooth fairy – these would stand in the hall for ever.

It was now three years since Susannah had died. From a distance you might not think that Guy had changed at all. His clothes were the same, just even more faded and washed. His curly hair, once the colour of wet sand, was now threaded with grey and white, and had the overall look of dry sand beyond the high-tide mark. But if you watched him walk you would detect more of a stoop, a slower pace. He no longer looked much like somebody who was 6 ft 1. There was something even more meandering about him now.

Up close there were changes too. His eyebrows had become two bars of white strands, etiolated seedlings left too long on a windowsill. His glasses, which predated Susannah, gold-rimmed and round, and once ubiquitous in academia, now marked him out as terminally past it. The lenses had a slightly misty milkiness which he didn't notice, so used was he to the cracked old glass of the greenhouses.

It would never have occurred to him to replace them. Susannah had made him an appointment and had planned to be there to supervise the choosing of the new frames; but after she had gone the date was forgotten. Reminders, new appointments, and then jaunty 'It is a long time since you last had your eyes checked' letters from the optician's lay unread on the hall floor with the free papers and the pizza and fried chicken delivery leaflets. Once the drifts started to impede the opening of the front door Guy would sweep them up, like so many autumn leaves, and put them in a box in the garage for recycling. They might stay there until the end of time.

7

THERE WERE TWO ENTRANCES to the garden. The first, the official entrance, was hard to find. You followed a mean little path behind the Geography building. There were signs to Astronomy, to the administration building, to the staff club, to the theatre and gallery, and to the departments of everything, but nobody had ever bothered with one to the botanical garden. The path behind the Geography building ended in a slough of pebbles, that after heavy rain would become just a pool. (Guy suspected an underground stream there, running towards the one that flowed through the garden.) Then if you managed to cross this, there was another path, made from cinders and clinker from the fires that had once failed to warm the first students' halls of residence. This cinder path led to the greenhouses where Guy worked, planting out seedlings, measuring sepals and calyxes, noticing the tiniest of variations in the most minute of details, and where Erica sometimes worked, busy with experiments of her own. She also spent rather a lot of time on other projects of her own devising, such as scooping potentially toxic berries from a pond, or watching pairs of goldfinches. She and Guy also worked in the corner of the sixth-floor lab that was theirs, and of course he had lectures to give and there were students to see; but the numbers enrolling on Botany modules were in decline. Guy tried not to think about it too often. If he had, he might have realised that his so-called Department of Botany was withering and in danger of being cut down completely.

The path continued past the greenhouses, several of which were now abandoned, and should, if Health and Safety came down there again, be made inaccessible with ribbons of red and white tape and copious notices warning of the dangers of broken glass and uneven floors. On very cold nights the greenhouses suffered more cracks. It might not be long before a huge bough from one of the oaks destroyed them all. The glass would splinter into the earth, but the poppies and the chickweed, the teasels and vetches would soon make good the damage, like the microscopic mesh of blood cells that work swiftly to cover and then heal a wound.

Beyond the greenhouses you could choose one of several paths. You could carry straight on and find some grassy banks and an orchard. The trees were neglected and now bore little fruit, and what there was fell into the uncut grass to be eaten only by wasps, squirrels and badgers. Susannah had collected apples for crumbles, pies and chutneys (so popular with her father), but the apples were all cookers, and so of no use to Felix or Guy or Erica, none of whom did much cooking.

The other paths led to little wooden bridges (although 'bridge' perhaps was too grand a word for them). They were constructions of once sturdy beams, nailed together and made slightly less treacherous by sheets of chicken wire. The stream ran several feet deep after heavy rain, but in high summer, or in the now common times of drought, it was reduced to a shallow (but still pleasingly noisy) few inches. On the other side of the stream was an open grassy area, which Guy thought of as the meadow. Many years back the garden's designer had called it a lawn. There was a huge hollow stump of an oak, beneath which dwelt the badgers. Then behind the meadow were the terraces of collected plants, the botanical specimens and trees; Californian nutmegs and maidenhair trees, crimson, yellow and golden maples, several cabbage trees (*Cordyline australis*) and Spanish daggers (*Yucca gloriosa*), smoke trees and sumacs, and a precious white camellia with almost blue-tinged flowers, which Guy had planted. The inventory would have gone on for many pages, but even Guy and Erica didn't know exactly what was in the garden. So many parts had become overgrown, and some slopes were becoming forbiddingly treacherous or too swampy for adults' heavy feet. Snowy, the university cat, was one of the few beings to know every inch of it.

If you walked the length of the meadow you would come to a series of ponds, fed by the stream, and beyond these to a completely wild area of woods that ended abruptly in a fence and the gardens of the road where Erica lived.

You could follow one of two steep paths up the terrace, and whichever you took, you would find yourself at a wire mesh fence and a gate into the car park of the university doctors' surgery. The gate was never locked (it should have been) but almost nobody knew about it. The fence was covered by a climbing, rambling plant, which in late autumn revealed itself to be a Chinese gooseberry. The fruits were almost as round as apples, and as hard as stones, but were, none the less, kiwis.

Guy wasn't actually in charge of the garden, and he had no dealings with the committee that was. The grounds staff came in occasionally to cut the grass of what had once been the lawn. The garden was so tucked away, and invisible from the university buildings, that hardly anybody went there. Why waste resources on something of no commercial use or public relations value?

Now that he was seven and in the Juniors, Felix went straight to the garden after school, knowing that his dad would be there. Each day he hoped to meet Snowy, who was very friendly. Felix would climb a tree, or just sit still until he and Guy spotted each other, or sometimes he would walk around, tapping things with a bamboo stick. It looked as though he were practising for a future as a blind person. He wasn't the sort of child to slash at things.

'Dad; we could make one of those bamboo forest things, like in France. One of those mazes. Do you remember that one, Dad? It's in the photos . . .'

Yes, he did remember. It had been Susannah's birthday and she'd chosen, as her birthday trip, to visit a chateau with fantastic, innovative gardens. There had been pairs of giant wooden legs, as tall as the trees themselves, hidden in the forest, a herd of golden deer made from twisted wire, a potager of giant vegetables, the biggest pumpkins in the world; so many wonders now preserved in Susannah's neatly catalogued albums.

Guy couldn't imagine that those things were all still there, that he and Felix might be able to go there again. They had been the only people at the café (how he admired the French nonchalance when it came to tourist attractions). They had eaten sorbets – peach for Susannah, cassis for him and raspberry for Felix – and he remembered how one of the boules had tumbled from Felix's cornet and landed with a splat in the gravel. Felix had wanted to fit it back onto the cone and attempt to eat it, dust, gravel and all. The waitress, who had seemed haughty when they sat down, immediately brought him another. Perhaps, he thought, people shouldn't be so kind to children nowadays, perhaps it would be best for children to learn early on that all will come to dust, even framboise ices.

Then he thought of Felix in his stripy T-shirts and legionnaire's hat with Tintin on the back and thought, no, let it all melt away slowly.

The bamboo maze was one of their favourite bits. Making one would be quite simple really. But much easier to start from scratch and do it with neat planting, rather than attempt to hack into an established bamboo thicket like those that were growing up on some of the slopes in the garden. Guy considered that he would need a serious machete for that. He didn't have one good enough in the tool shed. Perhaps the grounds staff would have one, but they probably wouldn't let him borrow it.

The floor of the French bamboo maze had been soft. Yes, it had almost certainly been planned, and done by clever planting. Perhaps one day they might . . .

*   *   *

A place where Felix often sat and waited was the huge tree stump that they called the Badger House. The tree had fallen during the 1987 hurricane, and been dragged away by a hired tractor, but the badger's sett beneath it had survived. In fact it had been there for many hundreds of years. Felix had never seen the badgers, but Guy had promised that one day they would come by night and watch. For now Felix left tiny offerings at their portals: half-eaten apples, minute pictures he had drawn on Post-it notes (he weighed these down with the smoothest pebbles he could find), a piece of chalk or string, a sweet if he had been given any at school. Some of the other children brought them in to share on their birthdays, and Felix, unaccustomed as he was to sweets, could take them or leave them for the badgers. He had seen badgers eating peanuts on wildlife shows, so Smarties were probably OK for them, and so were Magic Stars. Anyway they disappeared. He hadn't considered the possibility of pigeons or rats, or that sweets might be bad for badgers.

Felix loved the way the wind moved in the trees. It started as a whisper, was it even a sound? It became a growing swish. Then the whole gust would come as if by magic, as if from nowhere, becoming visible as it moved through the treetops. He loved it when the branches moved. He loved the Beaufort wind scale. He had copied it out from his encyclopaedia and put it up on the wall by his bed.

He often hoped for a 'scale four' when (if only he were at sea) there would be 'fairly frequent horses', or a 'six' which would see 'large branches in motion' and mean that umbrellas would be used with difficulty. He sometimes longed for a 'twelve'. The countryside would be devastated.

The wind seemed to move all around him, and then it would be gone. He would wait for the next gust. He would imagine himself sat on his globe, the wind circling him. He thought of the maps in his atlas.

This gust in the trees right now, where had it come from? It must have come from all the way round the world. From the South Atlantic up to the Gulf of Mexico, across the sea and land to him and then away again. Did winds get worn out, he wondered, or did the same gusts keep circling the planet? He was glad he didn't live on Jupiter where the storm of the Big Red Spot would suck him in and destroy him.

When a gust reached him he would sometimes whistle with it, or put out his arms to greet it and call out 'Helloo!' and 'Goodbye!' Would his words go right round the world with the wind and then come back to him?

His globe was on the little table beside his bed. Once Esther at school had told him that if a butterfly flapped its wings in South America, there would be a hurricane in Europe. He kept on wondering about this. Surely there were millions of butterflies constantly flapping their wings in South America, and these would include giant blue Amazonian ones with wings the size of school dinner plates. Maybe only certain butterflies could cause hurricanes.

If he jumped up and down, would a volcano erupt in Iceland? Or a geyser suddenly spurt upwards in Yellowstone Park?

Perhaps some of his mum's words were in the wind. Perhaps when they'd walked to nursery and laughed in the garden the sounds had been taken away and gone around the world. Perhaps if he opened his mouth the words and laughter would go back in.

Sometimes Erica would come and talk to him or show him things; often he would have noticed the things himself, unusual fungi, when the frogs spawned, or the first buds on something . . . He liked to see what Erica was doing in her greenhouses, and often she gave him sandwiches or apples. She liked the same sorts of things that he did, things that were very plain, cheese on big hunks of brown bread with bits in, hard-boiled eggs out of a paper bag (she told him that her family had twenty-four hens), apricots, cream crackers with butter and Marmite on (Snowy would lick Marmite off his fingers). Sometimes Erica brought him things that were just for him. Often it was a gingerbread man from the baker's, or a carton of Ribena, or, if it was a Monday and Erica's mum, who made cakes, had been to visit, there might be home-made things like chocolate brownies. He was pleased when those Mondays happened. Food at home was unswervingly the same.

One day he said, 'Dad, do you think we could sometimes have something that isn't actually breakfast, or to do with breakfast?'

Guy looked at him blankly.

'Er, not to do with breakfast?' What did he mean? They had lunches and dinners whenever necessary, didn't they? True, the menus didn't change. Cereal, toast, eggs, beans, bagels, potato cakes, Scotch pancakes, cereal for pudding, Ready Brek for dinner. What else was there to eat really? With the amount of cereal they got through, Felix should have been rich in cereal packet toys, but Guy tended to buy only dull ones like cornflakes and Weetabix that usually came without them.

'We have fruit,' said Guy, 'and bagels are an any-meal food.' It was true, most of their meals were kind of toast-based: grilled tomatoes and mushrooms on toast, cheese on toast (well, that was definitely tea-time fare), vegetarian sausages on toast. But really, what else was there to eat?

'I know, Felix, let's have tea in the staff club café. We can have something different for a change.'

When they got there most of the tables were empty. Felix chose one by a window that looked out onto a very small and neglected quad. Guy had never seen anyone go into it although there was a bench there, and a pond with koi carp. Too much blue-green algae was thickening the water. A lack of shelter and water snails, Guy surmised. Perhaps he could get one of those bundles of barley straw and lob it in.

The café closed in half an hour. Pizza was all gone. Likewise the cassoulet, all jackets, mushroom stroganov and a spinach risotto that they probably wouldn't have liked much anyway. But they could have an All-Day Breakfast.

'Make that two,' said Guy. 'And a hot chocolate. And a jasmine tea.' He didn't notice the café lady's lip curl slightly when he asked for his wussy drink.

'I'll bring it over,' she told him. Honestly, she thought, these professors. He didn't look capable of managing the tray all by himself; he'd probably trip over his own feet.

'Is that your little boy?' she asked, noticing Felix, and softening.

'Yes.'

'Mum's day off, is it?'

'Kind of.'

They exchanged smiles. As he sat down, Guy realised that it wasn't jasmine tea he wanted, but a beer. He looked out at the dark green water and the empty bench. For a moment he wished that he smoked.

Then he saw Erica coming towards them, swinging her arms. Could there really be room here for limbs that long?

'Hey Guy, Felix,' she said. 'Waiting for your tea?'

Felix said, 'You can sit with us if you like.'

Other people might have noticed that there was a perfection in the way that Erica moved and in the way that she was proportioned. Her skin was tanned to the colour of well-oiled pine. All those years of working out-doors in the sun or in sweaters that other people might have found too itchy had given her the smooth, brown, hairless arms and legs of an artist's manikin. Her face was oval. She consisted of a set of symmetrical planes. Her shoulder-length dark brown hair was kept back in a single stubby bunch, as thick and straight as a child's paintbrush. Her clothes were completely predictable: jeans or cut-off jeans and a man's green or brown Shetland cardigan or jumper, worn with a plain T-shirt or a very soft shirt. She was without logos. She wore hiking-type boots or espadrilles, depending on the season. There was nothing unnecessary or extra about her, apart perhaps from the length of those limbs.

8

GUY HADN'T OFTEN BEEN ILL, or at least off school as a child. His mother's rule had been that if you could walk, you went to school. Nowadays he would have been the winner of many Headteacher's Certificates for Perfect Attendance. An exception in his record of unbroken terms was when Jennifer and he had caught chickenpox and then, just weeks later, measles. How the days had dragged! Even the Misselthwaites couldn't be sent to school if they were covered in spots.

Once the first horrible phases were over, the days had seemed endless. Daddy was always at work. Mummy was not a natural nurse, and had been irritated by their presence. Even though they were still covered in spots, she treated them as though they were malingering. She bought them Ladybird workbooks, full of sums which were really too easy, join-the-dots, and exercises in producing line after line of cursive 'C's and 'S's and 'O's. Guy and Jenny's elbows were sore from propping themselves up and reading. Guy thought that he'd read every book in the house. He was weary of the Land of Counterpane.

One morning, in soft brushed-cotton pyjamas that really could have done with a wash, he slowly got out of bed. His legs were skinny and pale and wobbly. He made it to the downstairs bookcase and sat down too quickly, feeling as though he had fallen. The bottom shelf was all atlases and reference books that were so heavy they made his wrists ache when he only looked at them. Not quite so heavy and in a faded cover the colour of the school hamster, and bound with cloth that was even softer than his pyjamas, was *Ons Suid-Afrikaanse Plantegroei*. It was a while before his tired eyes saw that it had an English title too, *Our South African Flora*.

'Guy! What are you doing out of bed?'

'Just looking for something to read.' He had the feeling that his mother only wanted him in bed so that she could keep him contained and away upstairs. 'Please, please, can I read this? On the sofa?'

'Well, all right, but I suppose Jennifer will want to come down too.'

'I think she's asleep,' Guy lied. Jenny was doing French knitting. Just looking at it made his arms hurt. She had a tail coming out of the Knitting Nancy that was yards and yards long. She was going to break the school record. There was so much of it that it filled a Spar carrier bag. How he hated that knitting! Sometimes he thought of snipping it into pieces in the night. He would do it with the pinking shears. What on earth could she make with it? Enough little mats to cover all the kidney-shaped dressing tables in the world, to stock all the school bazaar craft tables until the end of time. And Daddy made such a fuss of it. Called her his Spinning Jenny. All Guy wanted Daddy to do was help him with an Airfix model or something. But it was always 'Not tonight'.

'Please let me read this. I'm so bored.' He blinked and blinked, and fumbled in vain for his hanky. It wasn't that he was crying, it was just that water kept coming out of his eyes.

'Come on then. That was made by your great-great-grandmother and some of her friends. They were missionaries. Be careful. It's really fragile.'

He sat on the sofa with a blanket, a horrid, itchy, brown tartan one that he loved. You could plait the tassels.

'Is it nearly lunchtime?' There were another two hours to go. 'Why do we have to have lunch at one o'clock?'

In the end he had some Lucozade. His mum disappeared again behind the frosted glass door of the kitchen.

When the Welsh rarebit arrived at one o'clock he let it get cold. This was one of the most beautiful books he had ever seen. And very old. His mother's name (before she had married Daddy) was written in the front in writing that was worse than his. He bet she would have been in trouble for that.

'This album,' he read, 'when completed, contains 100 cards issued by arrangement with the United Tobacco Cos. (South) Ltd., Westminster Tobacco Co. (C.T. & L.) Ltd., Policansky Brothers Limited, for the benefit of smokers of their products.'

The missionaries must have been dedicated smokers, or at least friends of dedicated smokers, for the album was complete.

The inside front and back covers were landscapes in sepia tones of what the South African veldt of the imagination looked like. Some gentle-looking deer, or maybe antelope or possibly gazelle, were grazing beside extravagant flowers with a backdrop of mountains. His fingers itched for his coloured pencils, but Mum would definitely be cross. He read:

The flora of South Africa is celebrated for its great size as reckoned in number of species; for its endless botanical interest; and also for its richness in plants of beauty and distinction.

The illustrations in this book have been made from a few of the vast number of subjects which the South African flora presents. They depict plants from various parts of the Union, though the Cape Province with its outstanding floral wealth . . .

The words blurred in front of his tired eyes. Nobody yet knew that Guy needed glasses. And Guy, fortunately for a small boy, knew nothing of what was currently happening in the land whose plants were about to enchant him, or that 'Kafir' was now a term of abuse. He looked at the Afrikaans pages. Maybe he could teach himself this language by switching backwards and forwards between the two texts. Or maybe not. The pictures were the thing. He was simultaneously bewitched and soothed by the vivid colours and the exotic names. He had hardly seen any of these plants before. The gardens of England had yet to be overrun by Osteospermum. Here was *Erica foliacea*, and many other members of that family. He read that the flowers of Erica 'though relatively small, are produced in great numbers and are remarkable for their beauty of detailed form and colour'.

It was the start of a long love affair. He gazed and gazed, and tried to decide which one he liked best. Was it the peacock flower, or the wild pomegranate, or perhaps the Kafir honeysuckle or Port St John's creeper? Which one was the most amazing? Was it the stone flower (how he longed for one) or the carrion flower (he couldn't decide if he wanted one of those) or the Big Wooly Protea? Could you eat the cones of the Kafir bread tree?

He kept the book hidden from Jenny. After ten days he was better and ready to go back to school, and he had the whole of *Ons Suid-Afrikaanse Plantegroei* off by heart. There was only a week until the Easter holidays, and they were all going to stay with Granny and Grandpa Misselthwaite in Yorkshire. Guy was taking the book to show them. He had it safely wrapped (and still hidden from Jenny) in a pillow-case in his bag.

Guy often had daydreams about being left behind in Yorkshire, where time and outdoors seemed to go on forever. Grandpa had been one of the gardeners at the 'big house'. He had retired just before it was sold. He said that his own garden was nothing much, but Guy loved it. Granny knew just as much as Grandpa. Behind her bit of the garden (which was where the flowers were) was a little shrubbery where you could hide, and then the vegetables. Guy liked helping with all of it. Jenny didn't help much at all. Unless the job was picking things, she just sat around and watched. Guy knew that she was secretly frightened of worms.

The only rule Grandpa had was 'Be careful in the

shrubbery'. When they were little they'd thought that there might be monsters or bad men in there. Now they knew that it was because of Grandpa's camellia. It was called *Camellia japonica* 'Eleanor Clark'. The family at the big house had given it to Grandpa when he retired, along with a watch, but that wasn't quite so treasured. Grandpa said that it was the only camellia with a little natural blue in the white, and that it was very rare. He said that when he and Granny died, they must make sure that it was looked after. Guy had nodded and promised. When Grandpa offered him a just-snapped broad bean the pact was sealed.

9

M ISS BLOCK'S CLASS WERE going on a trip. Even Guy
couldn't fail to be unimpressed. It was a geography
field trip to the local shops. They had worksheets to
complete and boxes to tick. They would draw maps of it
all when they returned. Felix, as usual partnerless, was with
Miss Block.

'Block,' said all the parents. 'What an ideal name for a
primary school teacher!'

Miss Block had once been engaged. There had been a
chance of her exchanging Block for Benning. But she had
broken the engagement off when her intended had laughed
at the sketches she had made at her weekly life-drawing
class. Miss Block had really wanted to go to art school, but
somehow she had done a B.Ed. instead. She thought of
herself as a cautionary tale. This was her first proper
position, it was only a maternity cover job, but who knew
. . . it was a nice school. Perhaps they would ask her to stay.
She was desperately hoping that Mrs Partridge would find
herself unable to return after the baby was born.

Felix and Miss Block were bringing up the rear. There

would have been little chance of Felix running off, Miss Block speculated, she hardly needed to keep an eye on him. He was plodding along like a little old man; perhaps his shoes were uncomfortable. She looked down at them. They looked like the most sensible shoes in the class. Perhaps he was just bored.

'Do you come to these shops all the time with your mum?' she asked him.

'My dad and I don't go shopping to these shops. My mum's dead.'

'Oh Felix, I'm so sorry!' Why on earth hadn't they told her?

'It's OK,' he said, plodding on.

'When did she die?'

'When I was little.'

Miss Block thought that he was still very little. Only seven.

'It must be very hard for you and your dad.'

'We're all right.'

Perhaps he didn't want to talk about it.

'Miss Block?' Her spirits soared. He did want to talk about it!

'Will we be able to buy things in the shops.'

'Not really. We're doing a survey, aren't we? Counting things, that sort of thing . . .'

'It would be nice if we could buy things.'

The line of children had now reached the shops. They divided into groups. Felix stayed with Miss Block. They also had Poppy and Prue and Sultan and Zak in their group.

Question 1 – How many greengrocers are there?

Question 2 – How many shops selling newspapers are there?

Question 3 – Where would you go if you wanted to buy a kettle?

'Argos,' said Poppy.

'Argos Direct,' said Zak. 'You wouldn't have to go anywhere. You could do it online.'

'I think we could go to the hardware store,' said Miss Block, 'or to a shop that sells lots of different things, like Woolworths. The answers to the questions are here in these shops.'

On it went until:

Question 10 – ('Look, we're on the last one already!' said Miss Block. She found being off school premises whilst in charge of children horribly unnerving.) *Which shop is your group's favourite? Vote for it.*

They all liked Woolworths best. It was a pokey Woolworths, carrying only a limited stock, but the children loved it. It won hands down. It got all the votes except Felix's.

'What would you vote for then Felix?' Miss Block asked him.

'I like the stationery shop. Everything there is beautiful.'

They walked back a few steps to look. It was a bargain, cut-price stationer's. The window display was of wheels of felt pens, huge cases of two hundred, all different colours, and blue, black and green box files (buy one, get one free!), a shredder, an easel, portfolios (the manager was drifting towards artists' materials) and stacks and stacks of Black n' Red hardbacked notebooks, some indexed, some for accounts, some A4, some A5, and some A6.

'I have always, always wanted one of those books,' said

Felix. Poppy and Prue sniggered. A whistle blew. The children were counted. The walk back up the hill to school began. Felix and Miss Block took up their position at the rear again. They had to stop whilst Miss Block had a sneezing fit.

'Don't . . . worry . . . Felix . . .' she said between sneezes. 'Tree pollen.' When it seemed to be over Felix said, 'Oh, I thought you were just doing it to annoy.'

'Felix! What a thing to say!'

'Oh, that's just what Dad and me always say,' said Felix. 'You know –

> *Speak harshly to your little boy and beat him when he sneezes.*
> *He only does it to annoy, because he knows it teases'*

Miss Block smiled.

'And what else do you always say?'

'We say "Off with his head!" if we don't like someone.'

'Well, I hope you won't say it about me.'

'Oh, we only say it about people on TV. We don't really know very many people.'

That evening Miss Block went into the stationer's on her way home. She bought two A4 ruled Black n' Red books, two A5s and an A6 with columns. She didn't know what he might do with that one. She knew that it was unethical, so she saved them for Friday afternoon. The Monday was an inset day, and somehow that made it less risky. At the end of school on Friday afternoon she called Felix back.

'These are for you. I do hope your dad won't mind.'

'Oh, Miss Block. Thank you!' Felix gave her a really big smile. 'He won't mind.' Or notice, Felix might have added.

He took the books home and showed them to Guy.

'Look, Dad, Miss Block gave these to me.'

'Block? Do you really have a teacher called Block?'

'Yes,' said Felix.

'Block. Are you sure? Spell it.'

Felix could.

'Good God,' said Guy. 'Are you really sure?'

'I only wanted to show you the notebooks,' said Felix, rather cross. 'She said on the first day that it was block like a brick.'

'Oh, I dare say it was originally Bloch. German or similar. Ask her.'

Felix would do no such thing.

'Five books!' he said, thrusting them at Guy's stomach.

'Oh yes, very nice. Clearing out the stationery cupboard, was she? Funny time of year to be doing it. Usually do it at the end of term.'

'She's new,' said Felix.

'New brooms . . . new blocks . . . new block on the kids . . .' mused Guy. 'Wonder if she gets sick of people saying that to her.' Actually nobody had yet.

Felix took his notebooks and wandered away. Upstairs by himself he propped them up on his pillow so that he could admire their covers properly. Imagine having five! Just one would have been brilliant. He didn't know why he had wanted them so badly.

He loved the way that they were not only black and red,

but said 'Black n' Red' on their covers. Why would that be? Everybody could see that they were black and red. If it was to tell blind people that they were black and red, it should have been in Braille. Perhaps it was for people who were colour-blind, just in case they happened to hate black and red, but then why wasn't everything labelled with its colour?

Anyway, he loved them. They were smart, serious, and important. And they had hard covers that nobody could rip. He knew that Dad had one in the lab with A–Z, a little one with phone numbers. But in these you were allowed to put things in any order. He loved the way that the pages had margins. They had to draw margins sometimes at school and the ruler would always slip and spoil it. These had margins that magically swapped sides as you turned the pages and hardly showed through. It was several days before it occurred to him that he could actually use the books for writing in himself. He started with an A4 one. Miss Block had calculated correctly that if she gave him enough of them, he wouldn't worry about using them up.

Felix Pieter Misselthwaite
Age 7. This is my book. This was Dad's new pen.
Felix P. Misselthwaite. Felix P. Misselthwaite.
Today I asked if we could have a dog. Dad said maybe. I have a kind of pet already. Snowy is my cat who lives in the garden. A sharing cat. But I don't know who feeds her. Or maybe it is a him. Also Sea Monkeys.
Miss Block gave me this book. Her name is Miranda!!! Miranda Block. Miranda Block. Mrs Cowplain

called her that at playtime. I hope she stays at our school for ever.

I like Erica too. She is very beautiful and kind also. List of why
1. Does not wear stupid clothes.
2. Good at being very quiet in the garden.
3. Knows many insects and animals also more about plants than me. I like creatures better.
4. Brings things to do, like frisbees. Also cakes and drinks.
List of things I know about her
1. Three brothers older than me.
2. She has a sister who lives in France up a mountain with goats and a boyfriend. Also older than me.
3. Her mum has twenty-four hens.

Felix stopped writing. He wished he had some brothers or even sisters. They wouldn't be babies but at least four or five years old so that they could play and do things.

Erica had said that he could go to tea with her soon. He had never seen her house before. She had said that she would collect him from school, and that, another time, maybe in the school holidays, she would take him on a trip somewhere – maybe to a museum or an aquarium.

He wouldn't have minded if the the trip was to the house where her family lived. She'd said it had a river.

10

AT LAST IT HAD COME. Today was the day that Felix was going to Erica's house. He told Miss Block. He told all the children on his table at school.

'Big deal,' they said and, 'Who's Erica? Your girlfriend?'

'No!' said Felix, too vehemently, and they all laughed.

'Felix has got a girlfriend! Felix has got a girlfriend!'

He looked as though he might cry. Miss Block came over.

'Yellow table! Get on with your work! Leave Felix alone!' She couldn't resist smoothing his tousled hair.

'Felix has got two girlfriends! Felix has got two girl-friends!' they whispered as soon as she had moved away.

Erica was waiting for him in the playground. She seemed to know just the right sort of place to stand, not too near the door, as though he were one of the little ones, but not so far away that they wouldn't have been able to spot each other the moment he came out.

'Hey Felix!' she said, and gave him a quick hug, even though she didn't usually when they saw each other in the garden. 'Got all your stuff?' she said. 'No lunch box?' Felix had his anorak-in-a-bag, a navy blue one, and his school folder with a school library book and a three-week-old newsletter inside. Guy didn't know that these bags were meant to be checked for communications every day.

'I have school dinners,' said Felix.

'Are they nice?'

'Sometimes. As long as it isn't fish or jelly.'

'Hmm,' said Erica, 'I can imagine. Especially if they were on the same day. Or even worse than fish and jelly – jellyfish.'

Felix laughed.

'I like it sometimes, but it's a bit noisy. When I started I hardly ate anything because the smell made me feel so sick. I had to breathe through my sweatshirt all the time.'

'That must have made eating tricky.'

'If you are naughty, the dinner ladies stand you up, and then you don't get to eat anything anyway.'

'Well, I hope you never get standed up, I mean stood up,' said Erica.

'I only have been once. And that wasn't my fault. I got pushed and my drink went in somebody's sandwiches.'

'Poor you.'

'Don't tell Dad.'

'OK. But I'm sure he wouldn't be cross.'

'Anyway, it was when I was in Reception.'

'Then he definitely wouldn't be cross. They shouldn't be standing up people who are in Reception. It sounds very cruel. Did you get to eat your dinner?'

'No. But I didn't mind. It was fish and jelly.'

By now they had reached Erica's car. It was a pale blue Renault 4. The front seat was a banquette.

'Can I sit in the front? It's sort of like a sofa for driving. I bet it's really old. Is it vintage?'

'Kind of vintage. It hasn't got any seat belts in the back, so you better had sit up with me.'

'Is it really, really old?'

'Um, nearly thirty. One of my brothers has a garage that fixes and sells French cars. He helps me look after it. I've always just liked these Renault 4s. I might get a van one day. It would be great for moving plants.' She strapped Felix in. 'We could have walked really. I just thought it would make a change for you to have a lift home from school.'

'Thanks,' said Felix.

Four minutes later they were there.

'If you could cut across gardens or wade along the stream, you could probably make a shortcut to the botanical garden,' Erica told him. 'It's just there, behind those trees. Have you heard people say "as the crow flies"? Well, it's not far as the crow flies.'

'If I shouted,' said Felix, 'would Dad be able to hear me?'

'Maybe, but we won't try it. We don't want to worry him. Anyway, come in.'

'Wow,' said Felix, 'it's huge.'

'It is huge, but it's not all mine. Just the ground floor is mine. And the garden. We can have tea outside if you like.'

'Yes please.'

'Who lives upstairs?'

'A lady from Poland. Some music students. Luckily they play nice instruments, and a man who nobody sees very much. I think he might be the real Mr Nobody. He doesn't get much post. We aren't meant to have pets, but the Polish lady, her name is Anna, has a grey cat. He goes up and down that plank to get in and out of her window.'

'It's like a slide. Does she go up and down it too?'

Felix supposed that the etiquette of not going up slides wouldn't apply to cats or to private slides. 'Even in the rain?'

'Anna uses the stairs. Sometimes she sits out in the garden with me in the evening. She's only got a little balcony. I don't think Sebastian (that's the cat) goes out in the rain much. Cats don't like rain, do they?'

'Some cats can swim. One day I might have a dog or a cat and teach it to swim. I have a book with all the names of all the types. Otterhound is best-looking, but I wouldn't let it hurt any otters. Or a Burmese blue for cats. They aren't actually blue, but I would call it Bluey.'

He looked around, wondering what they were going to do. He had always wondered what people might do when they went to tea with each other. There were shelves and shelves, and piles and piles of books, but these were neat piles, not much like the ones at home. They had lots of strips of coloured paper poking out of them, like Guy's, but Guy just ripped up anything to make his bookmarks. Erica's TV was even smaller than the one at home. Felix hadn't known that they came that small.

Erica followed his gaze.

'Would you like to watch TV?' she asked. 'I know lots of people like to watch TV when they get in from school. I used to sometimes.'

'Um . . .' said Felix, not sure which was the right answer to give. He could see the remote. It wasn't lost the way the one at home was always lost. Sometimes they didn't watch TV because they couldn't be bothered to find it.

Erica flicked it on.

'I don't suppose you want to see these. Too babyish,' said Erica. 'Who are they anyway?'

'*The Fimbles*,' said Felix.

'Well, their suits look jolly static-y and hot. I wouldn't want to be in one of those.'

'They have a friend frog who's more normal-looking. And a kind mole who reads pretend books. He has this underground library with all these shelves, and he always says, "Now let me see, which one shall I choose? How about this one?" Then he always picks the same one because the others are all just drawn-on books, but he hasn't noticed. And the stories aren't ever real stories, they are just about these boring children who wash the car and go to the shops,' said Felix. Then he blushed, realising that he had betrayed himself as a *Fimbles*-watcher. Erica noticed his discomfort.

'I suppose this mole hasn't noticed that he only has one book because he's so short-sighted. Sometimes little kids' things are really funny, and kind of relaxing. I used to watch *Playschool* sometimes when I was much too old for it,' she said. This was quite untrue. Her after-school time had been a whirl of riding lessons and swimming and cross-country, violin lessons, even a brief flirtation with fencing. She had been a member of the local Young Archaeologists' Society, Friends of the Earth and Greenpeace. She had spent her summers building dry-stone walls and restoring canals. There hadn't been much time for under-fives' TV. Her whole family had been this busy. It had been one of those houses with cricket pads perpetually in the hall, terrapins swimming in the sink whilst their tank was cleaned, and everybody having somebody to tea.

When she had been Felix's age, Erica had sometimes wondered why she had been called Erica. It was such an obvious version of a boy's name. She had three big brothers: surely it couldn't be that Mum and Dad had really just wanted another boy?

What a relief it had been to discover that it was to do with 'heather' – her mum and dad had been very fond of the plant heather but thought that 'Heather Grey' sounded rather silly (too many colours); they liked 'Erica' better because it sounded stronger.

Erica herself was fond of the whole Erica family. The name 'Heather' did sound rather Sunday-schoolish to her, a bit like a kind rabbit wearing a frock. On balance, 'Erica' was better. Her mum and dad didn't tell her that she had been conceived at dawn in the heather on a walking holiday in the Lake District whilst her trio of brothers were still asleep in the tent. No wonder that she was such an out-doorsy, wholesome person.

Why had she offered TV? It wasn't at all what she had planned. Actually, come to think of it, she hadn't really planned very much, apart from the food. She could play chess or draughts or dominoes with Felix, if he knew how to play any of those, or she could teach him. Her nephews and nieces were all quite sporty. At home they always had big family games of rounders, even when it was freezing.

Then she remembered the *Twits* card game that her niece Lyddie had left behind. It was a complicated 'old maid' sort of game with positive and negative scoring. Felix would love it.

Here it was, tucked into the bookcase, but oh dear, it said, 'For three or more players'.

'Never mind,' said Felix, 'deal out some for Mr Nobody, and one of us can do him as well. That's what Dad and I always do when it says "three or more players".'

They had their tea in the garden.

'Please may I come back again soon?' Felix asked, when Erica took him home.

A few days later, inside one of the greenhouses, Guy was staring at the glass. An interesting pattern of lichen was growing across it. It seemed that Jack Frost had been at work, but with green and yellow paint on his brush. Here were some burnt and raw umbers and siennas, brown and gold ochres, and Naples yellow. There were so many shades of green. Impossible to categorise them all. Could there be names for all of these greens? He realised that he ought perhaps to be cleaning them off, that they would be blocking the light to the plants and his experiments inside. But surely it would be wrong to wipe them away, to scrub out their lives with some detergent solution. He couldn't bring himself to do it. He was coming to the conclusion that everything was just best left. Let the honey fungus take the apple trees. Let the stream silt up. Let bindweed strangle the philadelphus and the roses. Who was he to go destroying and interfering with the natural order of things? Let the meadows turn to scrubland, let the scrubland turn back to forest. There would be nothing but trees.

He didn't even notice Felix come in, and was startled when he heard 'Dad'. It was really only a whisper. 'Dad,' louder this time. 'Erica says she'll take me on a trip, maybe to an aquarium. Please may I go?'

'In a car?' Guy looked worried. 'Um.'

'Please, Dad.'

'Well, I'll have to talk to her about it.' Stupid girl, thought Guy. Why hadn't she discussed it with him first? It seemed rather underhand. He really didn't want Felix going in other people's cars.

'Please, Dad? It would be so cool to go somewhere.'

'We go places,' said Guy. 'We go to the library every Saturday . . .' And, er, that's it, he thought. Oh dear. The thing was, he never remembered to think about other places. Why would he? Who would really want to go anywhere? Wherever they went there would be families and other people's mothers and wives. Perhaps he and Felix should try another holiday, but somewhere there were no other people, or perhaps they should go camping. Felix was tugging at his sleeve again.

'Dad? Dad?'

'What?'

'You know it's Parents' Evening. You do have to go to Parents' Evening. They only gave me this today.'

Felix took the grey and crumpled slip of paper out of his pocket.

'They really only just gave it to me.'

Guy didn't seem to notice how unconvincing this sounded.

'Oh, tonight, OK,' he said. 'You can come too if you like.'

At least he didn't say, 'You'll have to come too, I can't think of what else to do with you.'

When they got back it was nearly bedtime. They had some toast and jam as they hadn't had much supper. Felix went to bed and wrote in his Black n' Red book.

Today it was Parents' Evening. Dad said I could come too. Lots of other kids went too, some whole families were there. Dad said I could wait outside but I wanted to go in and see Miss Block with him. Miss Block said I work very hard, but that I need help to get friends. I said I needed to have friends who wanted to be friends with me. Miss Block said we could talk about it more. Then we went home. Dad said that Miss Block was very kind. I said why don't you marry her then. He just said oh Felix as usual.

11

MADELEINE JONES WAS NOW part of a gang of girls that liked to wear fairy wings and little coronets of pink and sparkly flowers to parties. They would wear their normal clothes which might be anything from jeans and a tiny top (quite likely pink or velour and sloganned) or something vampy. It was funny how they'd all got into it. Madeleine thought it was because they liked to make people happy, and to be happy all together. They never wore fairy skirts (there were girls that did that too), but they did sometimes carry wands. They all liked shopping at Claire's Accessories. It was surprising how many things you could actually need from Claire's Accessories. Madeleine's friend Jo had a weekend job there, so sometimes they had things at discount, but stuff wasn't exactly expensive there anyway. Something glittery or with a few feathers, a sequinned clip or a wide new hairband could really make you feel better. It was like all the pleasure of eating sweets, but without the calories.

Anyway, that night Madeleine was wearing her new top – it said 'Princess' in silver and had the cutest little slits in the shoulders – that and some jeans and pink boots, and of course the fairy stuff.

They went to Bo Jangles and then to Belle-Bottoms, which was where they usually ended up. That's where she saw Thom who was in her History of Art seminar groups. She'd fancied him for ages, really fancied him. He came over and said, 'Not so ill met by moonlight, pretty Madeleine. What's with the fairy gear?'

And then they talked, and then he went back home with her. It had seemed really cool, as though he really liked her.

In the morning she'd got up early, before he was awake, and had a shower. Then she made these blueberry muffins that she often made on Sundays (all the girls in the house really loved them). They were just so easy.

She'd taken in a plate of them with some coffee.

He'd woken up and said, 'Oh God, what is this? Fucking fairy cakes for breakfast.'

She'd seen him looking around, at her room and all her things. And then he'd gone, and that had been that. She hadn't said a word.

She was left there in her lilac pyjamas with the Scottie dogs on, holding the plate of muffins, still warm in their silver paper cases. She remembered a time when she was sixteen and getting ready to go out, and her sister Steph, who was eighteen and was going to be a surveyor, and was totally unfrivolous, totally pared down, said to her, 'Don't you worry about wearing those earrings? What if something really bad happened to you? Or you were having a row about something really important with someone? What if you were in an accident? You'd be so aware that you were wearing those stupid earrings. And whoever you were with would be thinking, "What does she think she looks like in those earrings? Why did she think she ought to hang those ridiculous objects on her ears?" And they might say it, too. If they didn't say it, they'd be thinking it . . .'

Madeleine sat on her bed and ate one of the muffins. She put the rest of them in the kitchen for the others to eat. It was Saturday morning and nobody else was up yet. They wouldn't know if he had stayed the whole night or not, or what might or might not have happened. She went back to bed and cried silently for a very long time because she felt so stupid. She wished she could go round to his room and sneer at all his stuff. And she had an essay to write for the tutorial on Monday. The group that he was bloody in. He had hardly even talked to her before last night. She supposed that he would pretend that nothing had happened. Well, so would she.

That night when the other girls went out she said she had a stomach ache, and she had to do that essay. She made some chocolate brownies for no reason at all and left them out for the girls to eat when they got back. She didn't have any, not even one, she wasn't at all hungry. She sat in her room and finished the essay. Then she began to take things down; first the photos in the furry frames. (Why have them up when she could see her friends grinning at her every day, and she could remember what the people from home all looked like?) Down came the fairy lights from around the mirror. They were stupid if it wasn't Christmas, and even if it was. The disco ball could go to a charity shop. The Beanie Babies wouldn't fit in the only envelope she had. She raided Kath's room. She had some giant jiffy bags, Madeleine knew. Kath's mum was always sending her books. She stuffed all the Beanie Babies in to be posted home. (To be *really* pared down she should have chucked them out, but somehow . . .)

Then away went anything cutesy, anything sparkly, anything unnecessary. The next day she went into town and bought a white quilt cover. She decided to keep her curtains. They were red and white spotted, with tie-backs, and she had made them as part of her Textiles coursework when she was sixteen. She had got an A star. Nothing would stop her liking them even if they *were* a bit, well, toadstool house-ish. But all the other decorations could go. Goodbye hearts, pinkness, bead curtains, wind chimes, dream catchers, funny pictures, animals, fairy things. Goodbye all accessories.

Almost all her clothes seemed stupid too. The same rules applied. She took as much as she could to the Oxfam shop on her way to the tutorial. She supposed that some people might just see it as an excuse to get some new clothes. She would have the bare minimum. Everything simple, plain and not ridiculous ever again. This was nothing to do with Thom. It really wasn't because she cared at all about what he thought, she just wanted to clear things out, to have less stuff around her. It was nothing to do with him at all.

12

PROFESSOR JUDY LOVAGE WAS in her office, staring out of the window and remembering something that had happened over thirty years ago.

'Judy,' he had said, 'I have looked you up. It says that you are a native perennial of the rocky places near the sea. You were eaten by the Scots to prevent scurvy. You are often found on the coasts of Scotland and Ireland but are not elsewhere. I think I shall go to Scotland and Ireland. Perhaps we shall go together.'

'Lovage is just a herb,' she had said. 'Quite common. It grows in lots of gardens. But I would love to go to Scotland or Ireland with you. We could go in the next vacation.'

He had smiled and kissed her. And she had never found out if he had really meant that they might go.

If I had my time again, she thought, would I do things differently? Would I try to pin him down, to discover if his intentions were honourable? She couldn't imagine many of her students putting up with any vague suggestions of promises of a possible future. They would be emailing lists of ground rules to be agreed. Or perhaps they would just take it all in their very long strides. Such big girls, such Amazons she had in her classes nowadays. She hadn't used to be so small. And the schoolgirls she saw on the bus, they were huge, like great, grown women. Phoebe, she thought, Phoebe Enright who was due for her tutorial in five minutes' time, would Phoebe put up with any nonsense?

Professor Lovage thought that Phoebe was astonishingly beautiful. Phoebe had cropped auburn hair and eyes the colour of sea-washed agates. Professor Lovage even excused Phoebe when she wore little tops that exposed her midriff. Phoebe was this year's secretary of the students' DramaSoc, and was still high on her success as St Joan.

Phoebe thought that her eyes were nondescript. She had yet to be told that they looked like agates. Phoebe was on track, Professor Lovage thought, for a First, or at least a very high 2:1.

Three sharp knocks on the door ended Professor Lovage's contemplation of Phoebe's eyes. The students had arrived with their neatly printed-out essays. Here was Thom (as he styled himself), indolent, confident, planning a career in journalism. Professor Lovage thought that his sideburns made him look like an extra from *Planet of the Apes*. She imagined that he thought her to be a spinsterish bluestocking; but what cared she for his opinion of her? In came Max, puffing a little after the three flights of stairs to her office, clutching, she noted with distaste, a bottle of Coke. It billed itself as 'share-size'. Really, she thought, share-size! There would be no sharing of fizzy drinks in her tutorials.

'Here, Max,' she said, 'you can put your pop on this.' She passed him a glass coaster with a sprig of rosemary trapped inside it. A present from one of her many nieces. He looked bewildered. 'Or you could ask the staff in the department office to put it in the fridge for you.' She knew jolly well that nobody called it 'pop' any more. It hadn't even been called 'pop' when she was young.

Here was Phoebe with a pink rucksack printed with roses on camouflage. And finally Madeleine, looking rather wild-eyed, with her poker-straight beige hair flopping everywhere. Her nose looked rather too pink. The child has been crying, thought Professor Lovage. She would ask her to read last, if at all.

'Well,' said Professor Lovage, once they had all sat down and rummaged in their bags for pens. 'Plant Forms in the Gothic Cathedral. Phoebe, perhaps you would like to read first.'

She was aware that Thom rolled his eyes, clearly jealous. She would ask him the first question, and make it particularly challenging.

Later, as Max read his somewhat plodding essay, Judy found her thoughts drifting back to the weekend. She had visited Winchester Cathedral with Jemima, one of her favourite nieces. Jemima was an art student and, to Judy's delight, brought her sketch book. It meant that they could spend many hours in the Cathedral. Judy was constantly astonished at how quickly other people could visit a place. She would see them with their heavy steps in sensible walking shoes, laden down with umbrellas and cool boxes, guide books and money belts (perhaps they feared medieval cut-purses lurking in the Cathedral Close) pausing only for a few moments in front of each object of interest. But there was the gift shop to do, and they must make sure that they had time for that. Slow down, she felt like crying, look up! Jemima had kindly given her some of the sketches she had made of a Green Man, and these were in a folder on her desk. She would put them up on her pinboard. She had longed to hold the Green Man's face in her hands. She imagined that it would feel smooth and warm, as though it were alive, or might crease into life. Perhaps, she thought, perhaps. She had smiled as she traced the outlines of the monkeys and plants carved in the wood of a choir stall.

So many years had passed since she'd last held the face of a man in her hands. Eduardo Ricallef. His olive skin had felt thick and strong, his hair not green leaves, but short tangled curls. Truly black. And his eyes, a surprising dark Pacific blue-green. A cold ocean. She thought she could still recall exactly the pressure of his mouth on hers. Eduardo Ricallef. Chilean poet, visiting lecturer, returned to Chile just before the coup. Never heard from again. What had they done to that long smooth back? To those square hands that she had once said were the hands of a fisherman or a labourer, not a poet? Those eyes. She had to blink away the thoughts, the unforgettable images and words from too many Amnesty campaigns and newspaper ads. He had, or was, as the phrase went, disappeared.

She dragged her thoughts back to the business of Max's essay.

Judy had been named for Judy Garland. It had seemed to her mother to be a pretty and no-nonsense name. In her mother's mind, Judy was destined for white bobby socks and blue gingham. Judy had thought herself destined for ruby slippers. Now here she was in a pair of dark brown Clarks Springers. Not like spaniels, she thought, these shoes had only the shortest fur, closer to that of a smooth-haired dachshund than a silky spaniel; but they did indeed enhance her already springy gait. Judy Lovage, now in her mid-fifties, was as fit as a flea. She swam almost daily and cut quite a dash in her red and blue stripy boy-legged swimsuit. Tuesday evening was Pilates, Friday lunchtime was yoga. She looked on her once smooth and muscly thighs only with affection as their slow transformation into skinny shanks was completed. I had better keep clear of donkey sanctuaries, she told herself, or I may find myself being rescued.

It was easy to feel fond of one's legs when one saw some of those on display at the swimming pool. There was one man that Judy could not bear to look at. He seemed to take some sort of obscure pleasure from unnecessary walks up and down the side of the pool. She also saw him cycling and marching around in shorts. Quite unnecessary. He had a terrible varicose vein running the length of his left thigh. It looked exactly like a Celtic serpent or a symbol on a Viking rune. At first she had wondered if it might have been a tattoo, or some sort of African or Maori thing, even though he was white and middle-aged. Once seen, it was never forgotten. Why on earth did he want people to know of its existence? Judy would have had it removed, whatever the cost, or at least kept it well under wraps. Even if one kept it hidden, she mused, one would still have to live with the knowledge that in the event of one's death it would be seen by the undertakers and any medical personnel involved. She would have been unable to die in peace, let alone expose it daily at the swimming pool and whenever the weather was anything approaching warm enough for shorts. Not that she had worn shorts in public for a very long time.

Though perhaps, she mused, there was something equally dreadful about herself, and nobody was telling her. Perhaps people said, 'There goes that woman with the teeth/arms/feet/hair/hands/nails . . .' It could have been anything and she might never know. This was one of the perils of living alone. But then the man with the serpent on his leg might well be married. Perhaps his wife said, 'Don't be silly. Nobody notices things like that.' Judy suspected that this was not the case. To go striding round like that, the gratuitous wearing of shorts . . . he must either be unaware of the effect that his legs had on other people, or actually enjoy it.

Sometimes Judy found that being alone made everything seem unutterably pointless. It highlighted the futility of all of one's actions. Sometimes everything she did seemed silly. Why cook? Why garden? But generally work did not make her feel like this.

Ah, 'work and love, love and work,' she thought, looking down at her Strawberry Thief PVC-coated tote bag (another gift from another niece). Well, at least she had the work part of the equation. Loneliness was not a feeling she allowed herself. She went to the theatre and to concerts with friends. She visited her sisters and her nephews and nieces. But it could only be a matter of time before somebody gave her a herb-filled tea cosy in a William Morris print.

She remembered the first time she'd seen Eduardo. He was a large, easy, confident man, some ten years her senior. Her immediate thought was that he looked too happy to be a poet. He was sitting in what was then called the Refectory with a group of post-grads and fellow lecturers. It seemed that he had already made friends. He had his arms along the backs of the chairs next to him. Everybody was laughing. She had felt shy and superfluous, and had immediately planned to take her lunch and hide behind a pillar, but Stanley, the then 'heir apparent' of the department had spotted her and called her over. They had all already eaten. How desperately she had regretted choosing an egg salad. She also had a knickerbockerglory glass of fruit salad on her tray, the squirt of artificial cream already melting into a chemical coating for the slices of apple and orange.

Oh, the food we used to eat! thought Judy. Egg salad was available all year. It never varied. You got two very hard-boiled eggs, veined with blue; a few leaves of round lettuce; some bendy cucumber; a quartered tomato that might be mushy or bouncy, but would always be completely tasteless; maybe a radish, and a large pile of cress. The catering became more daring over the next few years, and raw mushrooms, heaps of coleslaw and iceberg lettuce were introduced.

So she had to sit there eating salad in front of her colleagues, some ingratiating post-grads and the visiting lecturer from Chile, Eduardo Ricallef.

'Ah, cress,' he had said. 'I have already eaten cress.' He spoke as though it were the English national dish.

'And did you like it?' Judy asked.

'I abhor cress.'

Poor Judy had sat there trying to eat it as neatly as possible, wondering if she looked like Ermintrude with sprigs of cress twirling out of her mouth.

Sometimes now the shops seemed too full of beautiful,

healthy things to eat, and she felt nostalgic for that sort of food. She would make what she thought of as 'corner-shop salad' – just round lettuce, cress, and cucumber – delicious. It could be served with eggs or grated cheese, sliced white bread or cream crackers. The only dressing allowed was salad cream. Sometimes it was nice not to have all those different kinds of leaves.

13

GUY WAS UPSTAIRS WORKING. The room that had once been the bedroom that he shared with Susannah was turning into an overflow study. He had a study as well, a tiny bedroom that was once 'the baby's bedroom', kept as a halfway house nursery for a while, and then turned by degrees into a study when it seemed that Felix was to be the only one. Would he really have been the only one? Guy wondered now. They had stopped talking about babies. Perhaps they should have had investigations. Perhaps that would have changed things. Actually, he realised, anything at all might have changed things. Just the tiniest thing would have been all it took. A phone call from a fitted kitchens company, someone pressing the button on a pedestrian crossing just in time to halt the car by a few seconds, a colleague of Susannah's at the library delaying her leaving by even the tiniest amount; anything at all might have saved her. But then if something had been happening with that man (Guy could still hardly bear to think his name), maybe Susannah would have left and taken Felix with her. He would never know. If only, if only, what if, what if. The words must be almost visible as they circled his head like flies or moths, or even bats. He was trying to ignore these thoughts to work on an article on variation in leaf unfurling rates in ferns. He could half hear the video downstairs. Felix had long since tired of *Atlantis*. (A pity. How cheered Guy had been to discover that the hero was a bespectacled academic.) He was watching the Disney *Alice in Wonderland* again.

Felix had read the book, the real thing, again and again. Perhaps, thought Guy, Felix liked to be baffled. He could hear the video, but he couldn't hear Felix laughing in all the usual places. He hoped that Felix hadn't fallen asleep. It was much too early. It would disrupt his pattern and make him wake up at 5 a.m. the next day.

Downstairs Felix wasn't really watching *Alice in Wonderland* and he wasn't asleep. He was looking at photos.

Here he was when he had just been born. That was his mummy and there was Dad. All his relatives must have come to visit him. There were lots of flowers in vases. He turned the pages. Here he was in a car seat, and a yellow chair, and a pram. Here he was eating a bit of toast that looked disgusting, and chewing a wooden thing with bells on. That thing was still in his socks and pants drawer. And then here he was with Marmalade, when Marmalade was new. Here he was on a mat on the floor. Those, those must have been Mummy's feet when she was taking the photo, pink feet with pink nails. But there were stripes on her feet. Felix didn't understand that these were tan lines from her sandals – they looked silly. Her feet looked like tapirs. He turned the page quickly. Perhaps those were somebody else's feet. He didn't want his mummy to have had silly feet.

There were pages and pages of him being a baby, lots with Dad and only a few with Mum. She was beautiful. She had long fair hair like Alice. Now he had learned to walk, but he was still wearing baby shoes. He had little boots made out of jeans material. On the next page he had shoes with yellow diggers on. There was a photo of just his shoes. He wasn't interested in his baby shoes. On he went. He stopped every time he found one of her, and looked and looked. If he stared hard enough he might hear her voice.

He had seen other people's parents at school assemblies with video cameras. If only they'd had a video camera. He went to the box of videos and pulled them all out on the floor and read their backs. Perhaps they used to have a video camera and his dad had just forgotten. But there was nothing. He turned them over and over. Nothing but proper videos and on the tapes you make yourself, well, he knew what was on those, *The Life of Plants* and *Chitty Chitty Bang Bang* was all.

He went back to the photos. Here was one that he liked. They were on the beach. Mummy was smiling so much that she had creases near her eyes. She was holding both of his hands. His arms were up and he was swinging in the waves. He was wearing some trunks that he still had but they would be much too small now, blue trunks with stars on. Mummy was wearing shorts and a white T-shirt. Her shorts had splashes on them. He was smiling too. Then there was another one of just her face. He slipped his finger into the plastic pocket that held the photo. When he slid his finger out, the photo came too. He smiled and slipped it up inside his school sweatshirt. It was his now. He could keep it in the Black n' Red book.

Alice in Wonderland was nearly finished. He put the photo albums back so that Dad would not know what he had been doing. He piled up the videos and put them back in the box. He could feel the photo prickling his chest. His dad was coming back down the stairs saying, 'Time for bed, Felix.'

'OK,' he said. He didn't even ask to watch the end of the film.

When Dad came in to say goodnight he asked, 'Dad, did we used to have a video camera and you forgot about it?'

'No, sorry, Felix. We haven't ever had one.'

'What if you could get one and make videos of things in your head that you had forgotten?'

'That would be good, wouldn't it? Maybe one will be invented one day.' Dad kissed the top of his head. Felix didn't notice him looking at the suspicious specks in it. Then sighing and smiling when he realised that they were grains of sand.

'Can I have the light on to draw in bed?'

'OK. Night, night.'

Guy went back to the ferns. Felix drew in his notebook, pictures of the beach. He looked at the photo until he fell asleep. In the morning he found that he had cleverly managed to hide it in his notebook under his pillow.

When Guy had put Felix's light out, and put the photo and notebook away for him, he sat on the stairs and drank a can of beer. He never went out. Sometimes it would have been good just to go to the pub, like a normal person. He could, he supposed, it wouldn't be that hard to arrange, but somehow it wasn't worth the trouble. It would seem so fake, so forced, like some sort of holiday camp activity. But if he did, maybe he could find a new mother for Felix, someone to help look after him. Perhaps Felix was right about Miss Block. Perhaps he should ask her out. Would she have him? It would be great for Felix. Would he be able to ensnare her? It would all be trickery, and quite unfair on the poor woman. He was damaged goods, too old, the leftovers at a car boot sale, the stuff that nobody would ever want, fit only to be flung in a skip or stuffed in a recycling bin. Somebody could prop him up in a wheelbarrow. Penny for the Guy. He knew that he couldn't make it through even one date with Miss Block or anybody else, let alone go any further. All that part of him had died with Susannah.

A few days later Felix glued the photo of Susannah into his special notebook. He drew it a border of kisses. It didn't look right. He realised that all the joined-up kisses looked like a fence, the sort of wire fence that has sharp spikes on it. There didn't seem to be much he could do to get rid of the horrible border without ruining either the photo or the notebook. It made him feel sadder every time he looked at it now, and stupid. A week or so later he had the good idea of making another border. He traced the edges of the photo and then cut the right shape out of a plain piece of paper. He knew it would be safest to leave this one blank, he didn't want to muck up another one, but you could still see the wire fence kisses through the paper. He decorated the new border with regiments of coloured squares. It ran out some of his felt pens, but he didn't mind.

Felix didn't really write that much in his notebooks. He liked gluing things in, pictures that he found, or stamps or beautiful leaves.

He also wrote lists:

People at school who do and don't like me.
Countries where I have relations.
Birds and animals I have seen.
Books that I like that I have read.
Things I would like for Christmas or Birthday.
Places I would like to go one day.

14

J UDY HAD BEEN ABOUT to eat breakfast in her kitchen. She was enjoying the colour that the rays of sunshine made as they shone through the jar of marmalade on the table. Should she have that or strawberry jam on her bagel? Perhaps jam. Her sister Peggy had made it. Stupidly she picked up the newspaper and turned on the radio.

'No, no, they can't take that away from me,' the radio told her.

Except that they could, she thought, and they did. In today's paper were photos from Iraq – sprawled naked bodies piled up, the Americans with smiles as wide as pieces of apple pie, Iraqi men hanging, handcuffed, to the doors of cells; another man, hands up in surrender, smeared with something unspeakable; the snarling dogs, straining at their leashes – yes, it seemed that they could and did take everything away from some people. On another page was a photograph of an Iraqi professor who had died suddenly in custody of compression of the brain stem, whatever that was. It seemed it was often caused by a blow to the head.

She turned the paper over, but it was too late. The images were there now – once seen, never erasable. What, she wondered, had led those Americans to behave like that? Had they seen pictures of the Holocaust as college kids and been impressed? She carried her coffee and her breakfast into the next room, but a fat American bagel smeared with strawberry jam was not so appealing now.

Of course, her thoughts were now on Eduardo. Had torture methods changed much in thirty years? Surely there was a limit to the imagination, to the number of ways in which one human being could torture another? The Americans were calling it 'abuse'. Abuse and humiliation. As if what they had been doing was not actual torture, not that bad. They were saying already, just days after the story had, as they put it, broken, that it was time to move on and draw a line under it.

What had happened to Eduardo? Where was he, or what was left of him now? They had taken that away from her.

There was a song that she could not listen to, Ella Fitzgerald's 'I Gotta Have My Baby Back'. Eduardo had never known the last chapter of his love affair with Judy. A few weeks after he had gone Judy, stricken with worry and longing, had realised that she must be pregnant. She did not mention it in her letters. It seemed too careless, and perhaps undignified, and who knew where the letters might end up, who might read them, what it might do to Eduardo in whatever situation he was in, how they might torment him with it. It occurred to her that some secret police might come after her and the baby. But it was still early days. She was still hoping. Maybe he was in hiding.

Perhaps, she thought, he might have a wife. Judy imagined somebody beautiful and clever and sparky, probably called something wonderful like Conchita. And if he was wilfully leaving her behind for ever, then perhaps she didn't want him to know about the baby at all.

She carried the secret close to her heart. There was no question of not keeping the baby; somehow she would manage. She told nobody. The weeks passed. The nausea faded, but too early. One night she woke at 3 a.m., that terrifying dark hour, her abdomen turning to iron. Each wave was like the aftermath of a steel-capped boot in her back. She tried to lie very still, then curled up to try to avoid the blows. Soon she was lying in a pool of red and black, the sheets stained into a terrible flag. She crawled across the room to the phone. An ambulance arrived and the uni-formed men took her away. It seemed that she had lost them both.

Can't sleep,
Can't eat,
Because I lost my sweet baby, sweet.
I just gotta, I just gotta, I gotta have my baby back.

That was how the song went.
Her sisters were very kind.

Judy sat in the botanical garden, on the bench underneath the banana tree, wondering why she didn't come here more often. What a strange and neglected place it was. Really, the university and the students were missing out. Here it was, a beautiful little oasis of tranquillity, completely silent apart from the birds and really only yards from the campus. She should encourage the nicer ones of her students to come here, but not too many of them. How easily it could be spoilt if it turned into a place to chat on one's mobile, or to party, or if the university realised the wonderful asset it had, and started to use it for receptions and so on.

She remembered coming here with Eduardo. It had been a much more popular place when she was young. Eduardo had been disappointed by the campus. She thought that he must have been expecting something a bit more historic, at least a few dreaming spires and some punts, a river for late night naked swimming. The best they could offer him here was some redbrick buildings, some interesting 1950s architecture and good train links to London. The botanical garden made up for the rest of the place, at least a little.

The lightest of winds made the bamboo whisper and creak, and lifted the corners of the essays that she was pretending to grade. She had on her tinted spectacles. The air was very warm for October. She was sitting between two hawthorn trees, and trying to remember which one of them was pink and which one white.

Judy could never decide which she liked better, the pink May blossom or the white. The same went for lilac; purple or white? But then why should one have to decide? Why, she wondered, had it been considered such bad luck to bring lilac into the house, also cow parsley? Both were supposed to portend a death, or even to cause one. She would look it up.

She knew that if she closed her eyes she would be instantly asleep.

She sat so still that the frogs in the pond returned to the surface, and remained there. A pair of goldfinches were already feeding on the niger seed she had put on the bird table. She had bought it at the hardware shop for her own garden. It had seemed selfish not to bring some in her pocket and put it out here. Now she would feel it necessary to return regularly to replenish it. How warm the sun was. She would just close her eyes for a moment . . .

She felt a very slight chill, a shadow passing across her papers. She opened her eyes and a boy was standing there. For a moment she thought that he might be a shade of some sort, a ghost. He was very pale, and he must have come up to her so silently that the frogs had not noticed his approach and plopped back below the surface. Judy saw that if this were a ghost, it was one with rather grubby knees. He was wearing a school sweatshirt, the cuffs of which were frayed and hung in damp and stringy fringes around his bony wrists. His hair was a bit stringy around the ears too, in need of a good trim. He was carrying a long stick of bamboo.

'Hello,' said Judy. The boy smiled. Judy knew that smile. It seemed to stop her heart for a moment. This, she thought, must be Susannah and Guy Misselthwaite's little boy.

'Would you like to see the newts?'

'Yes please.' She was glad to see that he hadn't come armed with a jam jar on a string. She could not possibly have condoned newt-catching, even temporary newt-catching, even for a school project. He led her down a very small path into the copse, ignoring the notices warning that this area was crumbling, and that there was a danger of further landslips, past some rather nasty azaleas, and then across a little stream where some of the pebbles were coated with a coppery deposit. Here was the pool.

'Here,' said Felix, 'this is where they live. Nobody knows except me.'

'Thank you,' she whispered, 'I shan't tell anybody.'

'You have to keep very still, and then you will see them.' They squatted down and kept very still. There were oak leaves in the pool, water boatmen, some unusual-looking snails (she would have to look those up too) and there, with their tails looking as though they had been snipped from some of the fallen oak leaves, were the newts.

'Wow,' she whispered, 'I have never seen so many together before.'

'Even my dad doesn't know they're here. I don't think anyone does.'

They watched in silence for a while as the newts went about their business.

'When I was a little girl we sometimes had newts in a tank at school, but they are very rare now. I think we should leave them alone, don't you?' Judy was very against the modern practice known as 'pond-dipping' whereby children were encouraged to scoop out anything they could, plonk it in some shallow plastic tray where the water temperature would quickly rise beyond that of the pond, leave the creatures there for as long as they liked, to be prodded and remarked upon, and then perhaps tip the water and most of its inhabitants back. Who knew what tinies might be left behind, their element evaporating for ever? 'He who torments the chafer's sprite weaves a bower in endless night,' she told herself.

'I'm not gonna catch them,' said Felix.

'Neither am I.'

They watched the newts for some more minutes.

'I've seen you in the garden before,' Felix told her.

'Well, you are very clever,' said Judy, 'because I have never seen you.'

'I can climb very tall trees, and I know secret places, but I'm usually at school.'

'Does anybody know you are here?' Judy couldn't stop herself from asking. Perhaps the boy had absconded from the After-School Club to find his dad. She had seen the children being shepherded (rather carelessly, she thought) from the school to the church hall by some students in nasty maroon polo shirts. Perhaps he was on the run from some team games, perhaps from some after-school bullies. You had to take your hat off to him really.

'My dad is in charge of the garden,' Felix told her.

'That's wonderful,' she replied. 'It is such a lovely garden. I wasn't sure that anyone was in charge of it at all. He is certainly doing a very good job. What's his name?'

'Guy,' said Felix.

'My name is Judy Lovage. What's your name?'

'Felix Pieter Misselthwaite. Pieter is spelt in Swedish. My mum was half-Swedish.'

'Yes,' said Judy. 'Well, Felix Pieter Misselthwaite, I'm very, very pleased to meet you.'

She extended her hand and smiled. Felix looked at it for a second and then realised that he was meant to shake it. 'I knew your mummy,' said Judy. 'I thought she was very beautiful and kind.'

'Really, did you really?'

'Yes. We often saw each other in the library, where she worked.'

'Oh,' said Felix.

Judy wished that she had something a bit more precise or detailed or meaningful to add.

'She loved you very, very much,' she said.

'I have to go now,' said Felix, and he ran towards one of the greenhouses where a silhouette that must have been his father was sitting very still.

When she got home and hung up her mac she guessed one of the reasons for Felix talking to her. Her favourite brooch, a turquoise enamel cat face, was pinned to the lapel. It must have been that, that and seeing her feed the birds; or perhaps it was just boredom or loneliness on his part, and a normal childish desire to impress and to share his important discovery of the newts. She hoped that she would see him again, and soon.

The next day, in fact, she went to the garden hoping to see him, but Felix wasn't there, or at least visible. She thought it was quite likely that he was hiding somewhere, amusing himself by spying on her. What a pity that she wasn't doing anything more interesting than marking the essays that she hadn't got through the day before. Max's essay seemed better on paper than when he'd read it out loud. Perhaps it was just his manner. He could do with some hints on presentation and delivery before he shuffled into the real world. She gave it 62 per cent. High marks indeed from her. She put it to the bottom of the pile and as she looked up, taking a big breath before the next one, there was Max himself off in the distance, standing on one of the little plank and chicken-wire bridges, looking at the stream. She could see that he was eating something, he must have come here for a tea-time snack, but she couldn't make out what, something in a packet. From where she was sitting it looked as though his messy brown hair was a cap of autumn leaves. It cheered her to see him in the garden. He was probably just killing time, but even so. She briefly considered making the 62 per cent into 63 per cent or even 64, but thought better of it.

Max. What had been in his parents' minds when they'd named him? Judy figured that young people called Max had probably not been christened. Hard to imagine the vicar saying, 'Max, I sign you with the sign of the cross . . .' and so on, but one never knew.

He was Max (not Maxim or Maximilian). A Max should be rakish and debonair. A Max should be in a tux and carry a neat little revolver. A Max should be somebody slick and mean and rich. Or a matinée idol, or Maxim de Winter. But here was this Max, Max Cooper. If Judy had brought her binoculars with her, or if she'd been hiding in the tree with Felix, she would have been able to see that he was eating a Mexican wrap. Max liked Tex-Mex food. He was a Pepsi Max sort of a Max. A portion of fries please. Regular, Large or Super-Max?

At school they had sometimes called him 'Potato Man'; affectionately of course. He wasn't bullied, more tolerated, and sometimes accommodated. Max Cooper, born and bred in Shanklin on the Isle of Wight, flat-footed and heavy-legged. At least at university PE was no longer compulsory, but it was bad luck for Max that being fit was now the thing.

Was he fit? He was not.

Although he had friends, he felt as though he would never be the hero who got the girl, rather the one dialling for pizza for everyone at 11.25 p.m. He would be the geek in the movie with a *panino* poised a hand's breadth away from his mouth when something amazing appeared on the screen, a well-intentioned but expendable nerd.

'He's gonna get it!' the audience would think when the super-volcano blew its top or the aliens landed.

But maybe things can be changed, maybe destinies can be escaped. He didn't want to end up back in Shanklin. Max was headed, and nobody really knew this yet, for Newfoundland, or perhaps, you see he hadn't made his mind up, for somewhere just north of Seattle. Somewhere where nobody made jokes about Mini Coopers and Max Coopers.

'You are still young.'

Thirty years on her sisters were still telling her that, just as they had done when what they saw as 'a decent interval' had elapsed after Eduardo's disappearance and the loss of the baby.

'You are still young.'

She had wondered when people would stop saying that to her. Now she realised that nobody had said it to her for a very long time. It had turned into 'but you aren't old', which meant, of course, that they thought she was. She was way past childbearing age now, but she had her nephews and nieces. She knew that at some point, a long time ago, her sisters must have been saying that it would soon be too late for her. She could have put it crudely, and told them that she'd had her fair share of offers. The university was teeming with unattached and recently detached men, as well as many who pretended that they were; but now Judy had succeeded in erecting such a barrier of aloofness and impenetrable tranquillity around herself that she was quite safe.

The 1970s had not surprisingly been the worst, full of threats. The 1980s had been pretty bad at times. There was still the twice-yearly horror of the departmental parties, but these were now much more sober affairs.

At one, probably Christmas 1976, a colleague from the History department, Martyn Swatridge, had tried to kiss her. He had either been an early pioneer of designer stubble, or perhaps just a bit of a slob. One minute she had been talking to him, standing closer than she would ever have chosen, the music being so loud. They had been discussing Hardy's poetry. Then suddenly he had lunged at her and clamped his bristly maw onto hers. It had felt like a giant beech nut, and before she could push him away, his tongue had started making horrible little lizard darts at her. She had run to wash her face and rinse out her mouth. He had stood outside the bathroom door for some time saying, 'Aw, Judy, Judy' in a way that she supposed was meant to be appealing. It seemed that he had mistaken her disgust for reserve or inexperience. There had followed several months of what nowadays would be viewed as harassment or even stalking. This only ceased when his passions were transferred to and, to Judy's great relief, returned by a Medieval History post-grad. Eventually he had married this unfortunate young woman, finding her, at least at first, to be infinitely malleable and bullyable.

The thing that upset Judy most about the whole business

was that she loved Hardy's poetry. Now whenever she read any of it she had to concentrate very hard not to think of this incident. When she trod beech mast underfoot, or cracked open a nut and found a tiny insect inside, she still thought of him. She found that pistachios were the most likely to contain some other life form, some poor little white worm, meant to be born in Persia, waking up in England. She suspected that she got more than her fair share of these.

Now at parties she mostly talked to the departmental secretaries and made it her business to look after anybody new. Good old Judy. But she left early. Men kept their distance. She was too tough a nut to crack now, and perhaps too old.

Judy found that whenever she was out, she would soon start longing to be home again. She had been in her little house for so long, renting it at first, and now she owned it. If Eduardo ever came back he would find her sleeping in the same room. Then the walls had been purple and scarlet. Now they were white, the only room in the house where colour did not reign. There was such comfort to be had in staying in one place, shutting your own front door, following the seasons in your own little garden, growing the same and some new varieties in your own little greenhouse year after year, watching your lilac tree grow, worrying that each storm might deal its fragile boughs a fatal blow. Strange that some woods were so much softer than others.

That morning she had been woken by a strange new bird noise, you couldn't have called it a song. She had been quite unable to identify it. It had sounded just like a parrot, or even several parrots, but small ones, probably parakeets. She had once seen them flying wild in Richmond Park. Now perhaps they had reached this neck of the woods. Should one be pleased? It would be hard not to be. She could imagine the local paper's reaction – foreign interlopers . . . economic migrants, asylum seekers . . . scrounging off British bird tables – and what would her garden birds think? She had wood pigeons on twenty-four-hour patrol, a pair of jays, goldfinches, and all the other usual garden visitors. There was no crisis in the house sparrow population in her garden. She supposed that the pecking order would have to be revised. And the languages of birds . . . would South American-born parakeets twitter in a different tongue to their London-born relatives? She often wished that she had studied Zoology rather than History of Art, or some environmental science that involved field trips to the seaside and knowing the names of different types of marine algae and rare birds. What larks, eh? She contented herself with organising the School of Humanities version of a field trip, their annual jaunt to the Jane Austen Society's AGM and summer picnic. She was pleased that these events were not among those that attracted Professor Martyn Swatridge. He was now much too busy with the higher business of the university.

15

SOMETIMES FELIX LONGED TO have somebody to talk to; instead he would just draw in a Black n' Red book, or think about things and whisper into Marmalade's fur.

Today I had to run really fast to the garden. Sometimes if I am too slow there are people behind me and they might see where I go. Once Bradley and Harrison in Year 5 came after me. Today it was Thomas Keane as well, so that was worse. They were laughing and throwing fun snaps so I ran and ran. Harrison's mum saw them and they stopped. I hid behind a car and I heard her say that it was Sweeties Day. They all have Sweeties Day on Fridays. I don't care about that. At least it made them stop.

If I think that anyone is watching I just lurk around until they give up, or sometimes I can disappear when they aren't looking. It's amazing how stupid people are. They don't see something that is really obvious to another person, such as an important path or gate that leads somewhere very important.

If I was bigger I would be better at fighting. Even then

I don't think I'd like fighting much, even if I could beat other people. At least I'm not too bad at running. And I'm very good at hiding and disappearing. I bet I'm the best at climbing in the whole school. I can climb really tall trees where the branches are in really tricky places. Most people would find my trees impossible. I'll probably be an actual climber when I'm a man, and climb mountains as well as climbing walls. There may be a new Olympic sport of Difficult Tree Climbing.

Sometimes I can be in the garden and spy on people. They sit under my tree and say and do things and never even know I am there. I used to spy on Judy quite a lot, but now we are friends and she has made friends with Dad too. She never did anything interesting, just read, ate sandwiches and apples, and fed the birds. She would bring work as well, the sort of stuff Dad has to do. I don't bother spying on Dad. He never does anything interesting. I like spying on students best of all. Sometimes I think of putting up signs saying 'Interesting Place To Do Interesting Things This Way!' as not many bother coming. But really I like it best when it is quiet . . .

Guy dreaded questions about how and why Susannah had died, so he hardly ever mentioned her to Felix. Even so, he hoped that Felix still had some recollections of her. Felix could remember her a little, and he had spent so long secretly gazing at the picture he'd stuck in his book and the ones in the albums that he thought he could remember much more than would have been possible. Felix thought that he could now remember being a toddler in a back carrier on a holiday somewhere, sitting on a wall in Portmeirion eating a very small vanilla ice cream, and being startled by those peacocks (although in the next photos, he had laughed at them and found a feather to keep), that he could remember riding on his dad's shoulders on a walk back up a long sandy path from the beach. He looked and looked. Here was one of Uncle Jon with a funny hat on. And here was one of Grandpa eating a big sandwich. Something had made the bread go yellow, and he had the yellow stuff on his grey beard. It didn't look very nice. Felix wished that there were more photos of Mummy.

The photos stopped suddenly when he was about four. Sometimes he had to close the album quickly and chew on his cuff to stop himself from crying. But sometimes, later, staring and staring out of the window, or just when he fell asleep or woke up, or suddenly for no reason at all except maybe magic, he got a picture that wasn't a photo.

He is sitting on Mummy and Daddy's bed. She is getting dressed. She is cross with her clothes, but not with him.

'I hate everything I have,' she says, and the piles of clothes on the bed get higher and higher, until he is surrounded. He is peeking out, at the top of a castle looking over the battlements.

'I don't know why I have all these colours,' she says. Most things are navy blue and black and navy green, the colour of the uniform they have bought him for school. He thinks that colour is nice.

'Why do I have all of this dark stuff?' she says. 'I hate dark stuff, and heavy things, and itchy things and tights.'

Some of it is pale brown. She calls it tan. She throws a pale brown cardigan, that isn't dark or heavy or itchy, so that it lands on his head. He kicks some of the piles onto the floor and they laugh and she tickles him.

'What I want is pink,' she says. 'I need pink.' Then she says it is time to get ready. She puts on her jeans and a white T-shirt and the pale brown cardigan and they go to nursery where it is colours again. If you wear something red, he thinks, looking down at his shorts, and something white like his T-shirt, you are sort of pink.

After snack and milk, which is in red beakers with two handles but no lid, he does a painting. It is all pink and red.

'Do you like pink, Felix?' one of the ladies asks. He just looks at the picture and his brush. The ladies all wear green sweatshirts. Some are thin and some are fat. They are all kind except for Diane who won't let you make spare bikes into trailers, even if nobody else wants to ride on them.

'My mummy likes pink,' he says at last.

16

JUDY HAD TAKEN JEMIMA to see *Tosca*, and then to Pizza Express. Jemima stayed the night. Judy loved it when she did. It was so often unexpected, but Judy found that it never upset her equilibrium the way that the presence of almost any other unexpected guest might have. Judy still loved the phrase 'unexpected guest', as used by magazines suggesting suppers or lunches or presents for them. She always had a bed ready for Jemima. The school of art where she was studying was only twenty or so miles away. Judy hoped that Jemima saw her house as somewhere to bolt to, to have some home comforts without any intrusion. She really was a bit jealous of Peggy, Jemima's mother. Imagine having Jemima all the time, for eighteen years, and even now for almost all of the long vacations. The things that Jemima did that drove Peggy mad – sleeping beyond noon, using the top of her chest of drawers as a palette and getting blobs of oil paint on the carpet, wearing grungy clothes, buying everybody she knew the same thing for Christmas; one year it had been jars of Nutella, and another year hyacinths; they had all been lined up on the table in the hall ready to go, not even with individual gift tags (that would only complicate things), just 'Happy Christmas from Jemima' – these things Judy just found endearing.

Jemima slept with such abandon, like a little child. She seemed to lack an internal alarm clock and needed strings of phone calls to rouse her if she ever had to be up for an exam or a train.

When Jemima stayed the night, Judy would tiptoe in with a cup of black tea (this niece was a vegan) at 8.30, knowing that it might still be there, undrunk, at midday. Judy loved the bizarre things that Jemima slept in; ancient long johns, with impossibly pretty and tiny little camisoles that would have given Judy very chilly shoulders. It seemed that young women were now inured to the cold – they wore these minute vests, day or night, whatever the season. Phoebe did it, almost all of Judy's female students did it, including many whom it did not suit. This morning Judy wished that Jemima had been awake to witness her aunt's heroics. There had been six daddy-long-legs in the bathroom. Judy had armed herself with a tray, six large glasses and six postcards and pieces of junk mail. She had caught them all, and carried them downstairs and out into the garden trapped inside the upturned glasses on the tray. Judy Lovage, Daddy-Long-Legs Liberator, looking like an elderly cocktail waitress in a bar for bats. It amused her, even though she was so used to this sort of thing. If you live alone you have no choice but to put out your own spiders and deal with anything that your cat brings in.

17

'HEY! FELIX! CATCH!' Erica swung a sturdy branch of Montezuma pine and neatly batted a cone towards him. But Felix didn't catch. His mouth seemed to slowly slip open, but his arms stayed hanging at his sides. He turned as rigid as a petrol pump. Here, thought Erica, is a child who doesn't play catch.

'Want to try again?' She batted another cone, more gently. This time Felix made an attempt to get it, and he almost did.

'I'm not very good at this,' Felix told her. 'Mrs Cowplain says I always seem to be looking the wrong way.'

'I expect you're just looking at something more interesting than her. I bet you could be really good if you wanted. You're really good at outdoor things, aren't you?'

'Only climbing and discovering.' He might have added 'and silently watching'.

'Well, those are the most important things.'

Felix looked away from her, then down at the ground, which in this corner of the meadow was studded with pine cones. Many had been gnawed to the core by squirrels, the copper-coloured damp interiors exposed, all kernels gone. Felix thought that they did look tasty. It might be like eating a cereal bar, or maybe some dried pineapple. They had done food tasting at school and had rings of dried pineapple. It was the chewiest thing in the world, but if you ate too much of it, and you hadn't had much breakfast, it would give you stomach ache.

'Do you want to bat?' Erica said. She offered him her stick. 'I'll throw one and you see how hard you can whack it.' The first one he missed. The second he hit so hard that it went whizzing right across the garden and landed on the roof of a greenhouse. Through the milky glass they could see the shape of Guy looking up, startled.

'Ooops,' said Felix, but they both sniggered.

'See if you can bat it higher than that tree,' said Erica, jerking her head towards a young willow. Another child would say 'Easy!' even though it wasn't. Felix seemed to be without bravado. But he did it. The arc was high and wide and true.

'Wow,' said Erica, 'you're pretty good. That was as big as a rainbow!'

'Do you want a turn?' Felix asked politely.

'OK.'

Each time one of them made a great hit they would shout as loud as they could, 'Rainbow!'

Erica worried that there were quite a few things that Felix might never learn to do. Swimming was one of them. Was riding a bike another? She wondered if she could mention it to Guy without seeming to be critical or interfering, two things that she definitely thought she was. Also, why was Felix in the garden nearly every afternoon? Shouldn't he be going to tea with people, or having them to tea? Or doing some activities. Perhaps she would invite him to tea again, or make a picnic for him and some of his friends in the garden.

'Felix,' she said, the next time she saw him, 'would you like to invite someone to tea in the garden? I could make you an autumn picnic. With maybe a friend or two. Or even three,' she quickly added, remembering how two could gang up on one. It wasn't that long since she had been at school.

'The other children are all always busy,' he said. 'They get collected and go to each other's houses and drama club and football, and piano lessons, and tennis, and cricket, and cubs, and Kumon maths. And the girls go to other stuff too.'

'Don't you want to go to any of those things?'

'I don't know.'

'You could ask your dad, I could ask him for you.'

What were the other mothers playing at? Why weren't they constantly inviting this motherless child to things? Suddenly she quite hated Guy. He was failing this child, big time.

'Do people invite you to things?'

'Sometimes. I just say I can't go.'

'Oh Felix, you could go! Of course you could go!'

'I just say I can't.'

'Why?'

'I don't know.'

The truth was that some of the mothers didn't even know

about Felix's plight. It had happened four years ago now. Nobody gave it that much consideration any more. Their swoops on the Junior School playground were too swift for them to take much in. Those who had previously tried with Felix had been met with so many rebuffs that now they no longer bothered. By Felix's age most children were dictating their own social lives. The enforced inviting of other children to tea was over.

It occurred to Erica that Felix might not be very popular. Some people just don't have many friends. After all, she had hardly any that she actually liked.

At least she had a gingerbread man in her bag for Felix, and one for herself. They sat on the badger house and ate them. Felix was kind of odd-looking, she supposed, compared to most contemporary children. He always looked pale and what her mum called 'peaky', despite all the time he spent outdoors. His shoes were lumpy and too sensible, and why were his cuffs always so frayed? Other boys of his age wore trainers with integral stopwatches. Their hair was in styles, and the girls, well, they were something else.

'You know, Felix,' she said, 'there are lots of things you could do, things in clubs, or by yourself. You could collect things, or be a metal detector, I mean someone who finds things. You could have your own garden.'

A coffee break in the lab. Erica and Guy didn't usually speak, just sipped in silence and looked out of the window, across their corner of campus to the waving trees that bordered the garden. Today, Erica had decided, things would be different. She pulled a sheaf of leaflets out of her rucksack.

'I was at the pool today and I picked up these for you. I hadn't realised that they did all this stuff for kids. There's lots here that you and Felix could try, and it's right on the doorstep. Very reasonable too. Does Felix like swimming?'

'Er,' said Guy, 'um.'

'I loved it when I was a kid. Often the kids who aren't that good at other sports are strong swimmers. Not that I'm saying Felix isn't good at other sports. He's really good at tree climbing and so on . . .'

'Um, yes,' said Guy, which wasn't actually an answer. He took another sip of his coffee and then looked back out of the window. 'I'm interested in hailstones,' he said. 'I wonder if anyone has studied their properties. And the air around hailstones. Have you ever noticed how peculiar it feels? Everybody knows about the importance of lightning in fixing nitrogen in the soil. I wonder if anybody has studied hailstones . . .'

'I don't know,' said Erica, and looked out of the window again too.

He left the leaflets on the table, which she thought was rather rude, but the next day they had gone. She didn't know whether it was the cleaner, or Jeanette being efficient, or whether he had actually taken them home.

'Oh cool!' said Felix. 'Dad, could we really go swimming? You have to do swimming at the beginning of Year 4. It would be so cool if I wasn't in the bottom group.'

'I guess we better had then,' said Guy.

When he phoned the pool it seemed that you had to book lessons several years in advance. Felix could go on the waiting list. They might get a cancellation. He set the leaflets aside.

18

GUY SAT IN THE greenhouse with really, it seemed, very little to do. He was thinking of the garden at home. The lawn was in a condition that other people would consider 'in need of a mow'. It was only a small garden; once he had left it to Susannah. Nobody would have guessed that it was the garden of a botanist. The fences were looking precarious and although the bulbs that Susannah had put in still faithfully came up along with some self-seeded annuals to greet, he thought, nobody, there was nothing much of interest there now. Those hydrangeas could go, so could the *Symphoricarpos albus laevigatus* that Susannah had called snowball trees (and had worried about in case Felix ate the berries). So could the berberis and the cotoneasters and the forsythia and the flowering currant. He almost hated some of those so-called 'useful shrubs'. And then that depressing, pointless expanse of greenish yellow, the lawn. Its usefulness as a habitat and its beauty were zero as far as he was concerned. In the middle of it stood a broken plastic slide and a very small swing. Felix hadn't been on them in years. They could go too. He really did quite hate that garden.

He supposed that in other situations a lawn might be required for games or entertaining. There were some deckchairs in the garage, if he remembered right, but they must be rotten by now. With a rush of decisiveness he decided to make a wildflower meadow. He would uproot the lot of it. Perhaps he could borrow one of the grounds staff's miniature diggers. Why not do the house while he was at it?

A wildflower meadow, yes, that was the answer. A few cuts a year, possibly with a scythe, that would be all that was necessary. He began to make a list of species on the back of some student's assignment.

And grasses, of course. And there was a particular variety of herb Robert that he would like, the Solent one. Now that would be quite something. He could leave it all to the birds and butterflies. At least he would be doing something good for once. The list finished, he looked up and saw a peacock butterfly caught in a strong gust of wind, its wings flapping uselessly. What was it doing out here so late in the season? Why didn't it just surrender to the breeze, and let itself be blown to wherever? Perhaps it had some purpose, some-where it was intending to go. Did butterflies make plans and have memories? He remembered being about Felix's age, going in search of a lost marble, and finding five peacocks spending the winter asleep on the back of his mum and dad's chest of drawers. He hadn't told anybody about his discovery for fear that they would put the butterflies outside and let them die in the cold.

Felix could help him with the wildflower meadow if he

wanted. Then suddenly Felix's pale little face was there, peering around the greenhouse door.

'Dad,' he said.

It must mean that school had finished again. Guy smiled. He looked down at the trays of spleenworts. He was meant to be logging variations in the circumference of their spores.

'Dad,' said Felix, 'might I have a bit of earth?'

Guy looked down at the seed trays on the shelves in front of him, full of compost but waiting for life, the four-inch pots stacked up and growing nothing but cobwebs, the sacks of compost that sat under the bench, where some of them had been for years. The last one he had opened had contained a secret hoard of tiny pearls, snails' eggs.

'Please, Dad. Somewhere to make my own things grow. Not in here, not one of those trays. Outdoors in the garden. A garden in the garden, I mean.'

'Yes,' said Guy, 'of course. I don't know why you didn't have one before. Of course you can have your own . . .' He had been going to say 'plot', but of course he couldn't. He hated the word 'plot' now, and all its connotations.

Susannah's plot was not the usual sort of plot. There was a tree in a woodland burial ground. He was surprised that it hadn't been called a 'Woodland Burial Centre'. There might have been scope for an exhibition and gift shop. It must only be a matter of time before such a place existed. Actually it had been very nice, if such a place could be called nice. A tree had been planted in her memory. He had made the unusual choice of rowan. Now he wondered if there might have been an element of spite in his decision. Perhaps he should have gone for oak, like most people. There was a bronze plaque which he had never seen, maintained by an annual direct debit. The woodland burial ground had seemed the only option, but also horribly appropriate, just a few miles from where that car had hit the tree, that sycamore. Nasty, tall interlopers . . . Perhaps he and Felix should drive out and visit it, the rowan, not the sycamore stump.

'A bit of earth. Where then, Dad?' said Felix.

Guy had forgotten that he was there.

'Oh, I was thinking of the woodland.'

'No, Dad, near the meadow, where there's nothing. Dad, I wish your thoughts didn't take so long!'

'Sorry, Felix. You can have it anywhere really. What will you grow?'

'Strawberries,' said Felix, 'nice things with pink petals. Big things like pumpkins. Giant. Nothing dark, or itchy.'

What was he thinking of? Dark, or itchy . . . burrs, nettles, borage, euphorbias, rue, not that that was very dark. Had he ever really talked to Felix about plants? He had somehow just expected the boy to be interested in them and absorb the information by osmosis, or perhaps, more accurately, by some sort of wind-based pollen dispersal method. Of course he must have a garden of his own.

'Where again?'

'I'll show you,' said Felix. He offered his father his hand and they went outside together. Felix had a place in mind, just below the terraces. It was sunny and sheltered and not too dry. A fine choice. 'Can I borrow your tools?'

'Of course. And we'll get you some seeds. Now will be a good time to start the digging, before it gets too cold.'

Guy's pleasure was tempered by a huge boulder of guilt. How could he have let his son get to be nearly eight and not have a garden of his own? Why had he not bought him some tools, good quality child-sized ones? He thought back to the Christmasses and birthdays since Susannah had died, many of them now merged into one, his forays into the city and his impulsive, impatient purchases of things that Felix often seemed to find baffling. But books. At least he made sure Felix had plenty of books.

They chose the place for Felix's garden and Guy fetched a ball of brown twine.

'I like this sort of string,' Felix said. 'I once had some in my stocking.'

They marked out the area with twine twisted around some short bamboo sticks that Felix quickly found. At school the following Monday, Felix had something to write about for 'What I Did At The Weekend':

'I have got my own garden now. Dad is going to get me some tools, or Erica or Judy if he forgets. Small ones but sharp. Also they will give me some seeds. The digging has started!'

Then there was a neat diagram, a plan of his garden with strips of flowers, a bridge, and a perfectly round pond with ducks, lilies, frogs and newts. An arrow showed where the fountain was to go.

The teacher, Mrs Cowplain (who you would have thought by now would have the imagination not to ask children like Felix how they had spent each weekend), put his book in a special transparent folder up on the wall, where everyone could look at it. 'Nice work, Felix,' she wrote. 'Very imaginative.'

'Ha,' said Esther, one of the girls on his table, 'Felix reckons he's getting a fountain!'

'I might!' said Felix, jutting out his chin.

19

Dear Prof Lovage,
[said the note pinned to her office door]
Please could I have a week or so's extension on my essay? I am a bit behind with work as I have had rather a lot of commitments to cope with.
Max Cooper.

Using an envelope or providing a better excuse would have got him the week straight away. It was nearly the end of term, nearly Christmas. Everybody had, Judy thought crossly, 'rather a lot of commitments to cope with'.

Dear Max,
[she wrote on the bottom of his note]
See me!
Judy Lovage.

She put it in an envelope and left it in his pigeon hole. She would give him the extension, but only when she had found out why he was behind. There would be no slip-sliding on her courses. There was also, she knew, a possibility that the boy might be in need of help, trouble at home perhaps, even though his note had been so annoyingly casual.

Max knocked on her door the next morning. He looked very tired, but clean and rather scrubbed. Some marks for trying then. When he plonked his rucksack down between them she caught a whiff of fried food and lager, old collected smells trapped in the fabric by the rain. She smiled at him encouragingly and tried not to show her distaste.

'Hello Professor Lovage. Um . . .'

'So tell me, Max, why do you need the extension?'

Bloody hell, thought Max. I'm only asking for a week. Why did it have to be such a big deal?

'Um. I've got a bit behind with my assignments. I've had to do lots of extra shifts at work.'

'Oh, and where do you work? I love to know what you all get up to. Students today work so hard. A few years ago almost none of my students had jobs during term time.'

'It's only T.G.I. Friday's,' said Max. 'It's really boring. But they're very busy, what with Christmas. God knows why. Can't think why anyone would want to go there for a party.'

'Death of the soul, would you say, Max?'

He rolled his pinkish eyes. He really did look very tired.

'You could put it like that. I've got to do lots of extra shifts.'

'Oh?'

'Well, want to really, I suppose. I'm saving up. I'm going to Seattle if I can.'

'When?'

'Well, I did want to go over for a couple of weeks now to

just have a look, then I can go in the summer when I'm done here, and maybe stay. That's the plan.'

'And what are you going to do in Seattle, apart from drink very good coffee?'

'Beachcombing.'

Goodness, she felt like saying, aren't there any beaches nearer? And to go at this time of year . . .

'Beachcombing?'

'A lot of exciting stuff is going to be washed up in the next few weeks. I want to be there. And try and make some contacts for the summer. Trouble is, I'm still a bit short. I've got the fare, but I need a bit more . . .'

'I haven't given an essay extension for beachcombing before. But I will. You can have a week.' (If you bring me something exciting back, she felt like adding.) 'Remember that your degree should be coming first at the moment.' She smiled. 'Now if you've time, tell me about this beachcombing.'

'Well, I grew up on the Isle of Wight, but I'm trying to get away from there, and I started when I was a kid. Just finding stuff on beaches. Then I found out about these people who track things. There are websites and whole networks, communities of people. Did you hear about the Nikes?'

'I must just be living in a backwater.'

'There was a whole container, you know, a massive one, with a huge street value, that went overboard. Anyway, they all washed up along this stretch of coastline. East coast, that one was. This guy took it upon himself to help people match up pairs. It was beautiful. There's stuff like this going on all the time. One of the first really famous ones was those

Weebles. Toys from the seventies. 'Spect you remember them.' He leapt to his feet, blew his cheeks out and demonstrated how they had wobbled but not fallen down.

'Yes, I'm ancient enough to remember the seventies. You are a very convincing Weeble.' Sadly, she added to herself.

'Thanks. Actually, they're back being advertised again. And did you hear about the bath toys? Thousands of plastic ducks and turtles and that, adrift for years, all the colour bleached out of them by the sun. They're tracked, and then at last they wash up. There were these containers of Action Men, lost overboard six years ago. They're expected to wash up next month, around Seattle, where lots of the top combers are. I just have to be there.'

'Yes,' said Judy, 'I can understand that.' She pictured the Action Men on the last gruelling leg of their journey, swimming bravely on towards the shore. 'I wonder which way up they'll float. On their backs, I hope. You must tell me. And whether they'll have acquired any additional scars.'

'There were all types lost,' said Max. 'You know, lots of different uniforms, soldiers and astronauts and so on. Vehicles and some horses and sabre-tooth tigers too. I had one of those. He was meant to be fighting the tiger, but mine were friends.'

'Well, I hope you find some.'

'Thanks.'

'Show me when you get back, won't you?'

After he had gone she pulled out her folder to see what Max was meant to be doing. She knew it wasn't History of Art. Although he was a third year, this was the first time she'd come across him. Ah, Nautical Design. She'd even had Engineering students pitch up on her courses before. They

155

were encouraged to do something to broaden their knowledge base. She suspected that for some people, her course
was the default option when all other possibilities were full.

Judy approved wholeheartedly of Max's beachcombing.
She wouldn't mind spending the holiday doing it too.
Would he swim in the sea as well? Would it be warm
enough there at this time of year?

Even in December, she was still part of the early morning
congregation of swimmers, the faithful of 8 a.m. She could
have held her own in the medium lane, but preferred the
ambience of the slow, well away from the ridiculous
testosterone-fuelled, splashing show-offs in the fast. Up
and down she went, forty lengths a day. She planned to
be one of those hardy old ladies, braving the breakers in
their cossies at places like Eastbourne and Ayr.

Her already neat hair was turned into an even neater
swimming hat by the water. Her round little head bobbed
up and down as she swam, as sleek and amiable as a seal.
Judy rarely went to the pool on her birthday (September 1st)
because she had made a promise to herself that she would do
everything in her power to swim in the sea each year on that
day. It was a promise that she managed to keep. Sometimes
she was abroad with one of her sisters, usually on a French
beach, but there had been Italian, Bulgarian, Portuguese
and Spanish birthday swims too. If she was by herself she
would drive to somewhere nice in Dorset. Lyme Regis was a
favourite. Once there had been a terrible storm on her
birthday. She considered swimming anyway. There were
twenty-foot waves crashing onto the promenade at Bourne-
mouth, threatening a floral clock. Swimming would be
suicide. She thought about it, then laughed and sat in the car

by herself and ate her salad straight out of its Tupperware box. She had a Thermos of strong black tea and listened to the lunchtime concert on Radio Three. She stood in the salt wind and the rain until she was soaked. Then she drove home and drank whisky in the bath and felt sad, but only until her niece Jemima phoned, saying that she was back early and alone from the family holiday. Would Aunty Judy help to sort out her university application?

They went to Pizza Express and Jemima explained how she had realised that she didn't want to study Archaeology that badly any more, she wanted to do Fine Art. Judy promised to help her through Clearing, and did the very next day.

Sometimes when Judy swam or paddled in the sea she thought of the water swirling around the planet. How long would it take to get from Cape Horn to England, if of course it came that way at all? She thought that Eduardo or Eduardo's friends or family might be swimming in the sea at the same time. Chile wasn't that far away really. Sometimes she thought that maybe he was not dead or disappeared. Maybe he just hadn't wanted to stay in touch. Perhaps he'd had a wife and children back home all along. She had been nothing but a dalliance to him. So what if a visiting poet and lecturer had an affair with an impressionable young academic. There was nothing new under the sun.

Of course she had written to the university where he'd been based. It was the only address she had for him. She heard nothing back, but found out that it had been temporarily closed, and many appointments had been terminated. She tried phoning but there were no numbers that worked. If by some chance, probably by misdialling, she did get through to anyone, they had no idea what or who she was talking about. There was no news. Then she realised that she might be endangering him, phone calls from a foreign woman, a known leftie and academic at a foreign university. One day a packet arrived containing some, but not all, of the letters she had sent him. They had been opened, of course. How strange, she thought, that somebody considered it worth returning them to their sender. Why not just sling them on a rubbish heap, incinerate them along with some books? It had a horrible Nazi finality to it. Unless of course it was he, or his possible wife, who had sent them back to her. She still couldn't bear to think of what might have happened to him, that he might have been tortured to death, or shot in the back or the head or through the heart.

But might he not be alive, with grandchildren and a vineyard? Could it be that one day she would see him again? Oh, what a stupid, stupid, naive woman I am, she thought, and forced herself, yet again, to think about something or somebody else.

20

OFTEN WHEN GUY WAS too tired to work, but couldn't sleep, he read online journals. *The Drifting Seed* (a journal about seeds and fruits dispersed by tropical currents, and the people who collect them) was a particular favourite. He liked little local websites of places far away that detailed sightings and habitats. It seemed that there were so many plants that he would never see. His own work wasn't really going that badly. He was contributing three chapters to an undergraduate textbook. His latest paper was nearing completion, though he didn't know if anyone would want it. Late at night he found that he couldn't have any more useful thoughts, or any thoughts at all that he wanted to entertain, but he still didn't want to go to bed.

So his late night Amazon habit grew. He endlessly filled and emptied his basket. Sometimes he clicked on books that he'd contributed to. They had pitiful Amazon rankings somewhere in the hundreds of thousands, or were marked 'This item is difficult to obtain', although it seemed that there were plenty of people out there ready to part with their copies. No matter. As the sole author of none of them he didn't need to feel too acutely ashamed. Sometimes he would actually order books, and they often travelled from across the world to reach him. He decided that he would do all of the Christmas shopping for Felix this way too. Perhaps he could get a consignment of happiness, a new mum for Felix, maybe a new life. In the New Year he would pluck up the courage, get his act together and ask Miss Block out on a date. Maybe a date that involved Felix so that nothing could possibly happen. Yes, he really would. He resolved to be ready for Christmas this year as well.

That first Christmas Guy had only remembered about stockings on Christmas Eve, once all the shops were shut. He had plundered his desk and the kitchen cupboards for suitable items, and come up with a ball of string, boxes of paper clips and drawing pins, a stapler in the form of a silver tortoise that he hoped Felix had never noticed before, a packet of envelopes, some cake decorations and balloons, which fortunately didn't bear the number of some bygone birthday. Thank God for the satsuma. Guy could recall putting in a couple of them, and an orange and an apple, and several pound coins. Dear God, what sort of a father was he?

Months later he had come across a box hidden under the bed. It contained a number of highly suitable things, as well as some Thomas the Tank Engine wrapping paper. It seemed that Susannah had kept a secret stash of spare presents. He turned them over and over, looking for clues, but even the receipts stored with them yielded up no evidence, apart from the fact that she seemed to buy toys in sales and books in three for two promotions at

Waterstone's. He used the whole lot at Felix's next birthday. That one had been a blip of success.

Christmas was almost upon them. The university term had ended. School had finished. Guy attended the Christmas assembly accompanied by Erica, who wanted to see Felix reading a poem he had written about aardvarks visiting the manger. Erica wore a red velvet dress with a square neckline. Guy had never seen her wearing a dress before. He thought that he should not comment on it. The teachers hadn't realised that Felix's poem was satirical. But the audience did. Erica and Guy glowed with pleasure as Felix read, and were so proud when he instinctively knew to pause for the laughter. The parents of Mary and Joseph in the Infants thought that their children were the stars. Guy and Erica knew better. The assembly had started at two o'clock, so they were allowed to go straight home afterwards. Felix gently swung his PE bag with one hand, and with the other he reached out to feel the velvet pile of Erica's dress.

'Daddy,' he said, 'can Erica come round on Christmas Day?'

'I expect she's busy,' said Guy, without even looking at her.

The thought of providing some sort of standard Christmas for anyone else filled him with horror. She might expect him to cook a goose or something. It wasn't that he and Felix would just have a frozen roast dinner each. He had got a bit better than that; but he suddenly saw the house as someone else might see it – the bags of things in the hall, the layers of dust and cobwebs (which he thought were not now getting any thicker), the lack of the right sort of stuff in the kitchen, the piles that never got moved. Anyway, the end of the table where he and Felix ate was only just big enough for the two of them. He would have to clear some space if anyone wanted to join them. There were bags and bags of seeds, dry crackles of brown paper, strung everywhere. Perhaps these could be passed off as environmentally friendly Christmas garlands. Then he realised that of course Erica wouldn't mind them. But upstairs! In his bedroom he had piled boxes and boxes of Susannah's things into the fitted wardrobe. It was all neatly sorted, but he didn't know what to do with it. Though of course Erica wouldn't be looking in there.

No, there was no possibility of anyone spending Christmas with them.

Anyway, how could a girl like Erica not have a boyfriend? Guy remembered seeing her with someone. What about that biker? He was doubtless her boyfriend; but of course Guy didn't know for sure. Erica's love life was not the sort of thing they ever talked about.

Erica saw his discomfort. She certainly didn't want any awkwardness, or for Guy to think she might have designs on him.

'I always go and stay with my parents at Christmas,' she said.

'Well,' said Guy with undisguised relief, 'that's settled then.' But it was only December 19th. Erica knew that she would see Guy and Felix again before she left for her parents' house and Christmas with the large and jolly family. Neither she nor Guy could bear to be away from work or the garden for that long. And there were hellebores coming out.

The next day her rucksack was extra bulky. As well as the sandwiches and so on, she had some parcels for Felix. There was a Swiss Army knife (that really cut), a compass, a book that she loved, *The Lord of the Forest* by B.B., and some Horrid Henry books which she thought would add a bit of frivolity to Felix's life. In another bag were boxes from the bakery containing gingerbread reindeer and chocolate truffles in the shape of Christmas puddings. She hadn't got anything for Guy. There was also a secret bag of crazy things from the Hawkins shop – slime from Mars, round dice, a tin monkey playing the drums that she was informed was for adult collectors only, a sparky-flashy wheel, things like that – and she told Guy that they were for Felix's stocking.

Judy had had the same idea, and came to find them in the garden. It was jolly cold in the greenhouse. She hoped that Guy wouldn't keep Felix there too long. She sent Felix to put some fresh water on the bird table. Once he was out of earshot she said:

'I haven't brought over Felix's actual present, because I was wondering . . . it would give me great pleasure if you could spend Christmas with me. If you aren't busy, of course.'

Guy thought about whether they were busy or not. It seemed that he was more or less free for the next thirty or forty years.

'That would be great,' he said. 'Felix would love it, and so would I.'

'Come for lunch, and stay for tea.' She would be able to

use the new William Morris print herb-filled tea cosy that had arrived in the post that morning, an early Christmas present from some nieces who were off skiing.

'Well, thanks, if you're sure.'

'Absolutely.'

'I'm afraid I'm a vegetarian,' Judy told him.

'That's fine with us. Anything's fine with us. Felix once said that I only ever make him things to do with breakfast.'

'I'll write down my address.' Judy took a neat little red notebook out of her bag, and then a neat little blue enamelled pen, the same blue as her cat brooch. 'Come about quarter to twelve,' she said. 'I know from my nephews and nieces that children can't wait for their food.' Before Felix returned from the bird table she gave Guy the bag of stocking presents. Here, he thought, is a woman who does everything right.

'Guess what, Felix? We're going to visit Judy on Christmas Day.'

'Cool,' said Felix. 'I've always wanted to go to someone's house on Christmas Day. Can I see your cats, Judy?'

'Of course.' Now, she thought, I had better get a tree.

Guy found that there were only a couple of duplicates in the Erica and Judy Father Christmas things. He put them in a box under his bed for future use.

Felix and Guy arrived early, but Judy was ready.

'Wow,' said Felix. 'Your house is amazing!'

'Thank you,' she said, pleased, and hugged him. She thought that it was really very ordinary, just a Victorian semi-detached cottage.

Everywhere Felix looked there were interesting things. Some of the walls, in the gaps between the pictures and the books, were painted as yellow as sunflowers. In other rooms they were bright blue, and the kitchen – he couldn't believe it – was bright pink, like a flamingo.

'I didn't know you were allowed pink kitchens,' he said.

'In this country,' said Judy, 'we are allowed to paint things any colour we want. We're very lucky.' She feared that she sounded maudlin.

'Have a chocolate football,' she said, pulling herself together and taking one for herself.

Felix walked around looking at the pictures.

'This one's my favourite,' Judy told him. 'My niece Jemima made it.' It was of a group of scarlet macaws. 'Macaws and toucans are from South America. But of course you already know that. Jemima snipped up pieces of Indian silk that she bought from sari shops. Really she used material from the wrong continent. But it doesn't matter. It's so beautiful. When she was your age she used to make pictures with the pretty foil from Easter eggs and sweetie wrappers.'

There was a real fire, and a very small Christmas tree.

'I'm sorry, Felix, I haven't had time to finish decorating it. Can you put this star on the top for me, and these little angels, and these chocolate pocket-watches?'

After he had done that he still couldn't sit down. Everything was too interesting.

'Would you like a proper look round, Felix? I think the cats are a bit overcome with excitement, they'll be asleep somewhere.'

Everything made him laugh and exclaim. Everything smelt nice.

'Hey, Dad! Judy's got squirty soap made of green tomatoes.'

21

'D AD! PHONE FOR YOU!' Felix thought it was exciting and important to get phone calls. He had leapt to answer it (it didn't ring often). Guy had the answering machine permanently on, and would never have picked it up. Whenever he could Felix intercepted the machine by answering before the sixth ring. He occasionally remembered to ask who was calling. Guy would often be fetched to talk to some poor soul in a call centre. They were all important to Felix, but they didn't come much more important than this one.

'Dad, phone!' he yelled up the stairs. 'And it's someone called Nicole from the swimming pool.'

There were lessons to be had and they started on Saturday. Felix wrote in his Black n' Red book:

I am going to do swimming!!!! It is on Saturdays for ten weeks. Not half terms. At 9.45 a.m. SHARP. We are getting some trunks at Tesco on Friday. I hope they have got some. I told Dad that Asda is open 24 hours if they haven't. I've seen an ad that tells you all the things you can get there, but Dad has not. I told them at school that I was doing swimming now. I hope I am fast straight away. I hope you don't have to jump in at the deep end.'

'Wasn't like this when I learned to swim,' said Guy. At Guy's school there had been an outdoor pool, in use from April to October, a watery grave for a billion insects, or quite possibly a gillion or a squillion. The bright turquoise lining had wrinkled under the children's feet. Guy had worried that he might accidentally tear it, and that the water would all leak out. How wonderful if it flooded the dinner hall, and all the tables and chairs and the dinner ladies with their huge pots and pans floated away . . .

The changing rooms were outdoors too, made of fencing panels. The walls were permanently WET! DO NOT TOUCH! because applying creosote each week was the main pastime of Mr McGull, the school caretaker. Swimming lessons had been a peculiar mixture of exhilaration and misery for Guy, and he wondered how Felix was feeling now. It was hard to tell much, the parents had been instructed to wait in the café. There was a huge wall of glass between them and the pool. Guy could see Felix doing what he was meant to be doing, but he was too far away for his expression to be read.

What varied shapes and sizes the children in Felix's group came in. Felix was, Guy saw now, quite puny compared to most of them. Some of the children looked so tough, with their muscly, tanned torsos, and their shoulders always back. How at home they all seemed in their bodies, and in the world.

Guy sipped his vending machine coffee; it was really rather good.

There was a girl from school who had always stuck in his mind – Sharon Coleman. Everybody always had to be very kind to Sharon Coleman. There were things about her that had annoyed him slightly. Sharon Coleman didn't have to write as much as everybody else because, the teachers said, her writing was so small. Sharon Coleman got changed separately from everybody else. She was very quiet and very good and very odd-looking. Thinking about it now, the poor girl must have had some terrible syndrome. She was what was then called 'a bit simple', and had some mysterious things wrong with her that nobody was allowed to ask about.

He hoped that, wherever Sharon Coleman was now, she was happy. Perhaps it had been the sort of syndrome that you went through, and that then sorted itself out. Perhaps it was just a matter of time. Guy also hoped that the Medical Experimenter in the Sky would forgive him the mean thoughts he'd once had about her. He realised now, watching Felix's swimming lesson, that those mean thoughts had all started beside the school pool.

Sharon Coleman's mum had always come – even when swimming was in the middle of the day – to help her get changed. Her mum had waited by the pool with a special poncho/robe-type thing with elastic at the top. It was made from towels sewn together and looked like a giant, bottomless PE bag. He could still remember the pattern of seventies flowers in shades of avocado and olive against an orange background. There must, he supposed, have been armholes or sleeves because her mum also brought a flask of something hot, and Sharon had stood there drinking a plastic mug of it whilst she dried inside her towelling tent. They could all smell her drink, even from across the pool – hot Ribena, tomato soup, hot chocolate – how they all longed for that hot chocolate. He wondered whether Sharon had told her mum which one to bring, or whether her mum just planned to surprise her. Perhaps the decision depended on the weather. Sometimes it was hot Bovril, but Guy wouldn't have cared much for that. (His own family sometimes drank cups of hot Marmite with squares of dry toast floating in it. He had never been sure whether he was meant to like this, or if it was a punishment for being ill.)

Sharon Coleman must also be past forty now, unless premature death had been another part of the package. He downed the last of his coffee. The lesson was nearly over, and he headed back to the changing room to meet Felix.

Felix appeared, freezing but happy, with cruel red weals under his arms where the floaty polystyrene pole had rubbed. Guy realised that they should have brought shampoo. Felix didn't like showers much anyway. Guy noticed that some of the children were wearing latter-day versions of the towelling tent. They had special robes in either red and white or blue and white stripes. Other children were using special kids' towels with funky designs of sharks or pirate flags. Felix was just using one of the towels that had arrived as a wedding present, getting on for ten years ago now. Susannah's brother had once called them the 'towels of the newly married'. Guy still thought of these towels as plush, luxurious and new. He saw now, in the harsh lights of the changing room, that they were showing their age, worn in some places and with long loose threads in others. He would bloody well get Felix one of those towels for kids in time for the next lesson.

22

'PROFESSOR LOVAGE. HI! I came a bit early to show you the Action Man.'

'Max, how delightful! Did you really find one?'

'Yup. Here he is.'

Max pulled him feet first out of his rucksack. A tiny shower of sand fell onto Judy's office floor. She smiled.

'He looks a little pale,' she said.

'Well, he's had a long journey. I'll show you if you like.'

Max took his laptop and a turquoise transparent folder out of his bag. It all looked, Judy thought, much better presented than his academic work. She didn't mind. She loved to find out where her students' hearts lay. Out came a blue and green map of the world.

'The Action Men went overboard here, off the coast of China. Some of them are still at sea, maybe for ever. Plenty have washed up, all along this coast. I can show you how it all works.'

He pressed the button to switch on his laptop. A cheery little tune rang out to indicate that it was ready. It startled Judy, who had yet to have need of a laptop.

'Do you like or hate that little tune?' she asked.

'I dunno,' said Max, 'I've never really thought about it before.'

With a few clicks, or really pokes, at what Judy surmised must be the mouse, the screen lit up in more blues and greens. She read 'Surface Drifts and Currents of the Ocean'.

She liked the idea that it was all just one ocean.

'Warm currents are brown,' said Max. 'Cool ones are dark blue.'

She put on her glasses and peered at it. How clever it would be if the lines started moving. Another click and they did.

'There aren't any in the Mediterranean,' she said.

'Well, there is a current past Gibraltar, but it pretty much just slooshes around in there. That's why it's so vulnerable to pollution, algal blooms and so on.'

'Mmm,' Judy nodded.

'One of my first ever finds was a sea-bean. You can see how they get here. Look. They come from the Amazonian rainforest, maybe go towards Africa, or straight up here and across from Mexico.'

'So,' she nodded and peered some more, 'Chile is in a very different system to Brazil.'

'Yeah. But I guess if you chucked something off the very tip of South America it might end up here. From Chile it would be more likely to go towards Australia or New Zealand or Japan.'

'I see.'

'Of course these currents are vulnerable to change. It hasn't always been like this. And then there are factors such as El Niño.'

'Does everything wash up eventually?'

'Nah, that's one of the problems. This patch here,' (he pointed to a spot halfway between California and Japan) 'that's called the North Pacific Gyre. It's like an ocean landfill site. Things get in there and the currents mean they can hardly get out. It's like eternal plastic soup. Environmental nightmare. It's huge. Seems impossible to clean up.'

'If seven maids with seven mops . . .' said Judy.

'At least,' said Max. 'But who knows, things change. Like our own Gulf Stream. Might get switched off at any moment.'

They nodded morosely. They had both seen enough *Horizon*s to know that the polar bears would be arriving in Glasgow any day now.

23

Now felix had something to write in his News Book every Monday morning. Bulbs were coming up. Spring had sprung. Mrs Cowplain had begun to look forward to his entries. She was a ham-fisted gardener, a buyer of boxes of bargain bedding plants, chosen by their price and size, rather than their variety or even their colour. She would stick them in the ground in very neat rows, and just hope for the best. She was an avid watcher of gardening shows (but more for Monty Don than for any information she might glean), a buyer of ornaments and statuary rather than perennials, a non-propagator. But she loved seeing Felix's little descriptions of what he had done.

She was quite disappointed the week that he wrote about his birthday instead.

My birthday was on Saturday. Dad and Erica and me ['I, Felix, I!' she wrote in red pen] went to the Blue Reef Aquarium where I have always wanted to go. I wanted to go in Erica's car but Dad said we had to go in ours. *What we saw*:

sharks
rays that you could touch
stingrays
pipefish
seahorses
velvet swimming crab
turtles
pufferfish
domino damselfish
fox face which is also called badger fish and can turn
    completely black
clownfish
blue face angel
convict fish
We had lunch in the café. Chips but not fish and chips!
Then we went to Judy's house for tea and she had made
my birthday cake. It was a fish tank with green icing
seaweed and smaller than usual smarties for gravel and
blue background icing and the fish were plastic toy ones
to keep. One day I am going to work at the Blue Reef
Aquarium.

Mrs Cowplain wrote, 'What a nice birthday, Felix. Well
done!' even though she suspected that he had made up some
of the fish names.

The next Monday was even worse. Felix wrote of how his
dad had been digging up the whole of the garden. She was
horrified. Did that mean all of his seeds? His raspberry
canes? The three conker trees he had been growing?

'Oh no,' said Felix, 'that's just the garden at home. My
garden's at the university. In the botanical.'

'Really? I didn't know it was there. Imagine that. Lucky you.'

'You can come and see it after school one day.'

'Well, you'll have to ask your dad, won't you?'

'He won't mind.'

'Well, I'll talk to him at home time.'

'He never comes.'

'Really?'

'I just go straight there. I don't mind if you want to come too.'

'Thank you, Felix. That would be very nice,' she said, and gave him what was intended to be an extra kind smile.

Felix often hated the way that grown-ups and, most of all, teachers talked. But when school finished, he hung back.

'Is it tonight you're coming, Miss?'

She hadn't actually meant it to be tonight, just at some unspecified time in the future. She had some steak in the fridge which she feared was dripping blood through its bag onto the coleslaw beneath. She had a feeling she had forgotten to put a plate under it. But why not?

'Felix, you mustn't go in other people's cars without telling your dad.'

'It's all right, Miss. We can't go in a car, we can only walk.'

'Even so, I do think I should talk to your dad about it first. Shall I ring him up?'

But the boy's father proved to be uncontactable. It was all getting more and more complicated.

'It's because he'll be in the greenhouses, Miss.'

Why was it that for the last hundred years children had called teachers 'Miss'? She was a divorcee, but she still liked to use 'Mrs'. Being called 'Miss' really got on her nerves. She could remember being told off for doing it herself.

What was worse, she wondered, setting off with a child without his parent's permission to make an out-of-school-hours, off-site visit, or letting the child wander off by himself to find an uncontactable parent in some vague and quite possibly lonely place. Blow the dripping steak, she was on thin ice either way. She might as well go with him.

Mrs Cowplain stumbled a little on the pebbles.

'Watch out, Miss, it gets slippery here.' As they went down the cinder paths Felix held back brambles for her. Damp ferns were speckling her skirt and her tights with diamonds. Soon she could see the silhouette of a man in one of the greenhouses. She jolly well hoped that it was Mr Misselthwaite.

'Is that your dad?'

'No, that's Erica. He'll be somewhere, don't worry. Then you can ask him if it's all right for you to come. But it will be. I think anyone's allowed to come here. It's just nobody knows about it.'

'And who is Erica?'

But there was no time for him to answer. Erica came striding towards them, wiping her muddy hands on her jeans.

'Hey, Felix! Brought a visitor?'

'I am Mrs Cowplain. Felix's teacher.'

'Erica Grey,' said Erica. She went to extend one of her muddy paws, but thought better of it. This was clearly a member of the clean and structured clothes brigade.

'I was hoping to see Mr Misselthwaite. Felix was going to show me his garden, but I really need to talk to Mr Misselthwaite first.' Erica saw Felix rolling his eyes.

'Dad'll be back in a minute. He always meets me here.'

She could see that it was actually jolly convenient for the school. One dead-end road to cross. Just five minutes' walk, or less if one were wearing more sensible shoes.

'Do you want to see the garden then, Miss?'

'Yes please, Felix.'

The white cat, familiar from so many News Book entries, appeared and began to circle them, rubbing against Felix's legs.

'This is Snowy. He's the university cat.' Felix knelt down to stroke Snowy properly.

The cat turned his attention to Mrs Cowplain, butting her with his hard and heavy head. She smiled and asked, 'Do you think he likes me, Felix?'

'Oh, Snowy's a right flirt,' said Erica. 'He likes everybody.' Mrs Cowplain decided to try not to take offence. Perhaps Erica was from Yorkshire, or another cultural group.

Mrs Cowplain saw too that her tights were muddy and had been laddered somehow on the perilous journey. The cat had decided that he really liked her. He jumped up on his hind legs and dugs his claws into her right leg, adding injury to the insult.

As if from nowhere, Mr Misselthwaite appeared. He was, she observed, not much taller than Erica, and similarly attired. Perhaps she had stumbled onto the set, if that was the word for radio locations, of *Gardeners' Question Time*. He had the same weather-beaten skin as Monty Don, and was just as messy, although his eyes were very pale, and his hair much lighter. She could pretend to herself that he was a negative of Monty Don. He was equally lean and rangy.

'Dad, this is my teacher, Miss Cowplain,' said Felix. 'She's come to see my garden.'

'Thought you were in trouble for a moment. What about Miss Block, you could have brought her. Would you like a cup of tea, Miss, er . . . Cowplain?'

'Yes please, that would be lovely. And I must apologise for the state of my tights. They seem to be quite ruined. Miss Block teaches another class.'

'Lovely' turned out not to be quite the word for the tea. It was from a Thermos, and many hours old, with the unmistakeable smell and taste of flasks and plastic cups. She sipped it as they walked along more of the cinder paths and then across a bridge of planks and chicken wire. Then they were in a large open meadowy place. She could see ponds and terraces with crumbling paths and lots of plants with Latin names, as well as some she knew – bamboo, roses and azaleas. It really was paradise. She thought of the school's mean little Environmental Area, and here was this, just five minutes' walk away! And here was Felix's garden, all just as he had described, Californian poppies, love-in-the-mist, big poppies, strawberries, raspberries, pumpkin plants, all coming up in neat little rows.

'These are alliums, Miss,' he told her. 'I'm trying to grow them really big. And these are the conker trees. They'll have to be moved when they get bigger.'

'Felix,' she said, 'it's beautiful. Your dad must be very proud. It's much, much nicer than my garden.'

She couldn't wait to tell them about it in the staff room.

24

T HERE WERE SIX CHILDREN in Felix's group. They weren't meant to know that they were sorted by ability, but of course they did. The Triangles knew that they got twice as long for everything, and always had an assistant hovering beside them. Some of the Circles and the Hexagons had to be kept apart or else they would 'muck about'.

Felix was, appropriately enough, a Square. There were six Squares. Being a Square wasn't fair. As soon as you had finished the worksheets, you got given extra. The Squares weren't always very nice to each other. There was Grace who was good at clarinet, ballet, rhythmic gym and practically everything; Chun who was always drawing funny pictures on her legs, and was good at everything else as well; Duncan who didn't have a TV at home and was kind to everybody; Esther who never stopped talking, and Joe who could do any sum in the world in his head and hardly ever said anything to anyone.

Nobody but Mrs Cowplain would have called them the Squares. She seemed to delight in it.

'Squares!' she would squawk. 'Have you finished that yet?' They usually had, as long as Esther hadn't distracted them too much. One day Mrs Cowplain got very cross and threw a white-board pen right at her. It made a big green line across Esther's picture, but Mrs Cowplain didn't even say sorry. She said:

'Esther, you are living proof that coming from a nice Christian family does not make for a well-behaved child. Now give me back my pen!' as though Esther had been the one who took it. The Squares thought that was very unfair; after all, Esther's mum was famous for being a vicar who came to do assemblies.

The trouble was, you never quite knew what Mrs Cowplain was going to do next. Felix would always blame her for everything that started to go wrong with the garden, even though it really wasn't her fault.

A few days after Mrs Cowplain had thrown the pen at Esther she came and sat down at the Squares' table. Uh oh, thought everybody, we're for it now. But Mrs Cowplain was smiling.

'Squares,' she said, showing her golden tooth, the one that Chun, whose dad was a dentist, said must mean that she was very rich and very old. 'Squares, we are starting a very exciting project. A science project. The Head has been discussing it with the head of the university, where Felix's daddy works.'

'And my dad,' said Joe, who hardly ever said anything, and for once Mrs Cowplain didn't say, 'Stop interrupting', which was what she usually said to everybody.

'Yes, and lots of mummies too, I expect. Anyway, we are going to have a garden there. Just for a while, near to the one that Felix has already. We have Felix to thank. It was his garden that gave me the idea.'

'Can we grow anything we like?' asked Duncan.

'Within reason. Anyway, Squares, I want you to go QUIETLY into the library and find some books about plants and gardens. Then the whole class will have a go at drawing some plans.'

'Why is it just for a while?' asked Felix. 'Gardens take years and years.' Everybody knew that.

'It's just for a while because the garden will have to make way for some very big, new university buildings.'

'That's not true, Miss.'

'Felix, I thought your daddy would have told you by now. I'm afraid your garden won't always be there. The university is going to put a sports centre there instead.'

'No, Miss, no.' He shook his head wildly. Then he threw up all over the Squares' literacy problems.

Mrs Cowplain looked at the telephone numbers that the school had for Felix's father. There was the home one, another that she recognised as a university office number, and a mobile. She could imagine Mr Misselthwaite's mobile phone. It would just ring endlessly beside some pond, or be propped up with a flat battery in one of those cobwebby flowerpots in his greenhouse. She tried the office number. By some miracle Guy answered after the fifth ring.

'Guy Misselthwaite,' he said.

'This is Mrs Cowplain, Felix's teacher.'

Guy's heart slipped to his boots.

'What's happened? Is he all right?' Inside his head a voice was yelling, 'No! No! No!'

'I'm afraid Felix has just been sick in the classroom and he's very upset. We really think you should come and get him. He's having a lie down in the Inclusion Room.'

'I'll be right there,' said Guy.

The microscope was left on, the specimens were abandoned by the scalpel, the chemicals were left unlocked; he ran. The lift wasn't there, he took the stairs three at a time. He could have been at the school in five minutes, but instead he ran for home. Felix might not be able to walk.

Nine minutes later he was parking outside on a double yellow and sprinting towards the place he imagined the office to be.

'I'm Felix's dad,' he gasped at the woman behind the glass.

'Oh yes,' she said, making no move towards getting up. 'He's a bit poorly.'

'Has he been sick again?'

'I really couldn't tell you. Sign here please, Mr Misselthwaite. That's a nice name. Yorkshire, is it? I suppose it's to do with "thrush", and "thwaite" is lake, I think.'

She pushed an A4 black hardbacked book towards him. 'Visitors' Book,' it said. Guy found the page with the columns for Date, Name, Organisation (where he thought for a microsecond and then wrote 'not too bad considering') and Purpose of Visit (where he put 'retrieving son').

'So, can I see him now, please?' He slid the book back towards her.

'This way.'

Guy was reassured to see that the school was what people

described as 'like Fort Knox'. She pressed an electronic buzzer and the door swung open. Then she led him off down a carpeted corridor. Jolly pieces of artwork and framed certificates and sets of rules and exhortations to good behaviour decorated the walls. If Guy had paused beside the photographic Who's Who he would have been able to deduce that he was in the company of Mrs Cartwright, Office and Special Needs Coordinator. The silence suddenly turned to a many-decibelled babble.

How did Felix stand this every day?

'Morning Play,' she said. Now he had to wade against a tidal bore of small people. At last they were outside the Inclusion Room.

Inside Felix was sitting up very straight in what had been chosen as a comfy chair. They had given him a nice wooden solitaire set to play with, and placed a bucket beside him. But shouldn't someone have stayed with him?

'Felix!' Guy said, close to tears himself. He knelt down and hugged him.

'Hi, Dad. I'm not ill or anything.' Well, he certainly looked ill. 'I won't be sick again. It was just what Mrs Cowplain said.'

What on earth had that dreadful woman said to make his son throw up? Dear God, was she reading them horror stories, showing them anatomy books? Reproduction? He assumed that Felix knew all that, although he had never told him. There were encyclopaedias in the house after all. Then he thought, oh God. Maybe she was talking about car crashes. Maybe it was Princess Diana or something. Guy had never, never mentioned Princess Diana.

'Little one, we'll talk about this at home.'

He scooped Felix up in his arms and carried him out of the school.

Mrs Cartwright scurried behind them.

'But you haven't signed him out!' she yelled as Guy strode away.

The children watching from the playground were very impressed.

'Felix Misselthwaite threw up all over the classroom.'

'It was really disgusting, like Weetabix.'

'Now he can't walk and his dad has to carry him to the hospital.'

It is hard to explain anything when you are crying as much as Felix, but in the end Guy got the story.

'Felix, this is completely ridiculous. Your teacher has no business to be saying these things. I really don't think that they would concrete over the botanical garden without consulting widely, including the Botany department, well, with us in particular.'

But with every word he spoke the realisation that all this could so easily be true grew within him.

'There's only one way to settle it,' he said. 'We will ring up the people in charge and find out.'

'But Dad, you're in charge of the garden. I tell everyone that you're in charge, and it is sort of our garden.'

'Well, not really. It's some committee or other.' Come to think of it he didn't even know which committee it was. Did Felix know what a committee was? 'It's like this, Felix. The Botany department, that's me and Erica and Jeanette, have what they call historical use of the greenhouses, that's all. Now you wait here while I find out what's going on. Do you want a drink? Something to eat? Feel sick?'

'Not really,' said Felix, in answer to everything. 'But can I watch TV?'

Felix found that there was real comfort to be had in watching *Programmes for Schools* when you are meant to be at school but aren't. Guy brought him some water in his old Bunnikins mug and some custard creams on a plate with an apple.

Guy thought about who to ring. He had never bothered to keep up with the machinations and changing structures of the university. He thought of how the place had grown over the last fifteen years. Huge buildings were being fitted into tiny plots of spare land between other huge buildings. Any house or shop or scrap of space anywhere near the campus was bought up. The teacher's story was all too plausible. They had been left in peace for too long.

He phoned Erica. She gasped and said she'd get on to it straight away. She said she knew someone in the V-C's office.

Erica didn't phone to tell them what she'd found out, she came round.

'Don't worry, Fe,' she said, 'we'll fight them off.' She made her strong tan hand into a firm fist in the air to show how tough she was. 'Have you ever seen those road protesters on the news? I was one of those once.'

'Cor,' said Guy.

'We can dig tunnels and live in them if we have to, climb trees and stay there for ever, lie down in the digger buckets.'

'All three of us,' said Guy grimly.

'And your friend Judy,' said Erica.

'And Snowy,' said Felix.

*   *   *

Judy, calm, self-contained, kind, clever Judy said that they must have a plan straight away. They were meeting in her front room. She had made some scones.

'This is completely ridiculous,' she said. 'Butter, Guy? Jam?' There were several kinds to choose from.

'Can I have lemon cloud on mine again, please Judy?' Felix asked.

'They really don't have a leg to stand on. They will need planning permission.'

'Probably already got it,' said Guy grimly. 'Blanket for the whole city. Can do just what they want.'

'Now don't be such an Eeyore, Guy,' said Judy, pouring tea. She poured a tiny amount for Felix and passed him the sugar bowl. She still had the rainbow crystals that she'd bought for his last visit. 'This is what we'll do.' She had her little notebook ready on the table. 'I might hold some of my tutorials in the garden. I have some aspiring journalists among my students. I'm sure that they will know a good cause, a good story, and a good stick to beat the authorities with when they see one. We may have to form our own committee.'

'I hate committees,' said Felix. 'They make me want to be sick.'

'Well, yes, but not while we're having tea,' said Judy briskly.

'When Mrs Cowplain told me I was sick all over the classroom,' said Felix. He was now quite proud of the episode, which had lent him some notoriety.

'That's enough of that, Fi,' said Erica. Guy had been studying the mug Judy had given him, with its design of cornfield flowers.

'I don't think these are quite to scale, do you?' he said to Erica.

'But very pretty,' Erica added quickly. Honestly, she thought, the pair of them!

'We must encourage the school to take up as much space and create as many gardens as they can. I heard an article on the radio recently about community gardens. We may have to go down that path.'

'Bloody hell!' said Guy. 'I'm going to have to move my grandfather's camellia.' He hadn't told anyone about it before.

'What, the almost blue-white one? Is that yours?' Erica asked him. He nodded.

'I'll tell you about it sometime.'

'There are so many precious plants, we couldn't move them all. But a community garden might be all right,' said Erica. 'Like shared allotments. Everybody coming in and doing a bit. Growing organic vegetables for school dinners, learning how to propagate, a community composting scheme . . .'

Guy had his head in his hands. They ignored him.

'Exactly,' said Judy, 'but we'll have to be sneaky. It might be best to be so sneaky that we don't actually have a committee at first. Make a series of clever manoeuvres so that they simply cannot make that decision. We have to establish things so that they just can't do anything to harm the garden. Make it so that they don't want to, or feel that it would be impolitic. But it'll take more than a community garden. Anyway, there are lots of other things to try. Maybe it could be a performance space, an outdoor theatre, people could get married there. They have to realise what a gem it is . . .'

'I thought we were going to dig tunnels and tie ourselves up in trees and lie down in digger buckets,' said Felix.

Judy smiled. 'That's the last resort.'

'I think it should be the first resort. Erica was a tree-saver.'

'A road protester,' said Erica. 'Actually only for a few months in my gap year.'

'We need some important people on our side.'

'Oh God, do we have to fill it with people? People are the problem, always the problem. We should be thinking about the plants,' said Guy. 'They're the most important. And there must be many that they wouldn't be allowed to touch. Rare and protected orchids and butterflies. Plus the badgers.'

'How do I know we've got badgers if nobody will take me to see them?' asked Felix.

25

'T HANK YOU, MAX,' Professor Lovage said. 'That was a very interesting interpretation of the sources. It can really bring something to the subject when you come at it from a different discipline. Now before you all go, I just wanted to ask if any of you have ever been in the university's botanical garden.'

'Yeah, I have,' said Max. Professor Lovage knew this of course. She had seen him there in the distance.

'Me too,' said Phoebe, 'but not for a while. But I've been meaning to go and see if it would be all right for DramaSoc to use. We're doing *A Midsummer Night's Dream* as Speed Shakespeare after the exams. I've been wandering about, looking for the right place.'

'It would be ideal,' said Professor Lovage. 'It is quite the loveliest place. Very quiet, very beautiful, quite overgrown, a good natural slope to make a theatre space . . .'

'I've never been there,' said Madeleine. 'I didn't even know there was one.'

'Take a look. It's tucked away behind the Geography building and down the back of the Students' Union. It's been there since the university got its charter, but now it's quite neglected – but that's part of the charm. Unfortunately there are plans afoot to expand across it, destroy it really, by building the new sports science and leisure complex there. I thought that some of you might be interested. Thom, you write for the Union paper, don't you?'

'I'm a co-editor. I'll take a look if you like, Professor Lovage.'

What swagger, she thought, a co-editor of the students' weekly rag. Well, if he can make it there, he'll make it, boom boom, anywhere. She smiled at him in what she hoped was a grateful manner.

'Thank you. It might be an interesting article, or even a campaign. You might like to talk to the botanists who work there . . .'

Somehow Guy and Erica found that they had both promised to take Felix to see the badgers on the next Friday evening, weather permitting. Felix wanted to take a sleeping bag and make a night of it, but Guy put his foot down.

'We will take chocolate, peanuts in their shells for the badgers, tea, jumpers, and that's it,' he said. 'We cannot spend the night there.'

'I think we should ask Judy, seeing as she's in the committee,' said Felix. And she'll bring a huge picnic, he added to himself.

They all perched, as silently as it is possible to be perched, on tartan blankets on one of the wide benches in the furthest greenhouse. A few days earlier the door of this greenhouse had been taped up, and a notice had appeared saying, 'Danger Do Not Enter'. It seemed that Health and Safety were finally on their case, but it had been easy enough to slip inside. This greenhouse gave the best view of the sett. Judy had brought a very big bar of chocolate broken into squares so that there wouldn't be any unnecessary rustling. Felix could see that her bag, which was made of some sort of soft carpet stuff, was looking even bulgier than normal.

'Judy,' he hissed, 'what's in there?'

'Only some emergency supplies,' she whispered back.

'I've got my emergency knife. Have you got a see-in-the dark video camera?'

'Shh,' said Guy. 'They won't come if they hear you, Felix.'

'Or you, Dad,' said Felix. But he said no more.

The sky seemed to be turning green and violet. They could hear distant pounding music and laughter from the Students' Union building. A flight of house martins went over, invisible from the greenhouse, but identifiable by their harsh little voices. One sees so few swallows now, thought Judy, no wonder the summers are so unpredictable. A pair of bats flew low across the stream. Judy felt Felix's little hand reach out for hers. He had never done that before. She held it tight. His head looked very heavy. She hoped he would be able to stay awake long enough to see the badgers, or to conclusively not see them. But then the first one appeared. It was quite huge, a big fat stripy animated doormat. She really hadn't expected them to be so huge. And then another appeared, and another, until there were five or maybe six of them, it was hard to tell, the way they kept popping back indoors for something. How useful to have a snout like that, she thought. The badgers soon polished off the peanuts. Felix's mouth hung open in wonder. Behind her, she sensed that Guy and Erica were as close to each other as it is possible for adults to be without touching.

'Kiss her!' she willed Guy, but she feared that he never would, and that Erica would never dare to be the one to make the first move. I think that these two may need a little push, she thought. Then, as she watched the badgers rooting and snuffling, and saw one of the cubs heading for a patch of lady's-smock under an oak tree, it occurred to her that maybe some magic was called for.

Outside a fine drizzle began to precipitate from the violet clouds. The badgers didn't seem to mind. It intensified the smells. Here in the greenhouse ancient scents of tomato leaves, old sacks, dahlias and strawberries began to rise, heady and soporific. Were there ghosts of smells? Of moths? Of birds? Was Susannah watching? Surely no mother could bear to part from her child? Perhaps, thought Judy, these were the thoughts that were holding Guy back.

She felt Felix lolling against her.

'I'm not tired,' he whispered. She stroked his hair, it felt like marram grass growing on a dune, and then his head lolled again. She wondered if Felix had a regular bedtime. That was it! She could offer to babysit so that Guy could take Erica to the pub (she could imagine them doing a quiz together), or out to dinner. That was harder to picture. They would probably both go in their work clothes and boots, leaving little patterns of dried mud in a trail across the restaurant floor.

Presumably Guy had once wooed Susannah; he couldn't always have been so completely hopeless and inept.

It grew darker, and the badgers became less visible. Soon all that could be seen were the white stripes, and even these were hard to distinguish from the shadows and plants surrounding them. Time to go. She would have been quite happy for them all to come home with her, but Felix must need his bed. Guy wrapped one of the blankets around him, and she offered them all more chocolate. Felix said out loud, 'But I'm not tired!'

'I expect they will be gone now, off into the trees somewhere, Felix,' said Erica. 'I'm sure we could come and see them again. Weren't they just beautiful?'

'What do they say at school for "cool" now?' Judy wondered.

'Cool, mostly,' said Felix. It used to be "wicked". And then if something happened that you wanted, you said "ker-ching!" That was from a show on TV.'

Their feet made a faint scrunch on the damp cinder path, doubtless enough to send any badgers trundling for cover, and quite possibly loud enough to bring one of the security guards with a dog to sniff them all out. Luckily there was a minor disturbance in the Union bar, and an improperly extinguished cigarette had caused a small fire in a bin outside the theatre. All available security personnel were occupied elsewhere.

When Judy got home there were still two hours left of the day. She heated some soup and ate it watching the news; but Friday night after-the-news TV shows were something that she could not abide. She turned the TV off and sat enjoying the silence. She decided to make a plan. She would have them all to supper, including Felix, and keep suggesting nice things to do, places to eat and go, until at last the bait was taken, or she would come up with some lovely evening out for them, something romantic. Then she would offer to babysit for Felix. She would be delighted to do it. She could imagine him in some very soft pyjamas, definitely green, probably with the legs and arms too short. Perhaps she would get him some new pyjamas, ones that fitted of course; but Christmas and his birthday were ages away. Perhaps she might just happen to see some in a sale . . . there must be so many nice things that one could buy a little boy of Felix's age, so many things she could get for his room. She couldn't imagine that Guy was that big on interior design or soft furnishings. A nice new quilt cover, perhaps with a design of boats, or maybe parrots – she was sure she'd seen one with parrots somewhere; a soft, brightly coloured cotton rug; a lamp – she'd seen a lovely shade, very jolly, a bright yellow sun in John Lewis . . .

26

Erica was on the phone to the Council. After several false starts she had been put through to somebody who explained that they were a Neighbourhood Visions Officer, or an NVO.

'Does that cover gardens?' Erica asked.

'It could do. If they are part of the neighbourhood's vision.'

'And do you deal with views or only visions?' Erica couldn't resist asking. 'Because we have some very fine views. And views on our views. They might enhance your visions.'

'Um,' said the NVO.

'The reason I'm calling,' Erica told her, 'is that I am interested in community gardening projects. I heard this programme on Radio Four recently, all about community gardens. Do you have anything like that? Shared allotments, that kind of thing? Or maybe groups of people' (preferably deprived, she added to herself) 'who might be interested in them? I'm a botanist at the university, and I have been concerned that local residents aren't making the most of our facilities. We have a very beautiful garden here that is hardly used at all.'

'And whereabouts are you?'

Erica explained. This Neighbourhood Visions Officer didn't seem to have much of an idea about the geography of the neighbourhood; but what she did have, it transpired, was an empty space on the agenda of a public meeting. It seemed that the community was a little short on issues for discussion.

A leaflet advertising the meeting arrived in the post for Erica the following week. She was to share the agenda with a spokesperson for the Primary Healthcare Team, and an item on pigeons. She realised that what she was doing was actually very dodgy. If the people in Public Relations found out about it, or the Powers That Be . . . luckily she had been billed as a local botanist, rather than as an official university speaker. She could also, she figured, pass herself off as a local resident, because she was one.

Judy Lovage – Moth Rescuer, was how she thought of herself in summer. Much as she liked moths and ladybirds and so on, she couldn't help but wish that there weren't so many of them in her little domain. She could quite believe in the theory of spontaneous generation. Even if she left the bathroom window shut at night, there would still be dozens of little creatures in need of rescuing by morning. Today she leant over the bath and spotted a yellow and black beetle. It looked confused and possibly trapped. There would be no having a bath until it had been saved. And here was a whole community of tiny flies. It would be impossible to pick them up and put them out of the window without killing them. But she felt compelled to try anyway. She didn't want to be someone who was making judgements on who might live and who must die, especially judgements based on something as arbitrary as size. She attempted to dust the creatures onto a tissue and then dropped the whole thing out of the window. She could retrieve it from the garden later. Annoyingly, the tissue landed on the outside windowsill and stuck there. She hoped that nobody would look up and see it. How embarrassing! Professor Lovage threw tissues (and they might even imagine that they were dirty) out of her windows! There were four moths to rescue as well as a couple of those wooden-looking T-shaped creatures. Finally she was done and could run the bath.

She lay back in the fragrant water. But when she opened her eyes, oh no! A lacewing seemed to be caught in a spider's web. Oh dear. She knew that these only lived for a day. What a way to spend it! She had to climb onto the loo seat to rescue it.

How foolish I must look, she thought, my body dripping bubbles everywhere. I am hardly Venus emerging from the foam now, more like some old moth flapping about.

Finally she relaxed in the bubbles with the week's theatre and entertainment guide in her hands. It grew wetter and more fragile as she searched in vain for the right thing to send Guy and Erica to.

Thom eventually found his way into the garden. He had picked a good moment. There was Phoebe from his Gothic Architecture tutorial lounging on the grass with a big floppy daisyish thing in her hair. She was in the middle of a semicircle of fit-looking girls holding copies of the same book. Ah, what a gorgeous spectacle! A rehearsal. He stopped to watch.

Thom couldn't believe that anyone had the patience for amateur dramatics, or any kind of dramatics at all really. There was so much faffing about, so many debates about the most minor of points, so much waiting. He didn't have much patience with a lot of fiction either, which was a bit of a drawback for somebody doing English and History of Art. Why waste all that time saying something in tens of thousands of words that could be said so much more succinctly in a few lines? Make it punchy. Give him facts. He sat under a tree and took out a notebook and his iPod. He pretended to be working on something, whilst he watched Phoebe and her attendants. In between takes he dashed off an article about conditions in one of the halls of residence, and then started one about the garden. He was trying to get his byline on every front cover until the end of term. He needed to thicken up his portfolio. He had been coming up with so many stories (there was a place for fiction sometimes) that this garden one might have to wait a while. After the actors had left he picked a stalk or two of some of the bigger, more successful-looking plants, and then went to ask the middle-aged guy in the greenhouse what they were. All he got was the names and a terse 'You shouldn't be moving those. Not even fragments. Very bad idea.'

Thom wrote the names down in his book, a real pro.

* * *

Felix and Guy were going to the residents' meeting with Erica. It hadn't occurred to Erica to dress up, and she was wearing her self-imposed early summer uniform of soft shirt, khaki shorts and espadrilles. Felix was still in his school clothes, and Guy was in his backwater professor's uniform. Guy had never mentioned Erica's attire before, but tonight seemed different.

'I thought you might wear that nice red dress,' he said, 'the one you wore at the school Christmas thing.'

Erica was astounded that he had ever noticed what she was wearing.

'Oh,' she said, 'I didn't think of dressing up. Anyway, that's a winter dress. I only wear it for Christmas things.'

He remembered how his mother used to get so cross at people who appeared on TV without smartening themselves up. You really would think, she used to say, that if you were going to be on *University Challenge* or *Ask the Family*, you might go out and get a haircut, and put on a tie. Or even just wash your hair. He suspected that it was a great sadness to her that they had never appeared on *Ask the Family*. His sister Jenny was once a relatively successful contestant on *Blockbusters*, though. She made two glorious Gold Runs and brought home a portable TV and a week's stay for two at an outward bound centre. She invited a girl called Jacqui from her Rangers pack to go with her. He was quite put out that he didn't get to go. Not that he'd have invited Jenny if he'd been the one to win it. Jenny and Jacqui had sat around in their uniforms after Rangers, looking at the centre's leaflet and planning which activities they would do.

He had stalked through the room on his way to get a biscuit.

'Isn't being old enough for Rangers an indicator of being too old for it?' he had asked.

They ignored him. Stupid annoying Guy. He didn't know that Jacqui looked rather wistfully at the space he left in the room.

The meeting was held in a church hall. There were rows and rows of grey plastic stackable chairs, the sort designed to make you feel as though you have sweaty legs. The building looked 1950s, and the long black, grey and yellow curtains, patterned in an abstract, geometric design, were probably the original ones. When Felix hid behind one of them and tried to twist himself round and round in it, he heard terrible rips, and pieces of the sepia-stained lining fell to the parquet floor. He quickly stuffed them behind a radiator, hoping that nobody had noticed. Then he twisted himself up again, making a gigantic pulled cracker or a half-unwrapped boiled sweet.

It was lucky that when the 25-foot-long brass curtain pole came crashing down a few days later, just missing the leader of the Armchair Exercise Class, but taking out her CD player, nobody thought to blame the little boy at the residents' meeting. The vicar threw the curtains into a skip, not realising that somewhere the fabric would be considered vintage, and that they might be born again, or perhaps reincarnated.

The Neighbourhood Visions Officer emerged from the kitchen. The urn was now on. She gave Erica and Guy a sticky label each for their names.

'Could you give Felix one?' asked Erica.

'Sorry, no. Child protection issues prevent me from doing that.'

'Oh.'

'Council officers were once encouraged to dress down for low-level public meetings too,' she said, looking them up and down. 'Where would you like to put your display boards?'

'Er, display boards . . . I haven't got any display boards,' said Erica.

'What, nothing? Are you going to do Powerpoint then?'

'Actually, I was just going to talk. And I have got this . . .'

Erica opened a cardboard box that had once contained the kick-step stool that Jeanette had ordered for the department, rather unnecessarily, Guy thought. He couldn't quite remember authorising it either, and they didn't even have much stuff up high. He could see that it would make a nice footrest though, more comfortable than an upturned bin or an open desk drawer.

When Erica opened the box a ladybird flew out and landed on the floor just in front of the Neighbourhood Visions Officer.

'Quick, Felix! Come and rescue this!' Erica said. He untwisted the curtains and freed himself, with an almost calamitous final tug. The ladybird, which was black and orangey-red with three spots on each wing, seemed happy to be caught.

'Do you have a garden here?' Guy asked.

Good grief, thought their host, who were these people? First they didn't have any display boards and then they had to rescue a ladybird.

'No,' she snapped. 'Isn't that rather why you wanted to come and talk to us?'

'Can I have this?' Felix asked, and before she could say anything he tipped her roll of sticky labels out of their cute blue box.

'Break off some leaves and put them in,' said Guy. 'We can take it back tomorrow.'

'Ladybird, Ladybird, fly away home, your house is on fire. But I expect your children will be gone before you get home if it isn't till tomorrow,' said the NVO, and she stalked off to take up her position by the door.

'What a complete bit—' said Erica, then quickly she remembered Felix. 'What a horrible thing to say.'

'I hope nobody comes to her stupid meeting,' said Felix.

But the first of the residents were arriving. Soon there were at least fourteen of them, all drinking cups of tea from unbreakable smoked-glass mugs. Guy had always thought that those mugs were somewhat obscene. Because of those mugs he'd been unable to attend more than one meeting of the church youth group where Jenny hung out, and had made so many friends. If it hadn't been for those mugs he might have had more of a faith, and a very different life.

The woman from the Primary Healthcare Team arrived with her mind-numbingly dull display boards and her Powerpoint stuff. She had a huge jar of children's teeth to show the residents too. These teeth had been extracted under general anaesthetic during the last year. It was all very bad. Any questions?

Somebody asked where she had got the jar, was it from a sweet shop? Actually it was. Somebody else wondered if anybody else remembered those sweet milky teeth, pink and white and soft and chewy, or those sweet milk bottles. They were nice. And were there any NHS dentists taking people on . . .

By the time it was Erica's turn to talk at least three more people had arrived.

'Now,' said the NVO, 'we have Erica, sorry I can't remember your surname. . . .'

'It's Grey,' interjected Erica.

'. . . who has come along with her partner and little boy to talk to us about the botanical garden at the university. Over to you, Erica . . .'

Felix nudged Guy. 'Aren't you going to say something, Dad?'

'It doesn't matter,' said Guy. 'Ssssh.'

'These,' Erica said, gently lifting some foliage out of the kick-step box, 'are plants that many people might consider tropical, or exotic, or unusual, that all grow in a garden only a few minutes' walk from here. Does anybody know which plant these leaves come from?'

'Banana!' shouted Felix.

'Yes, I know that you know, Fe.' This raised a general laugh from the audience.

'What about these?' She lifted out a garland hung with ivory flowers.

'Is it a kind of vetch?' said someone in the back row.

'Anyone else?' Erica asked.

'A type of clematis?'

'Head in the sun, feet in the shade. We all know that one.'

'Actually,' said Erica, fearing that she would sound like a know-all, 'it's kiwi fruit. It's been established in the

206

botanical garden for decades. Long before they were so commonplace at the greengrocer's.'

'Not much commonplace about the greengrocers for some people. Some people have to live in a food desert,' muttered the NVO.

'What about these leaves? I'll give you a clue, another fruit.'

'Mulberry,' said a man in the front row. 'Ask us another.'

She had wild hops, carob, strawberry tree, vines, figs . . .

'Anyway,' said Erica, 'this garden, the botanical garden at the university is just a few minutes' walk from here, and it's open to everybody. You don't have to be a student . . .'

'Don't talk to us about students!' yelled somebody.

'. . . or work at the university to go there. There are ponds, quiet places to sit, all sorts of birds . . .' (Don't tell them about the badgers! Felix and Guy willed her. She didn't.)

'I'm going to have to stop you there,' said the NVO. 'We have to move on to our main agenda item – pigeon control.' (Yeah, a bit interesting and a bit too pleasant, thought Guy.) 'But if you'd like to stay, people can ask you questions individually at the end of the meeting.'

Erica, Guy and Felix all thought that they wouldn't like to stay, but they did.

Erica had been planning to talk about the different flowers, the changes throughout the year, the ponds and streams, some history of the garden. Oh well. She had been hoping to gain some more regular visitors, perhaps establish a gardening club or a scheme for people without gardens to grow their own fruit and vegetables. The nucleus of it could form a vocal pressure group, something that the university could not ignore without great embarrassment.

The big debate on pigeons was this: Should they be culled? Should people who feed them be prosecuted? Should special pigeon feeders be set up at focal points around the area? And might it actually be a cultural issue? Guy and Erica hadn't realised that pigeons were a local issue at all. When the discussion got quite unpleasant, they both wished that Felix wasn't there. Luckily he was tending his ladybird and probably not taking it in. At last it was over. Guy was astonished that anybody had voluntarily turned out for the meeting, let alone sat through it all.

A breakdown of the list of those present would have revealed that there were actually two other council officers, two prospective councillors trying to establish their credentials, a lay reader from the church who was also responsible for locking up the hall if the evening ever ended, a couple who ran a cheerleading club and were seeking a grant for a minibus, a sitting councillor, a youth worker, and the chair of the city's Council for Voluntary Services. The local bobby who tried to attend couldn't make it. There must have been fewer than ten bona fide local residents.

Afterwards, some of the audience came to talk to Erica about plants. She could have run a very successful *Gardeners' Question Time*. They all told her that they would try to visit the garden soon. The Primary Healthcare woman packed up her display boards and was gone before you could say 'Obesity Epidemic'. Guy and Felix helped the NVO stack up the chairs. She gave them some chocolate chip cookies and was suddenly much nicer now that the meeting was over. Perhaps anxiety and dread had been making her so unfriendly.

27

A FEW DAYS LATER THEY were in the office when the phone rang.

'Erica, for you,' said Jeanette. 'Gloria Gregson from the Primary Healthcare Team. What on earth would that be about?'

'Thanks, Jeanette. Put her through.'

'Hello,' said Erica. 'Can I help you?'

'I was given your name by my colleague. You spoke at the residents' meeting together, I believe.'

'Yes . . .'

'University switchboard had a devil of a time trying to think who you were.'

'Oh,' said Erica, 'perhaps it was someone new.' She had a feeling that one day the phone lines to the Botany department would be cut. She and Guy would find the locks to the lab and office changed. Jeanette would be moved full-time to Biology, who were always asking for more of her hours. Botany would slip out of the prospectus and be forgotten for ever. She thought that it might take Guy a while to notice, he seemed to pay so little attention to what was going on around them. Perhaps they should be looking for positions elsewhere . . .

'Well, when I suggested Biology instead of Botany they found you.'

'We share some facilities.' Really, had the woman just rung up to point out how insignificant they were?

'It's about your botanical garden. Is it open to everybody?'

'Oh yes,' said Erica, quite aware that it was not her garden, and that she had no jurisdiction over it at all.

'I am working with a number of groups of people with mental health issues. We are hoping to establish some sort of garden project, but we lack the space. All we really have are a number of front gardens and forecourts at doctors' surgeries. I was wondering . . .'

They arranged to meet in the car park behind the Geography building two days later.

When Gloria Gregson arrived wearing eminently sensible shoes Erica decided to like her.

'I'm a Friend of Kew,' she told Erica. 'You have some really gorgeous trees. Would it be a good or a bad idea to have a plot near the handkerchief tree?'

'Um.'

'Actually we'd quite like a number of plots. You see, there's a Refugees' Group, and a number of different therapy groups. There might be issues around some of them working on the same ones.'

'I hope none of them are, er, dangerous,' said Erica. 'I don't want to be rude, but we do have a school with a little garden up the other end.'

'They'll be supervised through all of the gardening sessions.'

'Of course it's open to everyone, the garden,' said Erica, feeling as though she must seem like a bigot, somebody who would call a radio phone-in.

'I can quite understand your concerns,' said Gloria. 'Now, is there a shed where we can keep our own things? I have a budget for tools and so on.'

'Lucky you,' said Erica, 'but I don't know about sheds. It's all pretty dilapidated.'

'Well, I expect we could fix something up.'

'There are some long-term plans for development around here,' said Erica. 'Some question marks over the garden's future.'

'Oh, well.' They were now standing beside the stream. 'We'll have to cross that bridge when we come to it.'

Gloria Gregson tried to think of a name for the projects as she walked back to her car. Fresh Air, Fresh Start? New Ground? Tranquillity Garden Project? She couldn't think of anything good. The groups would of course be encouraged to decide their own title for it. Mustn't be pushy and controlling, Gloria reminded herself. How about New Leaves Together?

What have I done, what have I done? Erica thought as she walked back to the office. She wondered if there had been a point when she had actually said 'yes' to what Gloria was asking for. Gloria certainly seemed to think that she had.

'Erica,' said Guy, 'you are the sneakiest woman who ever lived. How are you going to get that past any committee?'

'Oh, somehow,' said Erica. 'How can they say no? Just a little corner of the garden on a temporary basis . . .'

'Pulling in a load of people with mental health problems, and letting them start building something together – a bit of a low-down mean trick.'

'Not really. I told her that there were plans afoot for the garden. I didn't actually say plans to completely destroy it, but they know it might be temporary. Anyway, I don't care,' said Erica. 'If it saves the garden.'

'I expect it will end up as a leisure centre with a few raised beds in the car park,' said Guy, staring into his tea.

Jeanette came in. 'Everything OK?'

'Well,' said Guy. Erica explained what she had done.

'Easy,' said Jeanette. 'Go through the Community Liaison Office. The secretary there is the V-C's sister-in-law. He never says no to anything from there. Plus it's such good PR. They'll bypass that old A D & M Committee, temporarily at least.'

'I don't think anyone would notice anyway,' said Erica.

'But we don't want you getting into trouble, do we?' said Jeanette.

Guy decided not to mention the kick-step stool, or the espresso machine that had now appeared, or even the new blinds.

'These health groups have given me another idea too,' said Erica. 'I think I'm going to write a sort of coffee-table book. Are there still things called coffee-table books? About doctors' surgery gardens and plants. I've always loved them. False castor-oil plant, cotoneaster, choisia, mahonia, inner city pyracantha, snowball tree, maybe flowering currant. I might have photos of real people, say doctors and receptionists and patients, and practice managers, saying why they chose or hate particular plants. Pebble and gravel things that manage to look dusty and dark and depressing whatever the time of year or day, whatever the weather. The case against flowers . . .'

28

Not long until summer half term. Erica was off to visit her mum and dad, there was to be a large family gathering, celebrating lots of birthdays. They were just the sort of family to have nearly all their birthdays close together in a big matey bunch in the summer. Parties were always huge outdoorsy affairs with lots of games and larking about. To an outsider they might have looked like a family of ponies, galloping and whinnying around their field.

'What are you doing at half term?' she asked Felix, hoping that he might actually be doing something, going somewhere, but also wanting to invite him along.

'Dunno,' said Felix, swishing a bamboo cane through the air. 'Nothing as usual.'

Erica could remember the acute boredom of childhood, even with her three big brothers and a sister, and endless activities; there were times when it was all just screamingly boring.

She didn't want to do what her mum called 'putting somebody in a position', but decided that she would act.

'Guy,' she said, 'um, it's my birthday next weekend, and there's going to be a family party. Most of the family have their birthdays around now, so there's always this big party. Next Sunday. Anyway, I wondered if maybe you and Felix would like to come. It's half term. But I'm going down the night before.'

'Um,' said Guy, 'we don't really go to that many parties . . .'

'It's just a big all-day picnic really, with drinks. And people usually play games. I just thought Felix might enjoy it. I've got lots of nephews and nieces, and as it's my birthday, it would be nice . . .'

'Oh, you meant just Felix! Sorry! Well, he's never really stayed away from home, but if he was with you . . .'

'No, I did mean both of you, really.'

'You don't have to say that.'

'But I did, really.' Erica wished she had never invited him now. Honestly, what a fuss about something so little. It wasn't that big a deal, was it? 'It's at my parents' house. In Wiltshire. They've got this big garden beside a river. We could drive down together if you like. On the Saturday afternoon.'

'OK. I mean thanks. Felix will be really excited.'

Guy told Felix about it at teatime. They were having Vegetarian All-Day Breakfast out of a tin, with lots of toast, and cups of water from the cooler out in the corridor because it made them so thirsty, and also because Felix loved using it so much. They had endless debates about whether the water from the blue tap was any cooler than that from the green one. They were eating off paper plates in the office where Jeanette had now installed a microwave and a toaster. Guy felt a bit guilty using them, even though he suspected that they'd been bought out of his budget.

'So how old is she going to be then, Dad?'

'Oh. It's impossible to say when women are that age. Could be forty-five, could be nearly sixty. You can't ask.'

'Nearly sixty! Erica! No way!'

'Oh, I thought you meant Jeanette. I was just thinking about the microwave and stuff.'

'Dad, how old is Erica? You can ask someone if they invite you to their party.'

'Oh, I don't know. About twenty-five, I suppose, or something. Very young.'

Twenty-five seemed a hundred years ago. He couldn't imagine what twenty-five must feel like now. He couldn't imagine what it must feel like to be young. He wondered if anything really bad had ever happened to Erica, or happened *yet*, he caught himself thinking. It sounded as though her parents were still married and living. She seemed to have plenty of siblings. There had been mention of a river. Potential for tragedy and disaster there. He couldn't imagine what it must be like to inhabit a world that was basically good and not full of menace. He looked out of the lab window and across the car park, all tarmac and concrete, towards the building site that was to be the Electronics department's next phase of expansion. There were too many students swilling Coke. Too many students arriving in their cars for lectures. A few years ago they would have cycled. He could see a fellow with elaborate facial hair fly-posting some vulgar doctors-and-nurses posters for the weekend's drinkathon. The only thing to please the eye was some ragwort breaking through the cracks in the paving slabs. Really, the world would be so much better off without human beings. Bring on the asteroid strikes. Then he thought of Felix. A flaw in the argument. Perhaps if the plants could just slowly win back control . . . let the bindweed choke the phone masts, let lichens grow across the windscreens, let fungi spring up out of every laptop, let buddleia flags wave from the rooftops, let grass grow high across every golf course! That made him snigger out loud, something he didn't do that often.

Perhaps it would do them good to get away. He quite liked Wiltshire. Even though he'd grown up with an idea of it as quite unpleasant. He'd had a wooden puzzle of the counties of England and Wales. Wiltshire had been large and mauve. The image on it had been a pink and black pig. Other counties had all sorts of things, lots of different things each, combine harvesters, important buildings, power stations, apple trees, mountains, even gold coins for some part of Wales. All Wiltshire had was a pig. The artist must have just got very bored. Wiltshire could have had Stonehenge, or Salisbury Cathedral, or army bases and tanks. There must have been plenty of things to put on besides that pig. If they were making that puzzle now they could even give Wiltshire great bustards.

He'd always known how fat Wiltshire was. They'd driven through it so many times on the way to Cornwall when he'd been Felix's age. Why not go to Erica's party and then on to Cornwall? He smiled. They would have a real holiday.

'We should get some puzzles or something up here for you to do,' Guy said. Felix was looking out of the window too now, sitting on Jeanette's chair, swivelling and swinging. Jeanette had a bad back and that green chair had been brought in specially. It had taken several visits from someone in Human Resources and a lengthy debate between them all about which green was the nicest. In the end Jeanette had asked Felix to decide. Green was his favourite colour, and he always went for the same shade if he had a choice. It was what people called 'sea-green'. Guy couldn't recall ever seeing a sea that colour. One would probably have to go to a South Sea island.

'I don't really do puzzles much any more,' said Felix. 'All my puzzles are too easy now. Puzzles seemed to stop after I was about five.'

'Oh,' said Guy. Here was yet another way that he'd failed without even realising. Non-provision of puzzles. 'Well, we could get you some harder ones.'

'No thanks,' said Felix. 'But I might have some more water. Do you want some?'

'Yes please.'

'Blue or green?'

'What are you having?'

'Green.'

'I'll have blue. I know, get one of each and we'll take their temperatures. I don't know why we didn't think of that before.'

'OK, Dad.'

By the time Felix had struggled back through the swing doors and the office door with the plastic cups full to their brims, Guy had fetched a thermometer from the lab.

'Cor, I wish we had one that long at home,' said Felix, carefully putting the cups down on the table.

'Right. Now the truth will be revealed. Write this down. Sample A, the cup next to the window . . . now Sample B . . . right, which is which? B is half a degree warmer. Is that the blue one or the green one?'

'Um, I think it's the blue one, but I got a bit mixed up when I had to balance them on the photocopier whilst I did the doors, it seemed to be a bit, um, hot.'

'The mystery remains unsolved,' said Guy.

29

I T WAS HOT. They arrived on the Saturday afternoon. There was a wooden five-bar gate at the start of a long drive. Felix got out to open it, and then shut it once Guy had driven through. It looked very heavy, but he managed. Guy had always loved doing gates like that. It was such a holidayish thing to have to do. If only, he thought, I could have a holiday from being myself.

He had been expecting people to look him up and down, but that first night it was just the Misselthwaites and Erica and her parents. They ate noodles with lime and chilli. He realised that Felix had never been given noodles before, or quite possibly lime or chilli either; but he ate them all up. Felix seemed predisposed to love everything. The moment they'd arrived Erica's mother, Rosemary, had taken Felix off to look at the river. Guy had been left standing there like a lemon, saying, 'Well!' and knowing that his heartiness was too, too transparent. Then Phil, Erica's father, gave him a mug of tea and Guy saw how deeply muddy and blackly creased his hands were. Ah, a gardener, or possibly a charcoal-burner. All would be well.

Felix and Guy were given a tiny spare bedroom in an attic. Felix was on an ancient camping bed that groaned at his every breath. In the end Guy hauled him, still sleeping, across the gap, and they slept together in the huge nest of ancient eiderdowns and blankets that Rosemary had thought necessary for an attic room in May. Guy could feel individual feathers through the old cloth, spiky and soft through the silkiness. Perhaps, he thought, we should stay here for ever. Then he fell asleep.

He didn't hear Erica at 2 a.m. standing at the bottom of the little flight of creaky wooden stairs that led to the attic. He didn't know that she was wearing her new cotton shortie pyjamas which were yellow with white polka dots. She was hardly breathing at all. After a while she decided that she was being ridiculous, and went back to bed.

The next day, the day of the party, was something else entirely. The people began arriving after breakfast. It seemed that Erica actually had about a dozen brothers, each one taller and more athletic-looking than the last. One by one they pumped Guy's hand, and introduced him to a partner and some kids. There was no way of telling them apart. There were aunts and uncles and grandparents and neighbours. And everybody had crazy non-names. They were all called things like Dagger and Spaniel and Plops. Guy thought that he might just have been able to pick out the neighbours. The people related to Erica all had the same long limbs. Then he began to suspect that some of the Greys had married some of the neighbours.

Rosemary was making salads. Erica was snapping peas. Felix helped her, thinking it exotic. Some giant pieces of flesh were being prepared for the flames. Somebody had arrived with wicker baskets of strawberries and blueberries. Convention on Walton's Mountain, thought Guy. He wondered aloud what would happen if it rained.

'Oh, it never rains on our parties!' someone told him. Guy helped himself to a beer and went outside. It seemed that Erica had tipped her family off. Not once was he asked the whereabouts of his wife, and he trusted that nobody asked Felix about his mum.

There were three giant barbecues going. He wandered away across the garden to stare at the sheep in the field next door. They were Jacob's sheep, all spotty and stripy; his very favourite sort of sheep. He hoped Felix would come and join him, although he had seemed happy doing those peas. Guy drank the beer and walked down to the river that ran, so obligingly, through the garden. There were trout in the shade of a willow, and watermint and kingcups were in flower. Perhaps if he sat here all day, beside these irises, nobody would notice. He could hear that a game of rounders was getting under way. Suddenly, on silent bare feet, Erica was there beside him.

'Are you OK?'

'Yes, yes,' he said politely. She was wearing a skirt. He didn't remember ever seeing her in a skirt before, let alone a spotty one in shades of pink and red, that was all crinkly.

'I used to come down here all the time to get some peace when I lived at home. There are water voles. Dad thought he saw an otter last summer.' She put her glass, empty but for a sprig of mint and some pink stickiness, down on the grass and took a step closer to him. Good God, thought Guy, she might be about to kiss me. He stood very still. Something made them look up. Felix was sitting by himself in the willow tree.

'Hi Felix!' said Erica, smiling, and not missing a beat. 'Would you like to come and play rounders?'

'Um, no thanks, I don't think anyone would pick me.'

'It's not like that. It's not like at school. Everyone is picked. It's just for fun.'

The yells and whoops and cries of 'Get 'im out!', 'To third base!', 'Butterfingers!' sounded exactly like school to Guy and Felix.

'Are you going to open your presents?' Felix asked her. 'We brought you a present but we didn't know when we were meant to give it to you.'

'Now would be nice.'

They walked back to the house together, Felix and Erica holding hands.

'I like your skirt,' Felix told her. 'It looks as though it would rustle, but it doesn't. I hate it if clothes make a noise.'

The present was wrapped in paper that could only have been from a sub-post office.

'It's something from Amazon,' Felix said. 'Dad is always ordering stuff on Amazon.'

'Wow! This is lovely. And some of these will be from *the* Amazon. Thank you. I've always wanted to read more about sea-beans.'

It was *Sea-Beans from the Tropics: A Collector's Guide to Sea-Beans and Other Tropical Drift on Atlantic Shores*. Guy had ordered it for himself weeks ago and then forgotten about it. It had arrived conveniently when a present for

Erica was required. He had thought it ideal, but was reluctant to part with it straight away. He hoped he might get to read it too.

That evening Felix and Guy left for Cornwall, driving west into the sunset and then the night. Felix slept. Wasn't there something in the life force, some animal instinct, some migratory pull to go west? Guy felt footloose and in control, like someone in a movie. Really, he and Felix shouldn't be so tied to routine. They could go anywhere. He had the radio tuned to some bonkers show that kept on playing songs like 'Everybody's Talking' and 'Rhinestone Cowboy'. Hours later he was almost sorry when they arrived at the hotel. Felix woke up enough to make it upstairs to bed.

'But Dad, I thought Erica was coming too,' he said as he fell back to sleep.

Guy had no idea why Felix thought that, but it would have made sense. He wished that she had come. He decided to ring her in the morning and ask her to join them, and maybe she could bring the sea-beans book with her.

He opened the window so that they could sleep to the sound of the waves.

Guy had Erica's parents' address and phone number on a Post-it note in his wallet. Rosemary answered the phone. He realised that perhaps it wasn't normal to be ringing at 8.30 a.m.

'It's Guy,' he said.

'Oh hello.'

'I was just ringing to say, um, thank you for the party. And having us to, um, stay, and . . .'

'Well, thank you. It was a pleasure meeting you both. How was your long drive?'

'Oh, um, er, fine. Nice actually.'

'Did you want to talk to Erica?'

'Yes, please.'

'Well, I'm sorry, you've just missed her. She's just gone out for a ride with someone.'

'A ride. Oh. Just tell her I rang please. It's not important.'

So she was back with that black helmet boyfriend. Oh well, thought Guy. I guess I never had a chance. Off on a motorbike going too fast around the lanes of Wiltshire. He realised where the thought was taking him. He ground his fists into his eye sockets to stop it all.

'Come on, Felix,' he said. 'Let's hit the beach.'

When Erica came back, smelling strongly of her friend Polly's horses, Rosemary said, 'Nice ride?'

'Great, but my legs are really achy. I think I'll have a bath. And I know I stink, even though it's a good stink.'

'Oh, Guy rang. Just to say thank you, I suppose.'

'That's impressive. Not like him to make a voluntary phone call.'

And that was that.

*　　*　　*

There must have been several bucketfuls of sand on the floor of their room, and it was only the end of the first day. Felix had the first shower. Afterwards he looked so clean and healthy that Guy felt proud. Their hotel TV had a cartoon channel, which Felix watched, constantly laughing out loud, whilst Guy made some tea in the stainless-steel pot. Felix's pyjama trousers were well on the way to becoming pyjama shorts. Guy realised that they would have to go clothes shopping again soon, and actually buy stuff. He also realised that he was quite looking forward to it, and he smiled as he crunched across the sandy carpet into the bathroom. Twenty minutes later, his shower done, he felt as clean and warm and healthy as Felix.

Guy hadn't noticed the full-length mirror in the tiny bathroom. A hideous old man emerged from the steam. What did he think he had been doing, feeling at all good about things? Fool. Dolt. He looked with horror at the man in the mirror. His curls were flattened into a ridiculous bathing cap. He hadn't realised that he was turning into a tortoise. He seemed to have swapped necks with Michael Palin. He knew that his eyebrows were turning white, but he hadn't really noticed his chest hairs going the same way. Forty-two next year, or was it forty-four? He couldn't remember. Who could love him now? Thank God he had Felix. He hoped that Felix was not so damaged that he would never be able to leave home, but equally that Felix would stay with him for ever. What could he do to ensure that Felix didn't make the mess of life that he had?

There was no chance of Erica coming to join them. She was off with the motorbike boyfriend. Guy remembered the tall, youthful silhouette swinging that helmet as though it were the Gorgon's head.

He shaved and put on a T-shirt that was older than Felix. He lay down on the bed with him and they watched cartoons until the sky turned dark.

30

Tomorrow, the eden project. Today it was the Lost Gardens of Heligan. They had seen Flora's Green with its 'luminous backdrop of living colour'. Guy wondered which colours could and could not be called living. At first he found it all too annoyingly busy, but soon the irritation of other people not only existing in the world, but having the audacity to visit on the day that he had chosen, was washed away by the loveliness of it all. They passed through aisles of metal hoops for fruit trees and climbers in the Vegetable Garden, and decided that when they got home they would try eating one of everything they saw – asparagus, globe and Jerusalem artichokes, cardoons (which Felix now wanted to start growing), sea kale – it would make a change from Felix's usual repertoire of cucumber, carrots, sweetcorn and green lettuce. Felix said that now he would eat purple and brown leaves too. There was a whole world of fruit and vegetables out there, waiting to be tried. The wisteria in the Sundial Garden was just 'going over'. They looked in awe at the bee boles.

'I wouldn't mind one of these,' said Guy in the head

gardener's office. Or a pineapple pit, or a peach, banana or melon house. They had lunch in a café and then went skidding through Sikkim and down towards New Zealand and the Jungle.

'What does that say?' asked Felix. There was a notice, faded blue ink inside a colourless plastic wallet, drawing-pinned to a tiny postbox on a tree.

'You can read that, can't you?' The notice was a bit high. Surely Felix didn't need glasses already? Another corrupt gene passed on, Guy thought, cleaning his own glasses on his shirt.

But Felix was just being lazy.

'If You Can Correctly Identify This Plant,' Felix read, 'We Will Give You A Job.' An arrow pointed towards a camellia, next to the tree. There was another plastic wallet with a bleached-out photo of the camellia in flower inside it. The slight blue tinge to the edges of the petals was just visible. Guy examined the leaves, and recognised at once the way in which the veins were just slightly more pronounced than in other white japonica varieties.

'That's a *Camellia japonica* "Eleanor Clark",' said Guy. 'It's the one your great-grandfather looked after, the one we have now in the garden. I have never seen another one like it until today.'

'Go on, Dad, tell them! You might win something!' The thought of Guy winning anything at all was exciting. 'Quick, Dad. Let's go and tell someone. Find the boss. There might be a prize. Even some money!'

'Look, I expect they're all busy. I'll just write a note and put it in there. I think that's what you're meant to do.' Guy felt for his little waterproof plant-spotting notebook. It seemed that he had left it back at the hotel. How odd that he hadn't noticed the lack of it before. He had a receipt from the café. That would do. It took him a little while to get all the information down, then he lifted Felix up to post it in the box.

'Come on. Let's go and see something else.'

They crossed a little wooden bridge. The boardwalks were fresh-looking, the chicken wire that rendered them non-slip scrunched pleasantly under their feet. Tree ferns towered above them.

'We have that gunnera, don't we?' said Felix.

'Mmm. But not quite so much of it.' Guy found that he was looking at the shoes of their fellow visitors, as well as at the plants – sensible old people's trainers, beaded flip-flops, Birkenstocks, kids' sandals and flashing trainers, up ahead of them a sad over-cautious family must be sweating in those wellies – perhaps humanity wasn't always that bad. If you took these gardens, for instance . . .

'Dad, are these stink cabbages?'

'Yup.'

'Is this the stink?'

'I think it could be stronger than this, earlier in the year.'

'We've got some, haven't we?'

'Yes, but only a couple, not nearly this healthy. I think they like it better here.'

'Most things like it better here. Do you think there are any cats like Snowy?'

'I expect so, hiding somewhere.'

Felix looked down at his map. 'It says that there are badgers' setts, but I can't see exactly where. Anyway, we've got one of those in our garden.' He was temporarily indignant that this garden was an 'attraction' and theirs was not. 'So what's the big deal about this one?'

'Perhaps we should be selling tickets too,' said Guy.

'Do you think that would be cool, Dad? But we'd have to have loos and a guide book and an ice-cream place and postcards . . .'

They climbed a steep path, leaving the Jungle.

'This isn't anywhere, is it?' Felix asked. He wasn't quite sure where they were on his map now, so he gave it to his dad.

'It's Cornish woodlands, under a Cornish sky.' If Guy lived here, he'd be all for Cornish independence. 'If we carry on up here,' he said, 'we should find somebody.'

At the top of the hill she was asleep in the woods, the Mud Maid. Felix gasped. They stood in a circle of people smiling at the sleeping form, a goddess of the woods, so green and brown and serene.

'Is she real?' Felix asked.

'Well, of course she's real. She's made of earth.'

'I wish I could touch her!'

They gazed and gazed. Guy's eyes traced again and again the triangles of her neck and clavicle. Felix started to laugh as the wind made ripples in her hair, which was montbretia, about to flower. At any moment her eyes might have opened.

'Do you think she stretches and moves about at night?' he asked.

'What do you think?' said Guy.

'She does,' said Felix. 'Do you think that's what it's like being dead?'

'Yes. Exactly like that. And sleeping with no dreams, or dreams only of the people you loved.'

Shall I say it, thought Guy, shall I? Your mother is in the woods, Susannah is in the woods.

'Love goes on for ever, Felix,' he said. 'It doesn't die. It never stops. Your mummy's love for you is still here, surrounding you for ever.'

Felix said nothing, but he put his little hand – still sticky from ice cream, and grainy from earth and the stems and leaves he had been touching – into Guy's. The wind rippled the Mud Maid's hair again.

'I think she looks happy. I don't want to leave her behind.'

'Nor do I. But we have to, sometime.'

31

MADELEINE HAD NEVER REALLY known the pleasures of comfortable clothes. She had always gone for girly things, tight things, cropped things. She had been a teenager when man-made fibres had been making their comeback, and was of a generation that had no idea about the true horrors of crimplene, a generation that willingly showed its thong tops. Anything she owned that was baggy was so low slung that it was in constant danger of falling off completely, and so not in the least bit comfortable, only anxiety-inducing, and requiring constant vigilance. When she chucked all her things away she was left with these grungy low-slung trousers, several pairs of jeans, and the stuff she wore to the gym. It seemed that she had also thrown out all her summer clothes. Despite her new pared-down life, she needed to do a little shopping. The trouble was she couldn't really think of anything she wanted. I know, she thought, I'll get off the bus and go into the seventh shop I see, and buy some new things there.

She didn't tell anyone what she was doing. Her friends

would think that she had now completely lost it. Some of them had been quite cold since she'd started getting rid of stuff and stopped going out so much. Sara Louise had said she had a sort of consumer anorexia. Good, said Madeleine. Aimee had said that she had just turned boring and was too anxious about Finals. Madeleine was more than a bit anxious about Finals, but wasn't everybody? Also, she had started to feel that she had frittered all the time away, that she should have been doing something else, or gone somewhere else. The city and the university just didn't seem real any more. Maybe there was somewhere in the world that was real, somewhere where she would have more of a sense of being on the planet, or more of a sense of being somewhere.

She got off the bus at the usual stop and counted seven shops. The Gadget Shop or Scholl. Next door was Oswald Bailey, the UK's Best-Loved Outdoor Gear Shop. She smiled and went in. Maybe this was the true seventh shop. Maybe this was a message from her spirit guide. Go camping! Buy walking boots! Get some waterproof trousers! She had a good look round. She really couldn't bring herself to buy anything much, the T-shirts were all so shapeless, and she'd look like an igloo in one of those jackets. She went closer, maybe there was something to be said for having something completely waterproof. Those tartan shirts were really soft. She decided on a pair of sailing shoes, only £6.99, and a canvassy hat with a little pocket in it. She took them up to the counter. Then she saw what she really needed, a Swiss Army knife and a hand-warmer; you lit tablets of charcoal, put them in this neat little tin, and carried it in your pocket all day. OK, it was summer now, but that was what she needed, and it had been quite rainy lately.

She would once have been embarrassed to have been spotted anywhere near Oswald Bailey, but now she didn't even mind meeting someone at the counter. The someone she met there was Max. He might have been embarrassed that anyone had spotted him buying an XXL waterproof jacket, but he just smiled when he saw Madeleine.

'Off travelling?' he asked her.

She paid for her things.

'Maybe. I don't really know what I'm doing.'

'After Finals, I meant.'

'I know.'

'I'm going to Seattle,' Max told her. He loved to say it out loud. Seattle, Seattle, Seattle.

'Cool,' said Madeleine. 'Maybe I should go somewhere like that.' She didn't actually know where Seattle was. If it was in Washington, that meant it was on the east coast, right? But she had a feeling it wasn't. 'Why Seattle?'

'Fancy a coffee?' Max asked her, as though he was always saying that to people. They went into Starbucks, which was the first place they came to.

'So,' said Max, 'what brought you to Oswald Bailey?'

'Well. Just looking. Actually I need some summer clothes. I had this thing where I threw everything I had out, gave it to charity shops . . .'

'You don't look very Oswald Bailey to me.'

'Um, no. I don't really want to go shopping. I shouldn't have come.' She felt really stupid now. 'I wish we all just had uniforms like in Communist China. Or standard-issue overalls. Something like in 1984.'

'But Julia looked pretty fantastic in those. That bit where she takes off her sash and hangs it on the hedge . . .'

Madeleine felt embarrassed now. She hoped that she would look sexy in those overalls too.

'Or I wish you were just given your allotted things, they just appeared. Then we wouldn't have to be bothered with shopping.'

'Sometimes things do just appear,' he told her, as they reached the front of the queue.

'What are you having?' Madeleine asked him. Was this going to be some sort of meal? It was around lunchtime.

'Cappuccino and a doughnut,' he told the boy (who was probably a student in their year) behind the counter.

'Just an Americano for me,' said Madeleine.

They found a table.

'I've worked in cafés,' Madeleine said. 'At Gatwick, when I was a teenager. It kind of puts you off eating in them sometimes.'

The doughnut sat between them now and Max felt too ashamed to eat it.

'Sorry. I shouldn't have said that,' said Madeleine. 'I expect that one's nice and fresh and clean.'

'It's not as though you can keep doughnuts very long, is it? I mean, they go damp after a few hours, don't they?' Max had no intention of not eating it.

'It's not that I don't like cakes. I sometimes think I should have skipped university and just been a baker. I'd quite like my own tea rooms, or maybe a cake-decorating shop.' There was a part of her that was missing ribbons and fripperies. 'I don't really know what to do next.'

'A baker called Madeleine. That would be cute. You could call it Madeleine's,' said Max, licking sugar off his lips.

'Everybody would wonder if I'd put the apostrophe in by mistake.'

At the next tutorial Phoebe was selling tickets.

'*A Midsummer Night's Dream*. You have to come,' she told Professor Lovage. 'It's thanks to you we had the idea of where to stage it. It's Speed Shakespeare. DramaSoc is doing almost all of the proper rehearsals in a week after the exams are over. Here's a leaflet. Third week in June. In the botanical garden.'

'How wonderful. How much are they?' Judy reached inside her desk drawer for her purse. 'I'll take four,' she counted in her head – Judy, Felix, Guy, Erica. 'No, five. Maybe my niece will come. And are there concessions for children?'

'Um, no, sorry.'

Judy hoped that Felix would enjoy it. Knowing Felix, he could always just daydream if it was a bit over his head.

'And have you done the casting yet?'

'Not finally. People who want to be in it have signed up, and we've had a few read-throughs. I know I don't want to be Helena. I'd love Titania, but who wouldn't?'

'Who indeed? Well, I hope you get it.' She would look lovely with a crown of flowers.

'Want some?' Phoebe said, turning to Thom.

'Can't I have a press one, or a press pair?' How whiny his voice sounded.

'Oh, well, OK.'

'Madeleine? Max?'

'Um, maybe, I haven't got much money on me,' said Madeleine.

'I'll have two,' said Max. 'I love that garden.'

After the tutorial Madeleine and Max found themselves walking down the corridor together. Max took his bottle of Pepsi out of his rucksack. He'd been keeping it hidden from Professor Lovage.

'Max, you really shouldn't drink that stuff,' said Madeleine. She brandished the student girl's compulsory bottle of water. 'Think of all the delicious things you could put in your mouth instead.'

He looked at her. Her lips were as pink as a raspberry smoothie.

'Mmm,' he said.

Back in Professor Lovage's office Phoebe had some questions about her last essay. She had only got 68 per cent for it. Her First was in jeopardy. Thom, lurking outside the open door rolling a cigarette, heard it all.

Once Phoebe was satisfied that she could pull up the extra marks on the next one, Professor Lovage smiled.

'What are you going to do next year?'

'I've got a place at Central School of Speech and Drama.'

'How wonderful. That's what you want to do, is it?'

'I think so. Or live in Italy and go to the opera every week.'

'Well, that sounds sensible too.'

'I've been working all along, to try to keep the debts down, and there's nobody to keep me here.'

(We'll see about that, thought Thom, with a smile that made him feel like a silent movie villain. On silent feet he made his invisible exit.)

'Nobody at all?' asked Professor Lovage.

'No, I'm holding out for Valery Gergiev, you know, the Russian conductor. Or similar,' said Phoebe.

'Well, good luck.' What impeccable taste, Judy thought. But wasn't Valery Gergiev rather too old for Phoebe? She wondered what Jemima would say.

Felix had taken Marmalade to visit the garden, hoping to deepen their friendship with Snowy. He had given Marmalade a lead of string which made climbing trees with him easier. Also, he could hang Marmalade up so that from a distance he looked magically suspended. He could make him appear and disappear like the Cheshire cat, but nobody ever noticed.

The girl whose name was Phoebe was sitting under the tree. He liked her, and her name. He knew she was called Phoebe because she sometimes rang people up and said, 'Hi, it's Phoebe.' Sometimes she read, and sometimes she came with some others. She had a friend called Sophia, and a friend called Thom who Felix didn't think was her boyfriend because they never kissed. Thom was taller than Dad and talked in a show-off voice, so Felix didn't like him much. He thought Thom smoked drugs because he sometimes took a really long time to make cigarettes and then went quiet or laughed. (Felix had a leaflet about drugs from school.) Once Thom did try to kiss Phoebe, but she pushed him away. Felix thought that he might tell the police. It would be interesting to see what happened; but they might take Phoebe so he probably wouldn't. After they had gone Felix always looked for any leftover drugs, just to see what they were like, but he could never find anything.

Phoebe was always drinking water out of a bottle. She took the cap off, had a sip, put the cap back on, took it off, had a sip, all the time. Her friend Sophia always had Diet Coke and did the same thing. She always looked sad so the ads for Diet Coke must have been lying.

Today when Felix saw Phoebe coming he quickly picked some buttercups, even though he knew that you must never pick wild flowers, and some zigzag clover and tied them up with a piece of green string from his school sweatshirt. He left them on the bench but she didn't know they were meant for her. She picked them up and smiled and put them back again. All of the girls in Felix's class believed in fairies. Sometimes they talked about fairies all day long. He thought that Phoebe might believe in fairies too. Maybe she thought the flowers were to do with some fairies. Felix sat really high up in the tree and let Marmalade swing backwards and forwards, backwards and forwards, but nobody noticed.

32

'I DON'T THINK I'VE ever seen the garden this busy,' Guy said, staring out from the greenhouse.

'Well, you might sound a bit pleased,' said Erica. 'It is meant to be good for the garden. You don't have to be such an Eeyore about it.' She could imagine Guy making himself a little shelter of branches and staying in there until it fell down.

'You have no idea how much I hate A. A. Milne,' he said, and looked viciously down at his own hands.

'Well, sorry. But that doesn't have much to do with the garden.'

'Huh,' he said. 'I am pleased. It's just that it's a bit full of people sometimes.'

'Honestly. It really is our only hope.'

One of the mental health groups had adopted a slice of a terrace and rolled back the turf to make a bed. Another group had found the remains of a rockery and were busy weeding it, prior to its restoration.

'All we need now is bloody Gryff Rhys Jones,' said Guy.

'Might be a good idea. Think of the money. Then it

would definitely be saved, even if we didn't win. They couldn't concrete it over if we'd been on TV.'

'I was joking.'

'I know.'

The school group, who were now called 'The Greenhouse Gang', marched by carrying their little sets of tools. Felix was at the back with Miss Block whose class was working with Mrs Cowplain's on the project. They waved.

'Well, you can't disapprove of that,' said Erica.

'It's not that I disapprove. I was just thinking of the Lost Gardens of Heligan.'

'So what is better?' she suddenly demanded, flinging down her trowel. 'Lost or found?'

He stared back out of the window, then down at the bench.

'Well, um, found, I suppose.' He didn't sound that sure. Erica gave him a look. 'Or never getting lost in the first place,' he added.

Sometimes it seemed just completely hopeless. How could she compete with somebody who was dead? By not competing, of course. Maybe too much water had passed under Guy's bridge. Maybe she should leave, find a proper job. She could finish her PhD anywhere now. What was she doing wasting her time here? He was past forty. He didn't seem to give a damn about her.

'At Heligan,' Guy said, 'the paths were made of a mix of minerals so salty, you know, brought up by the barrowload from the beaches, that nothing, not even brambles, could put down roots in them. When they came to clear them they could just roll the brambles up, like giant carpets, like stair carpets, I suppose it would be, you know, that width.'

There was a long silence. Then Erica said, 'Guy, I really don't know what I'm doing here any more.' She left the cuttings she had been rooting and walked out. Guy stared down at the tiny plants she had been working with and then at her back as she walked away.

'Erica!' he yelled. 'Found is better. Or discovered! Or new! Erica!' But she didn't come back. Perhaps she hadn't heard him, perhaps she didn't care.

He couldn't leave the cuttings like that. He carried on from where she'd left off and soon they were almost all in their little compartments of earth. He stopped thinking about her. Just as he was doing the last one he heard a crash and looked up. Nothing. Perhaps it was an old tree, or a huge branch coming down in the wood. Perhaps a small clearing had begun. Perhaps the sun would break through, and there would be yellow brimstone butterflies. Perhaps, he thought, that was the sound of something that people imagine might make no noise if there was nobody there to hear it. He opened his mouth to ask Erica what she thought, and then he remembered that she had gone.

The children seemed to do such short little sessions in the garden. It was hard to believe that they could manage to keep their plot with its crops of lamb's lettuce, sweet peas, tomatoes and marigolds so neat with just a few hours' work each week. He could see them from the greenhouse. They had cleared some more earth and were arranging pebbles. It looked as though they were writing a message with them. He wondered to whom.

The children were soon marching back past the greenhouse. Mrs Cowplain at the front, Miss Block with Felix at the back. Guy stared. She was just as pretty as the last time he had seen her. She was wearing flat red shoes with ribbons that tied around her ankles. Guy remembered something that his Granny Misselthwaite had said: 'Red shoes, no knickers.' He smiled and wondered if it might be true. But why was Felix always at the back with a teacher? Why didn't Felix ever have a partner? Why hadn't he ever noticed this before?

'Look, Dad. Some of Miss Block's class are joining up with ours for this.'

'Ah, Miss Block. Hello,' said Guy. 'Your garden's looking very good. I can see Felix is really pleased to have you back.' He couldn't think of anything else to say.

'Actually it isn't Miss Block any more,' said Miss Block.

'She got married, Dad. Now she's Mrs, er, Something Else . . .' Felix couldn't remember. She would always be Miss Block to him.

'Mrs Adams,' she said, laughing.

'And guess what?' said Felix. 'She married a teacher. A teacher married her own teacher!'

'Well, er, congratulations,' said Guy.

'He is a teacher, but not at school. He's an artist and an art teacher,' said Miss Block/Mrs Adams, rather embarrassed.

'A teacher married her own teacher!' said Felix again.

'Come on, Felix, we'd better get back to school. The others are miles ahead,' said Mrs Adams.

It was less than an hour until school finished. Guy wished

that Felix could just stay with him, but before he could suggest it they were off.

'Bye Dad!' Felix shouted over his shoulder, and Guy was left all alone in the garden.

Why was Felix so pleased that this teacher was with him? Was that normal? Had he been starved of so much? Oh dear, thought Guy, I need to do something. He felt a pang that Miss Block was now Adams, whoever he was. And Erica. Oh God. He might lose her too. Why had she seemed so furious and stomped off, leaving those cuttings to die?

33

I T WAS RAINING. Jack Tresize, one of the Heligan
gardeners, was sneaking a ciggie in the Crystal Grotto.
The match caught sparkles of magic in the roof. One of
their jobs later that summer was going to be to clean the
crystals and restore the grotto to its fairy glory. He rubbed
at one of them with the corner of his sweatshirt. The
garden would soon be opening for the day; he had to get a
move on.

As he headed back to meet up with his fellow mowers, he
remembered that he was meant to check the box beside one
of their most mysterious camellias. There was never anything in it, or if there was it would just be some name that
had been dismissed ages ago.

Inside the box was a spider and a piece of paper, actually a
receipt from the café, all faded and a bit damp. He was
about to screw it up when he saw that someone had written
across it in the smallest writing he had ever seen.

I think that what you have here is a *Camellia japonica*
'Eleanor Clark'.

I'd be v. interested to know what you think. My grandfather had one of these, taken from a cutting of the only one he or anybody he knew had ever seen, which was in a collection at a big house in Yorkshire where he was a gardener. I transported a cutting from this, and it is thriving in the botanical garden at the university where I work. I do not know what has become of the original, and mine is the only one I have come across until today.

Professor Guy Misselthwaite.

[There was a university address and a phone number.]

PS Would be v. interested in a job.

Jack Tresize thought that he'd better give the note to the boss to check out. Lucky there was no date on it. He hadn't checked the box in ages. Funny how you could forget things in a garden.

It would be Midsummer's Day before the letter was posted to Guy.

34

MADELEINE WONDERED IF ANYONE in the history of the world had ever had a good time, a really good time, not just made a convincing performance of having a good time, at the graduation ball. She had, of course, nothing to wear. People just wore anything. It wasn't as though they wore ballgowns, but she knew that they did wear something that was something. After all, Madeleine thought, if you were never going to see most of these people again, apart from at the graduation ceremony, when you have to wear some hideous polyester-mix witch's cloak, you really ought to look good. But she had absolutely nothing to wear. She suspected that nobody cared whether or not she even went. She was sitting on her bed, staring at her almost empty wardrobe, when Jo came in.

'Aren't you ready?'

'I haven't got anything to wear. Maybe I shouldn't even go.'

'Well, if you hadn't chucked all your stuff away . . .'

'I still wouldn't have anything.'

'Come and see what I've got. There must be something

someone can lend you. Honestly, Madeleine, it's not as though you didn't know this was coming up.'

But really she was being kind. Jo helped her find something (Rachel's blue silk palazzo pants, Emily's camisole and cardigan) and Madeleine put on her own turquoise jazz dance shoes. Jo didn't even get annoyed with her when she wouldn't wear jewellery or much make-up; all she said was, 'Well, you look like somebody's sister, but at least you're coming.'

The graduation ball was meant to be all summery and tropical. The nearest it was to tropical was raining. It was in the guildhall in town, a big old dusty building. The auditorium had been decorated with sad pink cardboard flamingos and green crepe-paper palm leaves.

There were promotions on any drink that was even the slightest bit exotic, so everybody was drinking Vodka Reefs, the colours of tropical fish, and Bacardi Breezers. Madeleine knew immediately that she shouldn't have come. Outside were bumper cars and a ghost train so that people could pretend (as had been the custom for the last twenty-something years) that they were in the final scene of *Grease*. What was the point of having a youth if it had to be so identikit? She really shouldn't have come.

Madeleine wandered away from the others and decided to see how high up in the building she could get. She went up a few layers, past where they were showing films that everybody had already seen, and that lots of them would have written essays about. A vengeful fisherman in yellow oilskins loomed on a screen. She had to step over people crying (Already! The party had only just begun!) and snogging on the staircases.

At the very top of the stairs, looking forlornly at the so-called programme, was Max. Beside him was a can of Bud and a giant unopened bar of coconut ice.

'Shouldn't that be a Bounty bar? I hadn't thought that coconut ice was tropical,' said Madeleine, sitting down next to him.

'No, more fairground, or even seaside. I won it. Coconut shy.'

'Aren't you meant to win the coconut?'

'I think they were fake ones. Or maybe they didn't want to give them away this early. Would you like a bit?'

'No thanks.'

The staircase had an elegant, gliding metal handrail that spiralled down and down. If you looked over the edge you could see right to the very bottom, and could imagine exactly what it would be like if you jumped. The stairs at the bottom were polished marble with some unnecessary plush red carpet. Up here the carpet had ended, but it was nice to sit down on something so cold. The throng downstairs was so sweaty and alcopop-scented that Madeleine feared she was smelly too.

'I like your trousers, Madeleine.'

'Thanks. Actually they aren't mine.'

'I guess that's what they call "midnight blue".'

'Have you been in a bumper car?'

'They looked quite small. I thought I might not fit.'

'Of course you'd fit. You're not that fat.'

'My dad got stuck in a bumper car when I was about eight. It made me decide never to go in one, you know, once I was adult-sized.'

'How did they get him out?'

'It was awful. I was wedged in too. These fairground toughs, you know the sort, all really good-looking in an if-Elvis-had-been-a-weasel kind of a way, they were laughing, but they pulled me out. Dad was really stuck. In the end they dismantled the car around him. They had to switch off the electricity, so they kept going on about all the money they were losing. A crowd gathered. Dad and I had gone by ourselves, so I was standing there all alone, trying to pretend that he wasn't my dad, and that I just happened to be watching, so I felt pretty guilty even at the time, as though it was somehow my fault. I'd asked to go on the dodgems . . .'

'But all kids ask to go on the dodgems.'

'In the end they got him out. I think Dad and I might be the derivation of the phrase "Who ate all the pies?" Dad was so embarrassed he gave them almost all the money he had in his wallet, so we couldn't have gone on anything much else, even if we'd wanted to. We walked home. Luckily he had enough money left for some chips, as we were both pretty miserable.'

'I can see why you don't like bumper cars. But you wouldn't get stuck,' said Madeleine.

'You never know. What were you doing coming up here?'

'I just wanted to see how high it goes.'

'Actually it might go even higher than this. Through that door. Look.'

It was a very small door. Madeleine worried that Max might not actually fit through it. They would have to crawl, or do a sort of Cossack-dancing shuffle.

'I expect it's locked anyway.'

But it wasn't. They pushed gently and it opened.

'I don't think we should . . .' said Madeleine, but Max was already through. It was very dark.

'Prop the door open with something,' said Max. 'Here.' He handed her something. The bar of coconut ice.

'It's not big enough,' said Madeleine, 'I need something else.'

'Try this.' He shoved something else towards her. It was very heavy. A clock, a very old classroom clock. Madeleine wedged the door open with it.

'Now people will know there's somebody in here.'

'Better than not having any light.'

'It must be a storeroom. Props and things. Imagine bothering to carry them all the way up here.'

'Perhaps there's another way down, or a lift.'

There were stacks of wooden chairs, filing cabinets that were locked but sounded empty, and crowds of two-dimensional figures, the extras from *Alice in Wonderland*, standing around in dusty gangs.

'I've always been scared of those playing cards,' said Madeleine.

A stuffed wolf, on its hind legs and dressed as a pirate, was guarding rolls and rolls of orange carpet.

'Oh,' Madeleine said, 'I think we should go.' She realised that she sounded like Anne in the Famous Five.

'They can't have more than one stuffed wolf,' said Max, taking her hand. 'Let's see what's through here.'

They went through a pink velvet curtain.

'We're in the gods!' said Max. They were a hundred feet above the revellers. They sat on the cold floor and leant against a column to watch what was happening beneath them. 'Feeling hot, hot, hot' drifted up, but Madeleine and Max were quite cool now.

'Let's see where this goes.' They followed the row of seats, then went out through another door, through a fire exit and they were on the roof. A metal staircase led down the side of the building, like a New York fire escape in a movie, rusty and ready for the hero and heroine to go swinging down. But they didn't.

They could see the whole of the city, and smell the sea. The rain had almost stopped, or perhaps they were just so high up that the drops were blown away. Max put his arms around her. She could feel the strong, thick flesh of his face. His shoulders were huge. She felt enclosed. She looked up and kissed him.

'Come to Seattle with me,' he said.

'Um, I was maybe going to do a PGCE.'

'Do you want to be a teacher?'

'Um, no.'

'Then don't.'

She kissed him again.

'Come to Seattle with me.'

35

I T WAS TURNING OUT to be a bad day for Professor Martyn Swatridge. The Students' Union paper had come out with a story about the site of the proposed new facilities. Honestly, who did they think was in line to benefit from them?

NATURE RESERVE AND COMMUNITY PROJECTS
THREATENED BY NEW FACILITIES

The working group charged with finding a site for the long-awaited new sports science facilities and leisure centre have earmarked the university's botanical garden as the best place to put it.

The peace and tranquillity of the garden, home to many rare birds and unusual plants such as Japanese knotweed and convolvulus, could soon be shattered by the sound of excavators and workmen listening to Radio Two.

Our reporter visiting the garden found a party of schoolchildren hard at work on their little plots, as well as a group of vulnerable people with health issues tending their own beds.

The department of Botany uses the garden for its research, and DramaSoc is about to use it as a Regent's Park-style backdrop for its next production, *A Midsummer Night's Dream* starring the lovely Phoebe Enright, who is tipped for the top and heading for a leading London drama school, as fairy queen Titania. It could all turn into a bit of a nightmare for Professor Martyn Swatridge, chair of the working group. Rumours of tree protesters ready to mobilise may persuade him to think again.

Well, he'd be damned if he was persuaded to think again by some thrusting ignoramus on the student rag. First he'd heard about the kids and the loonies' gardens. Damn. Better go take a look.

It was Midsummer's Day. Felix had gone to the garden to meet Guy. They would be going round to Judy's for tea. When Felix arrived he could see that Guy was busy talking to some students in the greenhouse. The garden seemed full of people. The students who were doing the play were making a lot of noise. Felix thought that they were just mucking about, but actually they were getting ready. They had a honeycomb of pop-up tents for the costumes and props, and tables to use for selling drinks and programmes. They were sellotaping posters to the front of the tables and hanging decorations and strings of lights in trees. They were even using his special spying tree. He stood and stared. Nobody took any notice of him. He decided to go his secret way, down the secret path to visit the newts.

*   *   *

Professor Martyn Swatridge ran a hand over his bristly maw, and went into the garden. Funny how you could work somewhere for more than thirty years and still not know every corner of it. He gave the thespians a wide berth and sat down on one of the railway-sleeper edges of a raised bed. It looked bloody new. He read the sign:

'This is the Future and Hope Project Garden. We hope you will enjoy looking at it. We are a group of survivors of the mental health system. This is all our own work. The garden is here by kind permission and with the support of the university's Community Liaison Department. Thanks!'

Yeah, thanks a bloody lot, he thought. Bloody left hand not knowing what the right hand, his hand, is doing . . .

Runner beans were making the most impressive wig-wam he had ever seen. They probably called them bloody tipis now, or yurts. There were sweet peas and Californian poppies, tomatoes and strawberries and tiny, newly planted lavender bushes. It all looked very new, could only have been there a matter of weeks, and it all seemed very jolly and much better than his own sour, half-hearted efforts at home. I'll give them bloody raised beds, he thought. He was pleased to see a dandelion clock. He blew it hard at some of the rows of seedlings. Probably lettuces. Ha!

He could see another little plot on the other side of what were probably once some rather nice lawns. He went to take a look. This one had a line of jolly scarecrows to guard it. Marigolds predominated. He detected the work of small people. You wouldn't have caught his own kids doing gardening voluntarily, maybe if he'd paid them enough . . .

He decided to go to the top of the garden, to take in the whole picture. The path was steep and zigzagged. Bloody hell, was that a banana tree? And there were giant cabbages on sticks. A wild rose snagged his trousers, he slipped on some loose stones, grabbed at something and got a palm full of scratches. Some of these leaves were bloody sharp. At the top he puffed and struggled to catch his breath. There really should have been a bench. He sat down heavily on a bit of mossy tree trunk.

Well, the place was huge, but very sloping, probably subsidence problems. Plenty of room for anything though. He could see the students, some now in costume, a few Athenians and fairies and rude mechanicals. There were ranks of plastic boxes that must have been filled with ice and bottles. He started to get his breath back. An annoying pair of chalk-blue butterflies fluttered around his head. He tried to bat them away, but they took no notice. He sat very still and attempted to ignore them.

Perhaps the committee was going to have to go with another option. Maybe too much opposition to the plan here. More mileage in developing this as an environmental asset.

Then he saw a child, a little kid in school uniform darting around through the trees. Probably up to no good, nicking stuff, or damaging things.

'Hey!' he yelled 'What are you doing?' He galumphed down the zigzag path. The boy had disappeared into a copse, but he was after him. The wet leaves were too slippery, his left shoe went right under water. You couldn't even see where the paths stopped and the streams began. Bloody self and hasty hazard.

'Hey you! What do you think you're doing?'

He had the boy cornered now, just a little squirt, probably only seven or eight. He grabbed his wrist.

'What are you doing in here on university property, eh?'

'Um, um,' said Felix. All the things they'd always told him at school came flashing into his head.

Run, Yell, Tell!

Never, Never Go!

He tried to yank his wrist free, but the man was too strong. He had a horrible smell and grey and red skin.

'Well?'

'Let me go!' Felix tried to free himself again, but the man just held on tighter and caught hold of his other wrist too. 'Let me go!'

'You tell me what you were doing. Smashing things? Damaging plants, eh?'

Felix felt the blood stopping in his arms.

'My dad works here,' Felix managed. 'He's right there in the greenhouse.'

The man loosened his grip very slightly. Felix tried to kick him but his legs were all wobbly and he missed.

'Oh, he works here, does he? What is he, grounds staff? You shouldn't be in here, you know.'

Felix wondered if he could get past him, perhaps there was a way over the fence behind them that would come out at Erica's. Then he realised what he must do.

'DAD!' he yelled, louder than he had ever yelled before. 'DAD! DAD, HELP!' And Guy heard. He came running. Everyone in the garden heard, and some of the students came running after Guy.

'DAD! HELP!'

'FELIX!'

Guy appeared through the trees. 'You get away from my boy!' He pushed the attacker in the chest, really hard, saw him slip and fall backwards, his head was in the water.

'Dad, mind the newts! There are babies!'

'What the hell are you doing?' Guy growled. He was standing over the man now. He could put his boot on him, his leg was poised to do it.

The attacker sat up. 'Bloody hell!' he said. 'I thought he was a vandal. I didn't touch him. I never would . . . Got kids of my own.'

Guy had his arms around Felix, who was almost crying.

'Did he touch you?'

'He grabbed my wrists.'

'Look,' said the attacker, 'I thought he was a vandal. I was protecting university property. I'm on the Acquisitions, Developments and Maintenance Committee! I'm Professor Martyn Swatridge.'

'Oh you are, are you?'

Felix had now picked up a big stick. Guy felt like picking up a rock, but instead he let the attacker struggle to his feet. The back of Swatridge's head was wet and muddy. He had huge damp patches on his back and legs. His jacket was soaked. His shoes were ruined.

'What are you doing going after little boys in a garden?' said Guy. Some of his students had appeared behind him. Phoebe, Oberon and some fairies were there too.

'Look, I thought he was a vandal. I made a mistake. I'm sorry.'

He could see the looks of complete disgust on their faces.

'I'm all right, Dad,' said Felix. 'But I hope the newts are OK. His head went right in one of their ponds.'

'The newts will be fine. They'll have just thought a big log fell in or something. Felix, are you really OK?'

'Yeah, Dad.'

Swatridge was trying to leave. He could feel something in his hair, probably a glob of blood. When he put his hand to it, he discovered some sort of disgusting water snail. He tossed it back into the pond. He had to say 'Excuse me, excuse me,' to get through the students. They all turned and watched him leave. There were oak leaves sticking to his jacket. His trousers had thick stripes of muckiness.

'He looks like a tractor in a cartoon ran him over,' said Felix, and they all laughed, but Guy could see how uneasy they all felt.

'Who was that slimeball?' asked one of the fairies.

'Professor Swatridge. History department,' said Oberon.

'Would you like a drink?' Phoebe asked Felix. 'We have some nice pink lemonade.'

'Um, no thanks,' said Felix. 'I don't really like fizzy things.'

'We're going to tea somewhere anyway,' said Guy. 'We might as well go now. Thanks, all of you.'

As the students left he heard them muttering, 'Swatridge . . . History . . . followed the little boy into the woods . . . grabbed him . . . Lucky escape . . . Lucky we were all here . . . should be reported . . . locked up . . .'

Professor Swatridge took a long slow route back to his car. By going round the backs of buildings, and by cutting around behind the bike sheds and the bottle banks, he managed to avoid meeting anybody he knew. He took off his jacket and carried it, he raked at his hair. The trousers were hopeless. If only he were like some of his colleagues and kept a complete change of clothes in his office. Lots of them had toothbrushes and shampoo and soap, the philanderers and those who might sometimes find it necessary to sleep on their office floors. If he went home now, Patricia wouldn't be back yet. The kids didn't even look up when he went in.

In the shower he replayed the scene again and again. How could he have been so stupid? It would follow him like a vile stray dog on a holiday. It would thump along behind him like a knot tied in the tail of a rat, a knot that could never be untied. He would now have to make sure that the garden was left alone. The committee must back off, or the story might come out.

He emerged from the shower fresh and determined. He bundled the muddy clothes into a bag for Patricia to take to the cleaner's. On second thoughts, he would take them himself, although he'd have to find out which one they used. Then, in the comfort of his study, he composed an email to everyone on the working group.

From: Professor Martyn Swatridge
Rare and protected species of newt in botanical garden. Also unusual water snails. Development plans likely to result in costly public enquiry & defeat. Student body may be hostile following article today. Suggest we now explore other options. Believe local school may have excess playing fields. Derelict dairy buildings/site nearby also a possibility.

Just moments after he had sent it the phone rang. It was Dave Crickley (Sports Science).

'Are you sure we aren't giving up on this one a bit easily? It's not as though there's that much space up for grabs around here.'

'I've taken a good look at the site. It's really treacherous terrain. Real potential landslip problems. And with that stream. Could be disastrous. They've got the fucking newts on their side. We might have to think again.'

'Maybe. I'll have to take another look too. And get back to you.'

'There's more potential in the garden as a garden. Could be a real asset. Future agenda item here. Enhancement and proper management of botanical garden. Creation of possible small-scale attraction. Potential venue for receptions, etc. Would attract funding plus good PR. We could shunt more resources into Botany. But we'd have to get some fresh blood in. Really make something of it.'

'Shouldn't that be fresh sap, ha ha.'

'Yeah. Cut out the dead wood in that department. We'll talk next week.' Professor Swatridge put the phone down, poured himself a shot, and managed a small, slow smile.

36

THEY WERE SITTING IN Judy's garden, sipping cold beers, a pre-show drink. Felix was in Judy's old wicker rocker, which was peeling and cracked after too many summers. She should have been putting something SPF 15 or higher on it. It was so frail now that it wouldn't bear the weight of anyone much heavier than Felix. Next summer, thought Judy, I will get another. Felix, who seemed much less shaken than Guy, was gazing into Judy's pond.

'It really is the world's smallest pond,' she told him, 'but it is self-sustaining.'

'I like it,' said Felix. 'But I think you should get some fish.'

'I don't know what they'd think of the fountain.'

'You haven't got a fountain.'

'Oh yes, I have. A solar-powered one. A present from one of my sisters.'

'You've got millions of relatives,' said Felix. 'I wish I had some more. Mine are all gone or far away.'

'Oh Felix,' she said, and hugged him. But he just seemed

a bit startled, so she stopped and left him to the contemplation of the pond. She went back to where Guy was sitting, and decided that something had been unsaid too long.

'I knew your wife a little,' she said. Guy froze. 'Just from being in the library. She was lovely, wasn't she? I'm so sorry that you lost her. I do think you are doing so well with Felix. He's a delightful little boy.'

'Uh,' said Guy. 'Thanks.' Even at this distance of years he still felt liable to start crying if someone said something kind to him about it.

'It must be terribly hard for you,' Judy went on.

'Uh,' said Guy, and looked down into his beer.

'I was so sorry when I heard about it, and saw it in the papers. And I realised that I'd seen her on the morning that it happened.'

'Oh?' said Guy, suddenly sitting up.

'Yes. In the library, and then afterwards. I was on my way home, she was waiting at the bus stop. She told me she was going to get something for Felix for starting school. I remember thinking that she was very well organised as it was still only July.'

'Really? Did you really? You see,' he took a big gulp of beer to hide the crack in his voice, 'I don't know what she was doing. I've never known . . . why she was in that car. If there was something . . .'

But this is terrible, thought Judy. I have, perhaps, been sitting on a clue, something that can help him, something that he didn't know. 'She told me she was going shopping for school clothes,' she said firmly. 'I expect he just came along and gave her a lift, showing off that new car. I expect that was all.'

'Thank you,' said Guy. 'Thank you.'

'I'm so sorry. I should have said something before. I didn't realise it might be important. I'm so sorry. I should have mentioned it when I wrote with my condolences. I didn't realise.'

'Really, you weren't to know. It's only a tiny detail,' said Guy gruffly. He took another swig of the beer. 'You weren't to know. There were no clues that anything was wrong. It's just that I've never known . . .'

'Perhaps that was all there was to know,' said Judy. 'He happened by and gave her a lift.'

'I guess I'll never know,' said Guy.

For a long time they sat in silence, watching Felix watching the pond.

'I lost someone once,' said Judy. 'Two people really.'

'I'm sorry.'

'He was a poet, a visiting lecturer. Chilean. We were in love, at least I thought so. He went back to Chile. The coup happened. I never heard from him again. He seems to have been what they call "disappeared".'

'I'm so sorry,' said Guy.

'I sometimes feel that I am doing the dance that Chilean women do, La Cueca Sola, to show that their men have been taken away. It's the most elegant form of protest. The saddest too. Of course I'm not that elegant; but my arms are empty.'

'Oh, I'm so sorry,' said Guy. 'And you said two people . . .'

'Yes, Eduardo and a baby. I was pregnant. I had a miscarriage. He never knew.'

'How bloody awful.'

'It's longer ago for me, of course,' she said with a kind little smile, 'but you never stop being sad, do you, missing them . . . I don't suppose I'll ever find out what happened to him.'

'But it might be good to try,' said Guy.

'Or at least to see the place he came from.' Guy nodded. After a few minutes Judy asked, 'What are you doing this summer?'

'I don't know,' said Guy. 'I guess I ought to take Felix away somewhere. We went to Cornwall at half term, but we might as well go away again.'

Why not go with Erica? Judy thought. Why not get married? But she only smiled. Here came Felix.

'Would you like another drink?' she asked him. 'Or something to eat? That ice cream was a long time ago. I have some lemon drizzle cake. Actually, I think I'll just do us some sandwiches before the play. I thought that Erica would be here by now.'

'Yes please,' said Felix. Judy went inside. Guy blew his nose very loudly. Felix went back to the rocking chair and the pond. When the chair was upright he saw the pond, when he tipped it back he saw blue sky and house martins.

As Guy sat there he felt his chest loosen and sink. Guy breathed. He watched Felix watching the dragonflies and the fountain and the blue sky and the house martins, and he breathed. It felt an age since he had breathed out. He closed his eyes and breathed. He slept.

In the kitchen Judy buttered bread, thinking, I am an imbecile. The pain I could have spared that poor man.

Oh, but it was all supposition. Of course I didn't know what Susannah had been doing. Perhaps she had been waiting for her lover when . . . but most likely not . . . Oh, what a fool I am. I should have rushed in, I should have trod! If only I had mentioned my tiny bit of information before. If there were any way I could help make things right now . . .

She made some of the buttered slices into cucumber sandwiches, and spread lemon curd on others. It really didn't go with cold beer. I am losing the plot here, she thought. She opened a bag of vegetable crisps. Felix would think they were lovely, the colours if not the taste. She put a piece of Cornish Yarg and some crackers on another plate. Felix would think the nettles were funny.

'I hope this is substantial enough,' she said, putting the tray down on the little white wrought-iron table. The clatter woke Guy.

'Felix!' she called. 'Come and have something to eat.' They heard voices coming down the side passageway.

'Judy!' Erica called. 'Sorry I'm late. I've got a surprise visitor for Felix!' They came through the gate. The visitor was tall and blond. He carried a rucksack and a laptop in an expensive leather case. He had grown a beard, and was more weathered than when they'd last seen him.

'Good God!' said Guy, looking, Judy thought, as though he had seen a ghost.

'Hey Guy, and is this giant grown-up kid Felix?'

Felix stared. The man was familiar. He stared some more.

'Uncle Jon!' he yelled, and ran to him. Jon swooped him up and hugged him and swung him round. Guy got up, and they shook hands.

'I've a conference in Oxford. A night to spare. Meant to ring, but I wasn't sure if I'd be getting away in time. Thought I might just stop by to see how you are. Nobody at home, checked out your little department, Guy, and Erica here kindly led me to you.'

'Great to see you,' said Guy (and not so much of the 'little department'). 'Judy, this is Jon Ingram, Felix's uncle. Jon, this is Professor Judy Lovage. Gothic Architecture. Fellow gardener.'

'Nice to meet you, Judy. Nice garden you've got here. Nice verbascums.'

'Thank you. Would you like a cup of tea, a glass of beer? Erica?'

'Beer,' they said with one voice, and laughed. Judy didn't like the vulpine way this man was looking at Erica. Perhaps, she thought, he's a bit of a bad lot. And she certainly didn't like the way that Erica was paying him so much attention. Oh dear, oh dear.

'My niece Jemima will be here soon. We're all going to see *A Midsummer Night's Dream* in the botanical garden.'

'Please come, Uncle Jon,' said Felix.

'Sorry, mate, I can't,' he said, smiling. Oh good, thought Judy. Felix's face fell, but he soon realised it was a trick. 'I'd love to come but my rucksack's too heavy. Perhaps you could take something out of it for me.' Felix undid some of the many straps and found an airport shopping bag on top of everything else. 'That's for you, nephew.'

'Thanks,' said Felix, holding the bag as though that were the present.

'Open it!' said Erica. They all looked at him.

'Don't you think that there's sometimes a terrible

pressure in opening presents in front of people, knowing that you've got to gasp with delight and say that it's just what you've always wanted,' said Judy.

'It probably is just what Felix always wanted,' said Erica. Jon had clearly been asking her opinion. Felix opened the bag.

'Wow! A personal CD player! Thanks!'

'No, it's a personal DVD player. You can take it on the train, on car journeys, wherever.'

'Wow, thanks!'

'And there's these,' said Jon. 'I didn't know what you had, but you can exchange them or swap them with your mates.' Guy didn't say that they had no DVD player or DVDs at all. Felix didn't say that he didn't have the sort of mates that you swapped DVDs with.

'Let's see, then. What have you got?' asked Erica.

'*The Blue Planet*,' Felix read. '*Life of Plants. Aristocats. Lady and the Tramp.*'

'That was one of your mum's favourites,' said Jon.

Felix stared really hard at it as though it might have some special information to impart. He ran his finger around the edges and corners of the box, then put it back into the bag with the air of somebody who was saving a chocolate bar for later.

Madeleine was packing up her room. There wasn't really much stuff. She had chucked so much away. Jo came in, saying, 'I'm really stuck for boxes and bags and things. I seem to have tons more stuff than I arrived with. And what are we going to do about all the food and cleaning things? I can't fit any of that in. Maybe we can leave it for the next people.'

'We should chuck it all out,' Madeleine said. 'Nobody really wants other people's opened bags of rice and dysfunctional salt and pepper mills. If we leave it they might say we didn't clear up properly and not give us back the deposit.'

'They never give it back anyway, however good you leave it.'

'I was kind of counting on it.'

Jo rolled her eyes. 'Honestly, Madeleine. You're just so trusting. We won't get it back. Anyway, I just wondered, have you got any boxes or anything spare?'

'You can have this. Keep it.' It was a big black rigid bag on wheels with an annoying little tag saying 'Metropolitan'. Metropolitan. As if! It had been £19.99 in a catalogue-returns shop in Crawley. 'I kind of hate it and I don't want it any more.'

'Are you sure? Don't you need it?'

'You know how I've been trying to shed things.'

'OK. Thanks.' Jo wheeled it away. Madeleine could hear the case bump downstairs and away out of her life. Hooray!

But once she had gathered all her books, and retrieved all of her things from the other rooms in the house, she found that she could have done with that bag. Too late. She would have to go scrounging round some shops for cardboard boxes. They would all have been taken already. Or worse, she might have to buy some of those giant stripy nylon bags at a pound shop. Just what she didn't want to do. She hated the way people were always buying those bags, and then managing to get rid of them, and then buying them again.

There must be something she could use . . . The curtains! Down they came, the red and white spotty tab-top curtains she'd made herself. The very thing. She shook one out flat on the bed, put the other on top of it for strength, and then bundled everything in. She tied the tie-backs together to make a rope to gather it all at the top. There. All she needed now was a very stout stick to hang it on, and a very strong shoulder to put it over, and she could be off to seek her fortune. She texted Max to say she was ready. They were going to watch the play. The next day they would be off to stay with his parents on the Isle of Wight for a week (she wasn't quite sure why, except that they could stash their stuff there). After that, they would leave for Seattle.

They took rugs to sit on, and an extra one for Felix in case it got cold. Judy opened the hamper straight away. She had plastic champagne flutes and elderflower cordial (not fizzy) for Felix, who had edged himself closer and closer to her, until he was almost sitting on her lap. Guy had brought the wine. He wondered if they would have a little changeling boy in the play. After what had happened to Felix that afternoon, he hoped not.

Judy had brought as many lovely things as she could think of that could be eaten silently. Erica had brought honey cakes. Jon stretched out on one of the rugs next to her. Judy thought that he was taking up too much space. How dare he just pitch up like this and interfere with her plans? Erica stretched out her long legs next to him. They could be the winning contestants in the Longest Legs in the World competition. Guy sat morose and forgotten on Erica's other side. Damn, thought Judy, damn. And Jemima hadn't shown up at all. Erica seemed to be laughing at everything that Jon said. It was all very annoying. Sometimes Judy felt very alone.

'Oh, look at that moon!' said Jon. He raised a glass to the new moon, and smiled as though he had been responsible for hanging it over the greenhouse roof. The play started.

Then Judy heard a small familiar voice behind her whispering, 'Sorry, sorry.' She turned away from the tedious Greek lovers and there was Jemima, tiptoeing her way across other people's picnics. She gave her a tiny wave and a smile. Oh dear, she looked all red-faced and puffy-eyed. Judy made a space between herself and Jon, and poured Jemima a glass of fizzy wine, hoping that it wouldn't make matters worse. She saw Jon offer Jemima a Camel Light and Jemima accept it.

'Aunty, I don't really smoke,' Jemima whispered, dragging deeply.

'Nor do I,' whispered Jon. 'It's just occasionally I feel as though I should buy some Duty Free. I walk past it all so often.'

'Oh, do you like travelling?' Jemima asked.

'Do it all the time. I love it.'

'Sssh,' said someone in front of them. Judy would have said 'sssh' too if she hadn't been so pleased to see Jon turn his attention away from Erica. But Erica didn't seem to care. She was eating a honey cake. By and by Quince and Bottom exited. The first act finished.

'What was wrong, best niece?'

'You can't say that, Aunty!' Jon and the wine certainly seemed to have cheered her up.

'Actually it's awful. I was meant to be going travelling with my friend Tasha this summer. I've got all the money saved up and everything. Anyway, she texts me today and says there's a problem. We were going to book the tickets tomorrow. I've been researching all these different deals. Anyway, I text back "What problem?" And then she rings me and says that she wants to go to Mexico with her dumb boyfriend instead, but get this, I can go with them if I like. She knows I won't say yes. So that's it. No summer. Mum won't let me go by myself – she says it's the other side of the world, and I don't really want to go by myself anyway.' She started to sniff. 'Everybody I know has already got all their plans made. They're all sorted. I really wanted to go . . .'

'Go where?' asked Judy.

'South (sniff, sniff) America.'

'I'll come with you,' said Judy. 'I don't expect you want your aged maiden aunt along, but I'd love to. As long as we can go to Chile. But I'm sure you don't want me . . .'

'Aunty, I'd love it. It would be so cool. Let's do it!'

They clinked glasses.

'Of course your mum will have to approve your travelling companion,' said Judy, pouring them more wine.

Thom and his mate Will were watching the play, or kind of watching. They were smoking and looking at the sky and swigging from bottles of Becks. They looked across and paid attention whenever somebody pretty or scantily clad came on. This was quite often. Thom still had major designs on Phoebe Enright. During the second interval he slipped backstage, which was not easily done, but he took his reporter's notebook with him as a prop and a means of gaining access.

'You shouldn't be back here,' said Moth. 'You can't come backstage during a performance.'

'Press,' said Thom. 'I just wanted the view from the wings, or of all these wings. How do you think it's going?'

'Bugger off,' said Moth. He smiled at her, but it did no good. Behind the rude mechanicals, Titania was adjusting her costume.

'Hey, Phoebe! How do you think it's going?'

'Very well, thank you,' she said without even looking at him. Her costume seemed to be a little tight around the arms, the wings had been slipping, but not enough for anybody else to notice.

'Would you like to expand on that? I'm writing a piece.'

'Don't you think it's a little crass to be backstage before the show is even over?'

'So what happens afterwards, party for cast and friends?'

'Just cast and friends,' said Peaseblossom.

'What the hell is "Peaseblossom", anyway?' he asked. He turned to Cobweb. She was wearing a sparkly grey crocheted poncho over grey velvet shorts and a little black vest.

'Tell me, Cobweb, do you think there is a role for fairies in today's society?'

Cobweb gave him a tight little smile. 'Look, Thom, we don't want to talk to you.'

'How about a drink together afterwards?' he said, looking only at Phoebe.

'Go away,' said Peaseblossom.

'Yeah. Fuck off,' said Cobweb. And they put themselves between him and their queen.

'Two minutes!' somebody yelled.

He sloped off, back to where he had been sitting. Will had disappeared, leaving a pyre of empties. He was all alone. Sod it. He might as well just go home.

Felix drifted off to sleep in the final act. His head was in Judy's lap. She put the extra blanket over him. 'Have sweet dreams,' she whispered. With gentle fingers she stroked a kiss onto the curve of his cheek.

Erica poured some more wine for Judy, herself and Guy. Jon and Jemima had been quaffing it; they had taken their own bottle and were keeping their own glasses topped up.

'Thank you,' said Guy. 'I wonder what the badgers make of all this.'

'I expect they're hiding. Let's go and see.'

Erica got up, and Guy did too. Judy caught his eye and gave him a smile that meant she would look after Felix. Erica led the way, then Guy caught her hand. He had known that it was brown. Now he felt how warm and smooth it was too. Her long fingers entwined around his. They walked together into the green and lilac dusk, down to the stream.

'Erica, Erica. I feel as though I haven't seen you until now.'

'I was here all the time.'

It was enough. It was a beginning.

Eventually the sound of applause called them back.

Felix was half awake as the play reached its end. He sat up for Puck's closing lines:

Give me your hands, if we be friends,
And Robin shall restore amends.

'What does it mean, Judy,' he asked, ' "restore amends"?'
'It means,' she said, 'that they will try to make everything
all right.'

ACKNOWLEDGEMENTS

I would like to thank Victoria Millar, Alexandra Pringle, Sarah Lutyens, Susannah Godman, Mary Morris, Jessica Leeke, Holly Roberts and Arzu Tahsin for their help and encouragement. Thanks also to John Dean for the mystery plant anecdote.

A NOTE ON THE TYPE

This old-style face is named after the Frenchman Robert
Granjon, a sixteenth-century letter cutter whose italic
types have often been used with the romans of Claude
Garamond. The origins of this face, like those of
Garamond, lie in the late fifteenth-century types used by
Aldus Manutius in Italy. A good face for setting text
in books, magazines and periodicals.